Wolfgang

GOLDENROD

ABOUT THE AUTHOR:

Wolfgang E. Franke was born in Horstmar near Dortmund, Westphalia in 1915 and received his early education in Kiel where he sold his first story at the age of fifteen to the KIELER ZEITUNG. After teaching in Duisburg, in the Rhineland, he was drafted into the Navy in 1939 and spent the last three years of the war in charge of the Radio Station in Trieste as Lieutenant Commander.

At the end of the war, he was captured by the partisans and spent the next four years as a prisoner in Yugoslavia - this provides background for his second novel THE BALTIMORE CONNECTION (forthcoming).

On release, Mr. Franke resumed his doctoral studies in biology at the University of Frankfurt but decided to emigrate to Canada in 1951 following the Canadian Government's search for pioneers to develop THE NORTH.

After gaining his B.A. at University of Toronto and an M.Sc. at the University of Ottawa he worked for a period in plant pathology and genetics. He then began his teaching career in Canada, became principal of high schools in Morrisburg and Essex, Ontario. From there he had a distinguished career in education becoming founding president of the Lambton College of Applied Arts and Technology in Sarnia, Ontario; president of the College of New Caledonia, Prince George, British Columbia and finally founding principal of the Great Lakes College, Toronto, Ontario.

Mr. Franke has had some eighty stories and essays published in many of the major newspapers and periodicals in Canada, and his writings have been broadcast in CBC Essays (beamed to Europe). He is now writing full-time.

He is an accomplished sculptor, artist and musician and lives with his wife in Toronto.

Wolfgang E. Franke

GOLDENROD

Trans-Canada Press
Toronto, Canada

Canadian Cataloguing in Publication Data

Franke, Wolfgang E. (Wolfgang Egon), 1915-

ISBN 0-920966-21-7 (bound) - ISBN 0-920966-23-3 (pbk.)

1. Title.

PS8561.R36G64   C813'.54   C83-098697-9
PR9199.3.F695G64

Original art and cover by Alan Wilson

First published 1983 simultaneously in limited edition hard-cover and in quality trade paperback

by

TRANS-CANADA PRESS
142-A Dupont St.
Toronto, Canada M5R 1V2
(416)968-2714

Printed and bound in Canada

To Rose, Sylvia, Dean

and even Norman

1

Ferdinand never looked at little Jenny directly, never made eye contact with her, partly because his left eye was peering inward. He had been the target of cruel jokes about his cross-eyes all the ten years of his life, especially since he had started to wear the wire-rimmed glasses that tended to slip down his nose every now and then. Jenny never poked fun at Ferdinand, and that was comforting. But partly he didn't look at her because Jenny wasn't worth looking at. She was just a piece of the environment. She was the neighbor's child always hanging around where Ferdinand walked. Jenny was six and wasn't even going to school yet. She hadn't been 'quite ready' when her mother had tried to enrol her at St. Boniface. "We'd better wait another year," Mother Theresa had said after a short and cumbersome conversation with the child. Mother Theresa was the Principal at the school.

Ferdinand tolerated the presence of the skinny girl in spite of his masculine superiority, because she would never challenge his natural leadership position which stemmed from being a big boy. Other kids in the neighborhood did just that, and it bothered him a lot. And furthermore, who else was around he could talk to this early in the morning? Everybody was in school except the little folk.

If Ferdinand had been asked why he wasn't in school, he would have looked sideways, pushed up the bridge of his glasses with his index finger and said, "Mr. Malcolm knows I'm home" or "My Father's sick, and my Mom says it's all right." That would have been only half the truth. Ferdinand couldn't stand it in school, to be honest. He stayed home for the flimsiest reasons. Mr. Malcolm hadn't clamped down on him - not yet -because of the unofficial feeling at the school that there really wasn't much to be hoped for as far as Ferdinand's academic achievement went. The boy was almost eleven, but he had climbed up to third grade only, and that with great reluctance on everybody's part.

Ferdinand kept a dozen pigeons in the attic. He knew more about breeding pigeons than any of the egg-heads in school. The only time in his whole school career he had ever seen a hint of approval on Mr. Malcolm's face was when he had given an oral account in class about his bird breeding efforts. He told the class how to build a cage, what to feed the birds, how to tell a male from a female, when to start the mating, and when to watch for the bursting of the eggs when the incubation time was up, how to rear the young and to eventually sell them in town. There were lots of boys in town who buy pigeons, he said. He gained temporary acknowledgement as an expert in something, but when it came to written numbers and words in such lofty fields as arithmetic and geography, his aura as someone who knows dissipated as fast as it had arisen.

"I'm going to see the pigeons," he said to Jenny. "You wait here." He picked up a pebble and threw it down the embankment at a solitary linden tree, hitting it exactly in the middle of the trunk. The last time he had hit a tree with accuracy, Tommy Dudston had asked how he had done that.

"Whatcha mean, done that? I can do it every time I want to."

"I mean, do you aim at the right of it, being cross-eyed and all that?" The boys around them had hollered with laughter, and Ferdinand was hurt.

"I can punch you in the nose with my eyes closed," he said, holding his fist in front of Tom's face. Tommy knew he would too. He had not intended to poke fun at Ferdinand. Tom was a top science student, and he was genuinely curious about how a cross-eyed person can see straight. "I didn't mean to. . ." he said.

Ferdinand had then turned around and walked away from the boys, and the next morning had gone fishing at the bottom of the embankment where the Humber River meandered towards the lake. They called it a river, but it was only a pathetic little stream with car tires and old sofas sticking out of it when the water was low. There were hardly any fish left in there. The boys knew it was more like bathing a worm than catching a fish in the Humber River. But boys still went fishing in the river. You never knew, sometimes you did catch a fish. And even when you only hooked an old shoe out of the water, it was exciting.

Jenny didn't ask him how he managed to hit the tree trunk. "I'm going with you," she proclaimed.

"You go home," he said, pushing up his glasses.

"I want to see the pigeons."

"You can't."

"Why not?"

"You're a girl."

"Can't girls see pigeons?"

"Girls don't know anything about pigeons."

"You could tell me."

"No, you're too small, and you're a girl. It's for boys, big boys."

They went down Linden Street, past Mr. Wong's grocery store with the big Coca Cola sign over the window. Then they came to the spot where the sidewalk showed many unsightly bird droppings. They looked up the front of Ferdinand's house. On a little platform extending from the attic window they saw a couple of pigeons, one of them, its broad chest inflated, parading and fancily dancing around a demurely silent and rather disinterested, more slender bird. "Rookedecooh, rookedecooh," said the bloated one.

"See the one with the rainbow colors around his neck? He's the one making the noise. He's the father," said Ferdinand with visible pride. "I have another male that is blue and white. He's inside. See how the sunshine makes the colors change when he twists his neck?"

Now the father climbed onto the slender bird, flapping his wings wildly for a few seconds. Then he flew off the platform and, after dropping another whitish blotch on the sidewalk, he soared into the blue sky.

"It's working," said Ferdinand.

"What's working?"

"You go home now," the boy said abruptly, as if he regretted having talked to the little girl.

"I'm not going to. Let me see the pigeons in the attic, Ferdinand, please. . ."

"My father's home." Ferdinand sat down on the front steps. In a way he was flattered that someone showed interest in his hobby, even if it was only a little girl. He looked at her in her white T-shirt with Mickey Mouse on the front, and her clean skirt. Her dark curly hair framed a slender, pale face, out of which two coal-black eyes looked up at the boy.

"Your father would let me see the pigeons, wouldn't he?"

"Dad is in bed. It's his liver," said the boy.

Jenny didn't see the connection between the pigeons and his father's ailment.

"He came home this morning. Hadn't been home all night. . . Does your mother cry a lot?"

"She did, when my father died. Now she cries only when she peels onions." The girl sat down beside Ferdinand. They stopped talking, but Jenny saw the boy take off his glasses and rub his eyes with the back of his hand. When he'd put the glasses back on his nose, he said softly, "Have you ever seen your father drunk?"

"My father's dead, I told you."

"Oh, well," said the boy. Now there were streaks of dirt on his cheeks. Jenny offered to wipe them off, but Ferdinand rose to end the conversation. He felt there was too much talk between a big boy and a measly little girl. "I'm going to the attic," he said.

"Ask your mother if I can go up with you to see the pigeons."

"Mom went to work," said Ferdinand. Then he added in a bitter tone, "She works and he lies in bed, drunk."

"Oh," said the girl. She had no idea what it means to a boy when his father is drunk. She was neither surprised nor did she feel sorry for Ferdinand. Her own father had never been drunk before he was killed in a car accident. He made a hundred liters of wine every year, but he was never drunk. She had seen drunks staggering out of Dudston's Tavern late on Friday afternoon, and she had joined the little kids in their derisive laughter in the street when the police picked up a helpless wreck of a man from the gutter, shoved him into the olive green van and then slammed the back door with the small dark square window in it.

Ferdinand opened the front door but before he could shut it, Jenny had squeezed herself through. "I'm going with you," she said. Ferdinand was taken aback by her determination.

"Ssh," he said, motioning her to stand still and listen. There was heavy snoring coming from somewhere. The boy seemed relieved. He grabbed the girl and manoeuvred her on to his back. Then he carried her step by step up to the second floor. He opened the plywood door to the attic and climbed up the steep narrow stairs. "Not so tight," he panted. The girl loosened her grip around his neck. He let her down on her feet. She grinned mischievously, having won the battle. When she began to get used to the dim light, she admired the stalls in rows at the wall where the female birds squatted over their eggs and babies.

With the pride of a landlord, Ferdinand showed her a nest with three eggs. Two birds landed flapping on the platform outside, came through the opening in the wall and greedily fell on the food and water.

"Recognize him? He's the father we saw from the street." The female hopped on to the nest, huddled over her three eggs and looked stoically ahead. The male left through the hole and took off again.

Ferdinand emptied more feed into the dish. Suddenly he cried, "Oh, no !"

"What's the matter?"

He turned around slowly. In his hand he held a blue and white bird, stiff and lifeless. "He's dead," he said tonelessly.

Jenny didn't dare comment. She felt death was something formidable, something beyond understanding. And here in the attic it was so immediate. And the boy was mourning. The stillness was oppressive. She started to tremble. When her father died, she had been too young to understand, but she remembered her mother's tears vividly and she recalled Father Domenico's words when he laid his hand on her head. "You have to look after your mother now, Geneviève."

The boy held the little corpse in his left hand and stroked it with the other. He sat down on one of the two stools at the work table.

"He was a new sport," he said. "I was breeding ordinary pigeons and suddenly there was this new sport, blue and white."

They heard a commotion downstairs. Pots and pans were clattering in the kitchen. Then thundering radio music filled the house. The children sat beside each other, looking at the dead pigeon.

"Blue body and white wings. You don't know what that means. It's a new variety. If I breed a whole stock of blue and white, I'll be famous." He fanned out the feathers of one wing. "See how beautiful?"

"Is that your father downstairs?"

"Yeah, I have to go down," he said, laying the pigeon on the work table. "Why did he die? He had all the food and water he needed, and six females to choose from."

"What do you want me to do?" said Jenny.

"I shouldn't have brought you up here. What do girls know about pigeons! You didn't even look when I showed you the beautiful colors of the feathers. And I was stupid enough to carry you up here. Now what do I do with you? Father's up and around. His liver must be okay. He will leave for the afternoon shift any time."

Jenny had fear written all over her. "Are we going down?"

"I am going down. You stay here until I come back up." He climbed down the attic stairs. She heard the door on the bottom shut. She pulled up her legs on the stool, clasped her arms around her knees and watched the birds. Two more females left their nests, ate hastily and walked through the hole into the sunshine. Then they flew away. The dead bird's claws stretched into space.

Do birds go to heaven?

On the wall over the table Ferdinand had his tools neatly arranged, screwdrivers, pliers, wrenches, a hacksaw, three hammers, a drill and a little axe with a formidable edge. Ferdinand was a boy to admire, Jenny decided.

Now Ferdinand's father was bellowing downstairs. He sounded angry but she couldn't understand the words, the rock music drowned them out. She couldn't hear Ferdinand's voice at all. Now the music stopped. The radio announcer talked about Coca Cola. Then the radio was turned off.

"You lazy bum," ranted the man, "Why aren't you in school?"

"Mom knows," Ferdinand said meekly.

The man raised his voice to high pitch, "Don't listen to your mother. It's you that needs an education. She doesn't need it, you do. She's got too much of it already."

"I like Mom," said the boy defending his mother.

"Sure you like Mom, because she doesn't make you go to school."

"She works every day."

"You call that work? Sitting in a cozy office and answering the telephone? You call that working?" Mocking his wife he added in a squeaky voice, " 'Austen and Blimp, good morning. One moment, please, I'll put you on hold'...Ha, ha! You call that work?"

"She's never been drunk."

Jenny heard a wild scramble downstairs like chairs falling over, then two or three heavy blows and Ferdinand screaming. She trembled all over. Her chin rested on her knees. She could hardly keep her teeth from chattering. "Oh, Jesus," she prayed. That's as far as she got. She was confused. Then she heard the front door slam. Everything was quiet now.

Ferdinand came up, slowly, one step at a time, pulling himself listlessly up the railing. He held his broken glasses in his hand. He wasn't crying, his eyes were dry, but there was a far-away horror in them, the left one staring obliquely into nothing. He laid the two pieces of his spectacles on the table. Then he took the axe from the wall, placed the dead pigeon in front of him and with two hefty blows, cut it lengthwise in half.

Jenny had retreated to the stairs. She clasped her hands over her Mickey Mouse T-shirt, still trembling. Ferdinand held one half of the bird in his hand. Entrails were hanging from it. With the point of his axe he poked into the bloody mess and said, "It's his liver."

Jenny ran down the stairs, out of the house and home to her mother.

2

Mrs. Fabrini was only twenty-five when her husband died, but she had already brought into the world five little Fabrinis, three girls and twin boys. The boys were only two years old when Joe Fabrini was buried. To their Anglo-Saxon neighbors they all looked the same with their dark curly hair and pale skin, big questioning eyes and beautifully even teeth.

Joe Fabrini arrived here from poor old Calabria just two years before the Kaiser marched into France. He was immediately employed as a ditch digger. He had the muscles and also the enthusiasm for which newcomers were appreciated. It didn't bother him that he was called a wop, because he didn't know the meaning of the word. Much later, when he had learned some English, he told the foreman not to call him that any more. When the war ended, he was a foreman himself and his team operated six heavy machines. They were working on construction jobs. There was plenty of work for honest, hardworking musclemen. Veterans returning from the war preferred office jobs or went to university with government support.

Yes, Joe Fabrini did well in his new country. He now sent home some money to his parents in Calabria, and he had acquired a vacant lot on the outskirts of the city. He was thinking of getting married. But he couldn't get enough time off work to make the long journey home and such a trip would have cost a fortune. Of course, he would marry a girl from his village in the toe of Italy.

One day, Joe told Father Domenico that he would like to marry. Didn't he think it would be better if he got married?

"Do you have somebody in mind?" asked the priest.

"Yes, I do. But I was only a boy when I left the village. The Borghese family lived next door to us, and they had a daughter one or two years younger than I. She was a nice girl. Her name was Alida. . .Alida Borghese." He blushed but it was hardly visible in his weather-tanned face. "Sometimes I dream about Alida," he said, smiling.

"I'll see what I can do," said the priest. Joe was thirty-six and it was high time he started a family.

Joe had forgotten about this conversation when about six weeks later, the priest caught him by the sleeve as he left the church after mass.

"I've got good news for you," he smiled. "The Borgheses are pleased to hear from you. They have no objection to you marrying their daughter. I'll keep in touch with them and let you know what develops."

Joe stopped smoking and added the money saved to his bank account. He'd always wanted to quit smoking. Half a dozen attempts had no lasting results. Now he had a powerful motivation. He lived for the day when his future wife was to join him.

Well, the day came and Father Domenico took Joe down to Union Station where Alida was to arrive from New York.

They stood at the gate and waited in a crowd of excited people.

"I bet no one here is waiting for a bride he has never seen," said Joe, "or at least, not seen for twenty years."

The priest said, "There are always some Italians." He pulled a photograph from his wallet. "She's a pretty girl," he said with

Joe looking and nodding. "I have to tell you something about her, but I want you to meet her first."

"Looks kind of young," said Joe.

"It must be an old picture." Father Domenico grinned impishly.

"Yeah, they don't have pictures taken every year, Calabrians are still poor."

Now the train rolled in, hissing and puffing. And then the masses streamed through the gate. Shouts, embraces, kisses and tears. The two men studied the faces of all the women. Joe's heart was almost bursting. He held the photograph in his hand, trying to project from it maybe fifteen years into the future. Joe was looking for a woman in her thirties but when the flow of people subsided, no one had resembled the Italian woman he had in mind. Disappointed, he turned to leave. A girl with a cardboard box under her left arm and holding a small suitcase in her right hand ran through the gate and planted herself in front of the priest.

"Padre Domenico?" she said smiling while tears were streaming down her cheeks. Here she was, about seventeen, crying and smiling at the same time. She was glad to be able to speak Italian in this foreign country.

In the taxi she sat between the two men. Her cardboard box, her suitcase and her black overcoat were piled up beside the driver. Joe felt uneasy. He refrained from talking. There was something wrong here. The priest didn't seem to worry. He made small talk with the girl. Did she find it cold in Canada? Are the azaleas blooming in Calabria? How was the crop last year? She answered in monosyllables. Joe looked at her sideways. She was a pretty girl. She wore her black hair parted in the middle. It peeked from under a red fazzoletto which hugged her head. Her dress was light and summery. A gold cross hung from a chain on her breast.

Yes, she was a pleasure to look at. But who was she? Joe noticed a fine scent coming from her. It wasn't perfume but it was pleasant, almost intoxicating. She had the air of sunny Calabria about her. Joe hadn't been home for almost two decades. The close presence of this girl made him nostalgic about his roots.

Where were they going? Father Domenico had given an address to the cab driver which Joe knew to be in the Italian neighborhood. Now he said, "You will stay with Signora Pavarone until everything is arranged." Joe surmised that the arrangement he was talking about was the marriage. There must have been a mistake here, because this was not the girl he remembered from childhood. There was a slight resemblance but she probably had the features of the Calabrians. Calabrians look different from Neapolitans. When the taxi stopped in front of a neat little house with a tiny patch of a garden, they all got out. Joe paid the driver, the priest led the girl up the steps to the porch and Joe carried the luggage behind them.

Mrs. Pavarone was heavy-bosomed. On her upper lip flourished a faint moustache just fine enough not to suggest masculinity. No, she was very motherly, and the newcomer felt at ease with her. Joe unloaded the cardboard box and the suitcase at the door, and the landlady took the girl upstairs. When she came down again, she said, "Give her a few days rest. I'll take her to church on Sunday." Then she added to Joe, "That'll be three dollars a week for the room and four for meals. We'll look after the laundry and she can help with the dishes."

Joe fumbled for the money in his wallet. Suddenly he felt

he was a man with responsibilities and that gave him a certain satisfaction. It was a new feeling, a good one.

"Thank you, Signora," said the priest.

They walked the two blocks to the rectory.

"What do you think of her, Joe?"

"She's lovely, but. . ."

"Good. I meant to tell you, she's not the Alida Borghese you remember. She is Alida's daughter, Anna Frascati. Alida Borghese married Franco Frascati of Reggio long ago. She has seven children so far."

"You are playing games with me, Padre."

"Far from it, Joe. The Borgheses and particularly Signora Frascati remember you well, and they have a high opinion of you. If you want to marry Anna, everybody will be happy."

"Have they asked Anna?"

"You know perfectly well, that is for the parents to decide."

"What if she doesn't like me? What if she thinks I'm too old for her?"

"We'll see, I think she will like you. I wouldn't have taken those steps if I didn't think so. I know you, Joe. You are a good man and the Lord will give you His blessing."

"I'd want her to be happy," said Joe. He didn't sound enthusiastic, not even a little confident.

"I have been the broker in seventeen marriages between immigrants and Italian girls in the years of my parish work at the Church of the Blessed Virgin. We have now one hundred and fourteen additional members in our congregation as a result of my efforts." He laughed heartily. "I'm proud of that."

"Calabrians. . ." said Joe. He wanted to talk about their fertility but it was a tricky subject. He shunned the topic.

3

Giuseppe Fabrini had adopted the English 'Joe' as his first name after his arrival in the land of skyscrapers. He struggled, as newcomers do, between the feeling of loyalty to the home country and the desire to adapt as quickly as possible to his new environment.

Jenny was born half a year after Anna's eighteenth birthday in the apartment they had rented from Signora Pavarone on Weston Street. They both wanted to give their baby a name that would not betray her Italian ancestry. She couldn't be called a wop right away.

Joe asked Father Domenico for a list of men and women who had been sainted over the centuries. Anna and Joe huddled over the little booklet after supper. They came across an obscure Saint Geneviève from Paris. The name wasn't Italian, it wasn't a wop's name, and they found it exceptionally pretty. They practised pronouncing it the next few days. Yes, their first baby would be called Geneviève.

Joe made enough money over the next two years to build the foundation for a three-bedroomed bungalow on his lot, just west of the city limits. With his boss's permission he got the work done for a fraction of the usual price. When the lot next to him became available, he purchased it with a small downpayment.

After Maria and Sofia were born and Anna was expecting her fourth child, Mrs. Pavarone thought it was high time for the Fabrinis to move on to something bigger, and sure enough, the basement in the bungalow was ready just in time. The doctor had heard two distinct heartbeats under Anna's heart, and the great double event took place in the completely finished and comfortably furnished bottom floor of the bungalow. The roofless structure looked a little weird from the outside, and Joe started right away working on the upper rooms. Every day he worked until sunset and all Saturday. Even on Sundays, when the Lord wasn't looking, he sneaked in the odd little bit of work that didn't require loud hammering and such.

Everything had gone on with the 'Blessing of the Lord', as Father Domenico had predicted. Anna blossomed into a beautiful woman. She had learned English in night school classes, and now she was able to make reasonable conversation and to read the newspaper. Like Joe, she had had only two years of schooling at home. What they brought to the new country was not accomplishment, but the ability to accomplish. The opportunity to use their ability had been missing in the old country. Joe worked very hard and made good money with all the overtime paying time-and-a-half or even double. Anna and her five children were the pride of the community and Father Domenico smiled benignly when the family left church on Sundays. Anna would have liked to attend early mass every day but she could not afford the baby-sitter more than once a week. Her children were strong and healthy, well-dressed and impeccably clean. They were alert and eager to learn. Geneviève's English was as good as that of any toddler in the neighborhood. The last four children had received names that were equally common in both languages. Now Joe almost regretted having chosen the awkward 'Geneviève' for the first-born. Maria was Mary in English, Sofia became Sophie and Alfredo and Franco were adapted to Frank and Fred. Geneviève remained Geneviève. There was nothing like Geneviève in English. But in the street she was soon known as Jenny.

When the twins were two years old, the hammering and sawing in the bungalow above their heads was finished and the family moved in to the new quarters.

Oh, life had been so good for the Fabrinis and the future looked bright. On Christmas Eve, after a big day of parcel opening, carol singing, toys squeaking and rattling and a festive, sumptuous dinner, half Canadian and half Italian, the children soundly tucked into bed, Joe held Anna's hand and said, "We could never own a home like this in Calabria."

"You're a good man, Joe. You've worked very hard for it."

"I love you, Anna."

They sat in the gentle light of the electric candles on the Christmas tree and enjoyed the stillness. "I'll plant the lawn in the spring," Joe said.

He did not plant the lawn in the spring because on the first day after the Christmas break, his chest was crushed by the steering wheel of the truck when it rolled down the embankment to the Humber River. It toppled over three times, said The Toronto Star. Mr. Fabrini's body was pulled from the crumpled cabin of the truck which wasn't lifted out of the water until two hours after the accident.

They were looking for a drunken car driver. Mr. Wong had seen the truck swerve to avoid the car. But, in his shock, he had not registered the licence number. He had run down the embankment, then up into his grocery, totally out of breath, and told Mrs. Wong to telephone the police. Then he had run down again to the half-submerged wreck with the wheels in the air. The police arrived in minutes. He gesticulated wildly, explaining what he had seen. But he couldn't even say whether the car had been blue, black or brown, and he had no idea what make it was. He had seen it dashing from the scene on the wrong side, much too fast and swaying all the way. It had been early on Saturday morning and there were no other witnesses.

"Can't you remember anything special about the car?" asked the police inspector.

"No. . .except I got a glimpse of the dliver," Mr. Wong had trouble with his r's. "And I lemember his voice was vely hoarse. When he laced by me, he shouted 'dammit'. He seemed to wear a gleen baseball cap."

"He seemed to?"

"I'm not absolutely sure."

That was a pretty good lead but in spite of publication of this item in the paper and mention on the radio news, nobody came forward to help in the identification of the man who had caused the tragedy. Many people wear green baseball caps and even more shout 'dammit'.

4

Anna Fabrini was now sewing blouses for Teitelbaum and Company. Every Friday afternoon a young man with a station wagon collected the week's work and signed her book for thirty or forty blouses, neatly folded and carefully counted into a cardboard box. When one of the children wasn't well and needed special attention, or when she washed the windows and scrubbed the floors, or when she planted tomatoes in the garden behind the house, there were only thirty blouses or so to be picked up, but she had sewn as many as forty-four in a very good week. For one month, Teitelbaum had switched from cotton to rayon. Anna hated the slippery material. Her production lapsed to twenty-five and the money hardly kept the pasta on the table. It was now cotton again, thank goodness.

Sometimes, when her sewing machine rattled late at night, tears ran down her cheeks, even years after Joe had gone. At first she had considered going back to Calabria but, for the children's sake, she had stayed. Father Domenico had also advised her to fight it out in this country. She had a beautiful home with only a small mortgage left on it, and she owned the lot next door which she could sell at a handsome profit if she had to. But she got by with what she made and the prices for real estate were rising fast.

Jenny, at the age of seven, was finally admitted to the St. Boniface Separate School. Some time in December, her mother was called in by the Principal, Mother Theresa. Anna expected trouble because her daughter had been rejected the year before, and after she had entered school, Jenny had asked a thousand questions while she did her homework. There was probably something wrong with her. She had also shown an obsession with newspapers even before she went to school. She folded ships and funny animals out of newspaper. But the strangest thing was that she read the headlines aloud before she started cutting. Anna considered this an anomaly she had to worry about.

Jenny had never played with any of the dolls that Anna had given her on birthdays and for Christmas. They had been handed down in mint condition to Mary and Sophie. A girl not playing with dolls ! It was a disturbing thought.

Anna walked up the broad flight of stairs. The heavy carved oak door was hard to open. She walked on tip-toes over the highly polished venerable hardwood floor, past the Grade 2 classroom door. She heard the teacher's voice, loud and commanding:

"Who made you?"

The class answered in chorus, "God made me."

"Why did God make you?"

The class answered monotonously, "God made me to know Him, love Him and serve Him in this world, and be happy with Him forever in the next." Towards the end they were a little out of step with each other.

This sounded strange to Anna in English. But it still gave her a feeling of being at home, because in her school days and later in church, she had learned the same words in Italian. God was living in Canada as he was in Calabria, was there any better proof? She heard the teacher again:

"How many persons are there in God?"

"In God there are three persons, Father, Son and Holy Ghost."

Anna remembered that this particular sentence had always left her with a desire to find out exactly what this means. It was obviously the truth. There wasn't one man, woman or child in her village who didn't believe in the absolute fact of Trinity. Anna was firmly rooted in her belief. But she remembered with a smile that her only question to her teacher had been whether the Holy Ghost was a priest. The question had not been dignified with an answer. Neither had her mother attempted to explain the problem to her.

The Principal's face was pale. No trace of her hair was visible in the white frame under her black veil. She could have been twenty-five or fifty. All that showed was spotless dignity. When she started talking, her strong voice exuded natural authority.

"Mrs. Fabrini," said Mother Theresa, "I want to talk to you about Geneviève."

"I know," said Anna, "I have noticed it myself."

"Yes, she is certainly far ahead of her class. She is reading fluently, and she multiplies and divides where her classmates have difficulty adding and subtracting," said Mother Theresa. She spoke with the pride of an educator who feels at least partly responsible for such spectacular success.

Anna was taken aback. "Oh, I didn't know. She was constantly asking questions. She couldn't do her homework without asking questions. I thought she should have known her answers."

"The question is the beginning of serious study, Mrs. Fabrini. The more questions a child has the better."

"You think she is intelligent?"

"I know she is exceptionally intelligent."

"Why was she rejected last year?"

"She obviously gave no indication of her superior ability at that time, did she? Even physically she seemed to be somewhat backward."

"Oh, I'm glad to hear she's doing fine now. Joe would have been proud of her," said Anna. Silence fell over the conversation. Anna looked up at the crucifix above the Principal's desk. Her eyes were glistening. Then she said, "I'm pleased you called me in to tell me that. We have to thank the Lord for it, don't we?"

"Amen," said the nun. "But I wanted to talk to you about something else, Mrs. Fabrini." A frown appeared on her face. "It's about her social contacts. Geneviève has been seen with a boy much older than herself. I believe he's eleven or twelve."

"Ferdinand Bauers. Yes, I know, the one with the pigeons. She likes to be with him and the pigeons. She even went fishing with him in the summer."

"Don't you find it strange that your daughter should associate with a boy that age? She doesn't play with the boys and girls in this school."

"She seems to like his company. She even asked me if she could have an aquarium in the house because Ferdinand is not allowed to have one. He has very strict parents. Mrs. Pavarone has an old aquarium in her basement. She will give it to her for Christmas."

"Do you know, Mrs. Fabrini, that Mr. Bauers is an alcoholic?"

"No, I don't. I thought he had a sick liver. . .Poor man."

"I don't think the Bauers boy is the right contact for Geneviève. I took the liberty of obtaining the necessary information. He plays truant much of the time, and his academic record is poor."

"Jenny says he's a good boy, and she's enthusiastic about his knowledge of animals. It seems to have rubbed off on her," said Anna.

"That's just it, Mrs. Fabrini. Geneviève is being deflected from the right path."

"She's doing fine in school, you said."

"In almost every subject."

"Almost?"

"Brother Felix complains that she looks out of the window watching the birds in the garden. In fact, she listens to the birds more than to the Catechism. And so she might fail her religious studies."

"Oh, Jesus, Maria. . ."

"Ferdinand doesn't go to church at all. The Bauers are not Catholic. Do you see what I'm talking about?" When Anna looked puzzled, she added, "You see, don't you?"

Anna nodded. She had to go home. She had told her baby-sitter it wouldn't take more than an hour. She rose. "I'll do what I can," she said. She had the word 'domani' on her tongue. It suddenly came to her that she should add the word 'domani', but she didn't. Domani doesn't mean tomorrow even if the dictionary says so. When an Italian says domani, it means maybe tomorrow, maybe next week, maybe never, how do I know? When an Italian speaks to an Italian, there's no doubt about the meaning of tomorrow. No one presses for more precision. In this regard, Anna was an Italian.

The Principal accompanied her down the hall. Interrupting her thoughts, she said, "I'm glad you could come. We have to stand together against the evil forces in this world."

"Ferdinand is a good boy, Jenny says." Anna sounded as if she didn't quite agree with the judgement of the Principal.

Passing a Grade three classroom, they heard a man's voice:

"What are the seven deadly sins? Margaret?"

Mother Theresa held Anna back. "It's Brother Felix. He teaches Geneviève's class too." Her face under the veil showed she was happy with this teacher's work.

They heard a window being closed. A bright girl's voice answered crisply, "Pride, Covetousness, Lust, Anger, Gluttony, Envy and Sloth." This was shot out so fast, it sounded like a single word.

"Good," said Brother Felix.

Only last week, Jenny had asked her mother what Lust was. Anna had not known the answer. It had embarrassed her because of some vague indecency about the term. "I'll find out and tell you, domani. . ."

They had reached the stately entrance door.

"He's cross-eyed, unwashed and dumb," said the nun sharply. Anna was startled. It was anger she sensed in the nun's outbreak, and anger was a deadly sin. She looked into Mother Theresa's face. The dignity that had radiated from her at the beginning of the meeting was somehow diminished. Sharp lines descended from her nose to the corners of her mouth. But that could have been the bright daylight streaming through the open door.

All the way home, Anna thought about those last remarks. The Principal didn't know the boy personally. How could she hate him? No, she told herself, Mother Theresa had only Jenny's welfare at heart. She was going to talk to her daughter, domani, perhaps.

5

The goldenrod waved in the morning breeze down the embankment to the Humber River. It was one of those glorious October days when everything seemed ripe and satisfied. The first V-shaped flocks of Canada geese honked overhead, and clouds of blackbirds descended on tall maples and elms. Their noisy chatter filled the air. Ferdinand clapped his hands like a pistol shot, cutting off the birds' noise. With a flurry they whirled up and around, only to settle down again a minute later, resuming their palaver.

"They're getting ready to go south," said Ferdinand, leading the way back to the road. He worked himself up the embankment, pushing the goldenrod aside to let Jenny follow.

"Why don't pigeons go south?" asked the girl.

"They're tame. They have forgotten where south is. I feed them all winter. Why should they go south?"

"How do geese know where south is?"

"They're born that way."

"That means God made them that way."

"Maybe."

"Not maybe, Ferdinand, He did."

"If you know, why did you ask me?"

"My Mom says you don't believe in God, Ferdinand."

"How do I know? I don't know whether I believe in God. You know better, because you go to St. Boniface. I'm only in public school," Ferdinand said sarcastically. "But what does your mother care whether I believe in God or not?"

"She cares. Mothers care."

Ferdinand was now in Grade five. He had improved considerably in his school work. He was passing, if barely, in all subjects and he was almost excelling in science. He wasn't playing truant any more, well, rarely. He spent a lot of time with Jenny after school and on Sundays. His classmates said he was the only boy in Grade five to go steady. But only with a little kid from St. Boniface, they added with a grin. It was the little kid from St. Boniface who now heard snide remarks about the pagan boy with whom she had been seen coming from the river with a fishing rod in her hand. The only person who did not show any indignation or derision about being with Ferdinand was Mrs. Fabrini. Since Ferdinand had shown Jenny how to set up the aquarium on the kitchen counter in the Fabrinis' bungalow, she had invited the boy for a snack several times. She ignored Mother Theresa's warning but she had not felt at ease about letting her daughter play with a boy who was so totally unsuited as a companion. She had confessed her sin to Father Domenico in the confession booth. He forgave her, but he suggested she should find a girl of the proper age at St. Boniface to play with Jenny. Anna felt better as she always did after confession, and everything remained as it was.

Jenny had been easily promoted to second and third Grade with only a mild rebuke in her report card about her bare passing mark in Brother Felix's course in Catechism. "Geneviève has the ability to do better," it said.

On Monday morning, her class went across the street to the Church of the Blessed Virgin for confession. When it was her turn, Jenny entered the confession booth. Father Domenico opened the partitioning window, but he was hidden from Jenny by a curtain. As she had learned in Brother Felix's class she declaimed, "Bless me, Father, for I have sinned. I confess to Almighty God and to you, Father, that I have spent all Saturday with Ferdinand."

"Who is Ferdinand?" said the voice through the screen.

"Ferdinand Bauers. He's my friend."

"What did you do when you were with the boy?"

"Fishing."

"Nothing wrong with fishing."

"Ferdinand is a pagan."

"That's dangerous. Better drop him. Play with other children. Anything else?"

"May I ask you a question, Father?"

"Certainly."

"Is it a sin to tear pages out of a cookbook?"

"Why did you do such a thing?"

"I wanted to fold little animals and boxes and things. The paper is good for folding things."

"How did your mother feel about that?"

"She said it's a sin to tear up such a good book. And when I told Ferdinand about that, he said I had broken the eleventh commandment."

"There is no eleventh commandment."

"That's what I told him. But he told me the eleventh commandment says, Don't tear pages out of your mother's cookbook."

Jenny wasn't sure whether she heard a suppressed chuckle through the window. Father Domenico wouldn't laugh at her, would he? Not in confession, not in the Church of the Blessed Virgin.

Then she heard him say, "Play with girls, Geneviève."

"I will, Father." She didn't say domani. She wouldn't have said tomorrow either.

"For penance, say three Hail Marys."

"Yes, Father."

In the evening, she knelt down in her bedroom, facing the crucifix. She whispered,

"Hail Mary, full of Grace, the Lord is with thee.
Blessed art thou amongst women and
blessed is the fruit of thy womb, Jesus.
Holy Mary, Mother of God, pray for us sinners.
Amen."

Then she repeated the prayer. During the third Hail Mary, she listened to her two sisters' regular breathing in their double bed. Then she turned off the light and slipped under the cover. She had her own bed now, being a big girl. Ferdinand didn't have to confess. If he sins, he goes unpunished. It wasn't fair. But poor Ferdinand. He'll never get rid of his sins.

6

The only reason why Tim Bauers tolerated the pigeons in the attic was that he had started the bird-breeding business himself. That was after he and Mathilda had been married and moved into this house. Ferdinand was introduced to the hobby as a little boy, and had soon surpassed his father in mastering the tricks of feeding, breeding and dealing with pigeons. Then Tim Bauers had slid into drunkenness and had neglected to look after the birds. For the last four years, it had been the boy who felt responsible for them. Even when Bauers was sober, he didn't climb up to the attic any more, and Ferdinand had given up reporting to his father about his work and his plans upstairs.

Ferdinand and his mother dreaded the moment when the burly six-foot-two would stagger through the door and slump on the sofa to fall into his dreadful, snoring stupor. It took him twelve hours to come out of it. But when he did, Mathilda and Ferdinand stayed out of his way because he was given to violence not only when he was drunk but also during his hangover mood. Mathilda had thought many a time over the years of packing up and leaving with Ferdinand, but she was afraid of the uncertain consequences of such a step. She couldn't make up her mind.

She knew this sort of family life would leave permanent scars on her boy who had withdrawn into his pigeon attic. That weighed heavily on her soul. But she stayed and kept suffering. Little did she know that her life would change without her initiative.

It was Friday and the parking lot at Dudston's Tavern was filled. Cars began to spill over into the neigboring streets. Bauers parked around the corner. He felt strong. His pocket was bulging from the manila envelope with a week's wages in it from Wilson's Lumberyard. A man feels strong with well-earned cash in his pocket. His brick-red base-ball cap was boldly cocked on his blond curls. He was a Phillies fan. It never occurred to him to go home from work and lay the envelope on the kitchen table. Then, after supper, he could have taken a two dollar bill or even a five, walked the few hundred feet over to Dudston's and had a good time playing cards. Mathilda wouldn't have minded at all.

Love was dead in the Bauers' home. Mathilda was thirty-five but with her greying hair and tired eyes she looked more like fifty. She made only half as much money as her husband but at least her wages came in regularly and the bills were paid.

Harvey Dudston was not only a successful businessman, he also got along well with all sorts of people. He had no rough edges, not physically and not in his personality. But he could be firm when necessary. Sometimes he told a customer that he had had enough for the day, and he made it clear that this was his final word. He didn't want anybody passing out and lying under the table. Only once did he have to call the police to remove Tim Bauers because he threatened his waiter with a knife. But when the police arrived, things had quieted down again. The knife was in the cash register and no charges were laid. Bauers had behaved from then on. He never asked for the knife and neither Mr. Dudston nor the waiter had ever talked about the incident to anyone.

The Tavern was well-known for serving good liquor and in good measure, but its main asset was something no one could describe -atmosphere. And Harvey Dudston was the reason for that. Many of his customers came all the way from Markham and Scarborough. On Fridays, some steelworkers drove the forty miles from Hamilton with their pay envelopes, and that was just fine with Harvey. It was strictly cash at Dudston's with no exceptions. So bookkeeping was a cinch, and Mrs. Dudston was good at it.

Bauers was playing cards at the corner table with three guys from Hamilton. The light from the lamp over the table barely penetrated the cigarette smoke. Every now and then laughter shook the room and one of the players started to deal again. Before the new play began, they ordered more whisky and another chaser. All the other tables were occupied too, and there was a tight string of customers sitting on the stools at the bar. Others were standing behind them, glass in hand. The Tavern was filled with chatter which was highlighted by the occasional hollering from the corner.

It was an excellent day for Harvey Dudston.

Several people had poked their heads through the door, found it too crowded and left. But one man ploughed his way through the masses all the way to the counter where Dudston was ringing the cash register. It was the grocer, Mr. Wong. Mr. Wong didn't seem to have a given name. At least nobody knew it. There was something like respect in addressing him only as Mr. Wong and, since he himself called everybody by his family name, there was a distinct but polite barrier between the grocer and his customers. Of course he knew that behind his back, some people referred to him as the Chink. Some of them were sitting right here in Dudston's Tavern.

Talking between the shoulders of two customers, he addressed the owner, "Mr. Dudston?"

"Hello, Mr. Wong. Never seen you in here. What can I do for you? Whisky? Beer?"

"No thanks, I'm in a hully." He waved a ten dollar bill in front of Harvey Dudston. "Can you give me change?"

"Sure, Mr. Wong. How would you like it?"

"Thlee dollars in coins, please, the lest any way you like."

The cash register rang and Mr. Wong pocketed the change.

"Harvey," shouted Tim Bauers turning around from his card table. "We're dry again, dammit !"

"Coming," said Dudston. He directed the waiter to the table in the corner.

Mr. Wong was still standing there, his mouth open. He looked from the card table to Dudston and back to the table.

"Can I do anything else for you, Mr. Wong?" said Harvey.

Mr. Wong closed his mouth, swallowed and said, "Isn't that Mr. Bauers over there?"

"Yeah, the one with the red cap."

"The gleen cap," said Mr. Wong.

"The red cap, the Phillies cap, Mr. Wong."

"The way he turned his head and shouted 'dammit'. . .like thlough the car window. And it was the same hoarse voice. I heard him many times in my dleams."

Dudston was busy with the cash register. Of course, the cash register was the hub of all the activities in here. It was ringing constantly today, and that was a sweet sound. When he looked up he saw Mr. Wong slowly working his way through the chairs steadily towards the corner from where the 'dammit' had come.

"Can I talk to you?" he said to Tim Bauers.

Bauers looked up into the expressionless face of the grocer. "Can't you see I'm playing cards?" He took a long drink from his beer, wiped his mouth with the back of his hand, belched contentedly and slammed a card on the table, shouting "Ten of spades."

"Mr. Fablini is dead," said Mr. Wong, ice-cold and almost plaintively.

Tim Bauers jumped to his feet. His chair fell over backwards. He grabbed Mr. Wong by the throat. "Hey, Chink," he shouted, "Shuddup or I'll make you!" He towered over little Mr. Wong, shaking him like a dog shakes a rabbit. At that moment, the waiter slammed his tray on the nearest table and jumped on the aggressor from behind, trying to restrain him. This was the signal for the other three card players to join the battle. There was a wild mêlée on the floor.

From behind his counter, Mr. Dudston saw what was coming. He phoned the police.

It was hard to say who was the first to break off a chair leg. The fact was that the whole tavern was now full of men swinging fists and furniture. Tables and chairs crashed down hard, spilling drinks and ashtrays, and a howling mass of half-drunk customers was writhing, punching and wrestling on the floor.

Two women were screaming at the door. Their men were fighting somewhere in the mass of legs and arms.

The siren of a police car was heard outside. People scrambled up. Dishevelled men replaced tables and chairs, and when the two policemen entered, Bauers and the three men from Hamilton pretended they were playing cards.

The women at the door swamped the officers with voluntary information. Mrs. Dudston carried the cash register back from the kitchen where she had deposited it during the fight. Some people wanted to leave.

"Everybody stays here," said the officer. "Who's that?" He pointed to a little bundle of a man among the debris on the floor.

"It's Mr. Wong," said the waiter. He rushed to the grocer and turned him over. "Oh, no. . ." he said whimpering. Then he cried aloud once more, "Oh, no !"

At the hearing, it was established by the coroner that Mr. Wong had died of a broken neck and it was assumed so far that Tim Bauers was responsible for his death. But it was also clearly established that the grocer had provoked him by interrupting his peaceful conversation with three men from Hamilton. He had said something to him that must have been quite offensive. The steelworkers testified that they had not understood what Mr. Wong had said, his heavy accent and all that.

But then Mr. Dudston testified that Mr. Wong had been startled when Mr. Bauers had shouted 'dammit'.

The prosecutor then approached the bench and conferred with the judge.

"The Court is adjourned," announced the judge abruptly. The crowd filed out of the courtroom, disappointed. Why an adjournment?

At the next hearing, the connection was made to the driver of the car that had forced Mr. Fabrini's truck off the road and down the embankment.

The baseball cap came up, but the judge disallowed that argument because the testimony of Mr. Wong at the time of Mr. Fabrini's death had clearly been that the cap had been green, not the familiar red of the Phillies cap that Tim Bauers had always worn. As far as the voice heard from the fleeing car was concerned and its comparison with that of Bauers at the card table in the noisy tavern, "Well, it was a little far-fetched, don't you agree," said the defense lawyer.

Tim Bauers listened to all that with great intensity. When he was called to the stand, he testified that Wong accused him of owing the grocer forty-six dollars, and that he better quit wasting money sitting around the tavern.

"Did you owe him money?" questioned the defense lawyer.

"No, I did not. I owed absolutely nothing to Mr. Wong."

"Your Honor, may I submit an excerpt from Mr. Wong's store record?"

The lawyer placed a sheet of paper before the judge. "It clearly proves that the last month's bill at the grocery was duly paid by Mrs. Bauers," he said loud enough for everyone to hear.

Tim Bauers was winning.

He had been provoked by a liar. His reaction had been natural. Mr. Wong's death was accidental. The three witnesses from the steel factory in Hamilton looked straight ahead.

At that point, a police officer in uniform asked to be heard. He told the Court that as one of the investigating policemen he had taken the driver's license from Mr. Wong's pocket as he lay on the floor, and that he had read a remark on it which he clearly remembered, because it was rather unusual and hand-written. It stated under 'handicaps' that Mr. Wong was color-blind.

A murmur swelled up in the audience.

"Order !" said the judge. When the room was quiet, he asked the coroner, why a color-blind person was allowed to hold a driver's license.

"Most colorblind people cannot distinguish between red and green," testified the doctor. "They are no traffic hazard because the red light is on top and the green on the bottom of a traffic light. A color-blind person goes by position of the light rather than by its color."

Now one of the Hamilton guys conferred with the defense lawyer. He wanted to change his testimony. The lawyer argued with him in a subdued voice. Then he approached the bench and whispered something to the judge. The Hamilton man was asked to step forward. He reported what Mr. Wong had said about Mr. Fabrini before Mr. Bauers grabbed him. "I had to get that off my chest," he said.

The spectators broke into a turmoil. Old memories came back of the terrible accident two years ago, and of Mr. Wong's unsubstantiated talk about the drunken driver swaying along Linden Street. The judge banged his gavel.

It was the first offence for Mr. Bauers, the first and the second at the same time. Threatening someone with an open knife would have been another, but it didn't come up. Neither did prolonged wife-abuse or cruelty to a child. These wouldn't have been considered serious crimes and, of course, there was no complaint. But Tim Bauers' victims would have been important character witnesses. After all, two men had died because of him.

As it was, Tim Bauers was put away for five years. He was handcuffed and led out of the courtroom.

Mathilda was crying but her husband didn't look at her.

When she came home, she hugged her son and the two cried silently together. Ferdinand hadn't wanted to attend the trial.

He sensed that his father had been convicted. He stayed home from school for three days, and his mother tolerated it. She slowly told him the awful facts, a little at a time. When she came to the Fabrini disaster, Ferdinand took off his glasses, rubbed his eyes and said, "Jenny."

He finally pulled himself together and went to school. From his seat, he saw newspaper clippings on the bulletin board showing his father handcuffed between two cops, and a fat front page headline saying, "Mystery of the Green Baseball Cap Solved." Another clipping showed a family picture of Mr. Wong and two teenage girls standing and Mrs. Wong sitting on a chair in front of them holding a baby boy on her lap. They were all smiling happily. Another headline said "Bauers Responsible for Death of Two Toronto Citizens."

The class was frightfully silent. Ferdinand had not seen any newspapers after the trial and his mother had not felt like turning on the radio either. He was now all raw and sore inside. Mr. Malcolm entered the room. When he saw Ferdinand, he silently went to the board, ripped off the newspaper clippings and threw them in the waste can.

It was a fruitless lesson. The air was bristling with painful thoughts. Mr. Malcolm didn't ask Ferdinand any questions. The bell rang and they filed out into the yard. Ferdinand stood near the garbage can. He started eating the sandwich his mother had packed for him, but he couldn't get it down. Were all three hundred kids staring at him? Or was it only his imagination? He pushed his glasses up his nose, threw his sandwich in the can, shoved his hands into his pockets and slowly walked alongside the six foot chain link fence, kicking a stone forward with his foot. He felt tears trickling from under his glasses.

Normally, there were cliques of students playing ball or tag. Now they were conspicuously quiet and standing about in groups. Would the recess never end?

Finally the bell rang, and the building sucked in three hundred boys and girls through the door. Tom Dudston held it open on one side, Mr. Malcolm on the other. Ferdinand was the last to enter. The teacher put his arm around the boy's shoulder. Not a word was spoken as they walked up the terrazzo steps. Then, on his other side, Ferdinand heard Tom Dudston say, "Hey, Ferdinand, I'd like to see your pigeons some time. Will you let me?"

Ferdinand's face was contorted with suppressed grief. He couldn't speak but he nodded. Mr. Malcolm had to teach another class and the two boys entered their classroom together.

7

School was a breeze for Jenny. She still asked countless questions and her teachers as a whole appreciated a lively, inquisitive mind. Her mother at home had long ago stopped worrying about a possible mental problem. She started to enjoy finding the answers with her. St. Boniface educated Anna through her daughters. All three girls were doing well in school. If the twin boys hadn't been so mischievous, they would have contributed to the reputation of the Fabrinis as bright and brainy. Their academic record was suffering as a result of their pranks and laziness, but their potential wasn't questioned either. They needed their father, said Anna.

Mother Theresa had been right when she said that the question is the beginning of serious study. It was gratifying for a mother to feel that the educational philosophy of the school fitted her own vague ideas about life, and it was certainly easy for her to see the success of the educational process when her eldest daughter came home again and again with the best marks in the class. These were tangible results. Numbers in black on white; what could be more convincing? And Jenny enjoyed school. Anna would have preferred having a good education herself. Maybe when the children were a little older, she could take evening classes.

There was only this Brother Felix. He had felt personally offended when Jenny wanted to know what a womb was. She had said a few thousand Hail Marys over the years, one rosary with fifty-three beads for each prayer every day, recited while kneeling on the classroom floor. Brother Felix was kneeling with them, except when he left the classroom. Jenny didn't like him to leave because as soon as he did, some boys and girls started giggling and talking, and twirling their rosaries about. Didn't they know this was a sin?

There were more rosaries at home with Mother, Mary, Sophie, Frank and Fred kneeling on the dining room carpet every one of the forty days of Lent and many times outside Lent too. On Easter Sunday, however, there was jubilation and joyful celebration in Holy Mass and no Hail Marys! Jenny always looked forward to Easter Sunday in the Church of the Blessed Virgin. And then, of course, the children hunted for Easter eggs in the garden. Unfortunately, the eggs and the bunnies were more exciting to the boys than Holy Mass.

Now it suddenly dawned on Jenny that she had bypassed the meaning of 'Blessed is the fruit of thy womb' every time she recited the strange medieval language that had scared her off the content. It was hard enough to dangle between Italian and English. And then there was Latin which was even stranger. It was older than medieval English, Anna explained. Father Domenico spoke it in church and Jenny, washing the dishes in the kitchen, chanted it with delight as she had heard it at Holy Mass so many times.

"Agnus Dei, qui tollis peccata mundi" or

"Dominus vobiscum."

Jenny had no idea what it meant. But the sound of the words was reassuring and awe-inspiring, and the organ music touched Heaven, making a shiver run down her spine.

Jenny was a member of the school choir like everybody else,

and when she came home from a rehearsal, her mother heard her sing all day "Et cum spiritu tuo. . ."

She recited the whole Latin Mass word for word. She only regretted that she couldn't be an altar boy. She envied her little brothers. One day they would be able to give the responses to the priest at the Holy Mass. Oh, to be a boy !

But Brother Felix's class was so awfully boring. Jenny asked him what the 'fruit of the womb' meant, and he simply answered, "It means Jesus." When Jenny didn't look satisfied, he added, tapping his finger on the Catechism, "It says it right here, can't you see? Blessed is the fruit of thy womb, Jesus." Why did he turn so red in his face? For further clarification, he added, "You're only in Grade six. Wait till you come to Grade seven. You'll learn that 'Jesus' is an apposition to 'the fruit of thy womb'. An apposition after a comma simply is the same thing as the thing before the comma. Don't be so impatient, just wait and see. You will get grammar next year."

Religious Studies was Jenny's poorest subject. Expressed in numbers she was only worth fifty-six per cent. She just had to live with that.

Overall it had been a blessing to be born in Canada. In Calabria, at her age she would now be carrying a heavy jug of water on her head from the well to her home six times a day, as Anna had done, and beating the linen on the rocks in the creek and sweeping the donkey manure dropped in front of the house, pushing it on to a shovel and carrying it into the garden at the back of the house to make the cetrioli grow. She was about the right age to do such chores and she could by now make a good minestrone and slaughter a chicken for supper.

Anna was glad she had come to Canada. Of course, she would like to visit home one day and see her brothers and sisters, twelve of them by now, but as her own children grew up and spoke English better than she did, her roots on this continent became stronger every year.

8

The humiliation was wearing Ferdinand down. If it hadn't been for Tom Dudston, he would have broken under the burden of having his father in the Don Jail. The two boys built a pigeon stable in the attic over the Dudstons' beautiful apartment, and Tom taught Ferdinand to play chess. Sometimes they heard a drunkard's wobbly singing as he emerged from the tavern below into the street. A faint odor of stale beer and cigarette smoke and people's sweat seeped from the tavern up into every room of the building, even to the attic.

Ferdinand wanted to give Tom a few birds to start a brood, but Mrs. Dudston insisted that he take a dollar in payment.

"No, Mrs. Dudston," said Ferdinand, "I have a plan and I want Tom to carry it out. You see, I had this new sport, a blue and white male that appeared out of nothing in my flock. I think we can breed the new kind again."

"It was a beautiful color, Mom," said Tom, "with white wings."

"But it died," said Ferdinand. He didn't tell her about his furious autopsy on that terrible day and the way he scared little Jenny out of the attic. It had been the worst day of his life.

"Now see, Mom," said Tom, "Ferdinand went through his notes and he picked all the relatives of that blue-and-white and he separated them from the others."

"I know there's no other blue-and-white like that in the

whole world," said Ferdinand, aglow with fervour. "I've read all there is to read about pigeons. It must have been a mutation."

"What's a mutation?" said Tom's mother. Was she becoming interested? So Ferdinand and his friend explained their breeding plan to Mrs. Dudston who was more impressed by the enthusiasm of the boys than by their reasoning.

"If Tom breeds only this line, we may get another double-recessive," said Ferdinand.

"That's enough," said Mrs. Dudston.

"So you see, I'm not selling birds to Tommy. We're partners in a breeding project."

"All right, all right," said Mrs. Dudston, leaving with a smile. She thought it better for boys to pursue a hobby like that than to smoke behind a barn or steal chocolate bars at Wong's grocery.

One day, Mrs. Dudston came up to the attic waving a newspaper. "Ferdinand," she said, "you should get your eye fixed."

"I was born that way, Mrs. Dudston."

"I know, but there's a doctor at the General Hospital who can fix it. It says so right here in the Star."

"I can see all right. It doesn't bother me."

"Sure, it's all right. But let's face it. You're a good looking boy, and you would look even better, wouldn't you?"

Ferdinand smiled. After his mother left, Tom said, "Why fix it? You got used to it, as you said. We all got used to it. You look fine as is."

In spite of a thorough redecoration, Dudston's Tavern had lost many customers. At first, the waiter avoided walking over the spot on the floor where he had looked into the face of the dead man. It was now three years later, but the Tavern was still haunted, said some people. The younger men, of course, were not drinking at Dudston's at all because they were now fighting Hitler in Europe. The chatter around the tables and at the bar was mainly about the ups and downs of the war.

Ferdinand stubbornly avoided meeting Jenny. He didn't want her to be seen with the son of her father's murderer. Manslaugher wasn't murder but the community had referred to Tim Bauers as their first murderer, and every time people walked along the Humber River and looked down the steep bank, they thought of the man with the baseball cap and the husky voice who was now in jail on the other side of town.

It was an eerie feeling to have a murderer in your midst. And his son, well, you never know.

Anna didn't encourage her daughter to seek contact with Ferdinand but she overheard her praying for the boy.

Now some grass had grown over the matter. But in a few years Bauers was to be released. What then?

One evening Mrs. Dudston came over to see Mrs. Bauers. She offered to bear the cost of the operation on Ferdinand's eye. "It's only three hundred dollars," she said. Mathilda Bauers didn't think she could accept that kind of gift. She herself couldn't afford such a sum at all, but thanked her all the same.

"Ferdinand has been a good friend of Tommy's for three years, and we would like to do this for you," said Mrs. Dudston.

So, after school closed in June, Ferdinand's left eye was straightened at the General Hospital. For two weeks, Mathilda made the long trip to the hospital every day in her lunch time to hold her son's hand. When he finally came home, he looked into the mirror in the hall, grinned and said, "Oh, boy !" He didn't have to wear glasses any more either.

His voice was changing too, and on his chin and upper lip some fluffy stuff appeared. Well, you wouldn't say he needed shaving, but these were certainly signs of impending manhood.

In September, he entered Grade eight and plunged with renewed zeal into his studies. His report card at Christmas showed spectacular improvement. In science, he was ahead of his class, and his overall position was number four. Mr. Malcolm congratulated him in the hall on his achievement. He said Ferdinand was the talk of the day in the staffroom. But it was Tom Dudston's handshake that made him proud. Tom had been the undisputed number one in the class all these years and he had a genuine appreciation for his friend's success.

Mathilda Bauers had visited her husband only a few times. The conversation had been icy each time. She was considering a divorce. Ferdinand had lost his father years before he went to prison. If he were to give a specific time when the break occurred, he would have named the day when his father shattered his glasses while Jenny was waiting with the dead pigeon in the attic.

They had a little Christmas tree and Mathilda had cooked the goose she had received as a bonus from Austen and Blimp. They had red cabbage with it and roasted potatoes. Afterwards, she served an excellent apple pie. Mother and son couldn't bring themselves to sing a Christmas carol, but they listened to the radio. Ferdinand presented his mother with a lamp he had made. He had whittled the stem from finely grained pinewood. Two pigeons carved from white lindenwood were glued on the foot, and the shade was made of warm, translucent parchment. He plugged the lamp into the wall socket. When it lit up, his mother embraced him happily. She had given him a white shirt and a tie with red and black stripes. A choir on the radio sang Silent Night.

Suddenly the house bell rang. "It's Tom," said Ferdinand, "I knew he might come over." He went to the door. It wasn't Tom.

There stood his father, in striped prison garb. A maroon pick-up truck was parked at the curb with its engine running. Ferdinand saw a man sitting at the wheel. It was snowing, and the street was deserted. Bauers looked cautiously left and right. He pushed his son aside, giving him a quick glance, "Hey, Ferdi, you've grown." It sounded artificial. He had never called his son Ferdi, not even when he was a baby. He was in a hurry. He ran through the hall. Mathilda had come out of the living-room. She grasped her face with her hands and pressed herself back to the wall. The fugitive ripped the telephone wire out of its socket and ran upstairs. He had no words for his wife. They heard him rummaging through the closet and the drawers. Then he came down with his good suit on and a pile of other clothes over his arms.

"Give me some money, quick," he demanded. His wife went to the kitchen and he followed her. With trembling hands, she took her wallet out of her purse and opened it, but he grabbed the whole wallet and ran out of the house, past his son. "Merry Christmas," he said hoarsely. He slammed the door. Mother and son heard the car wheels spinning in the snow for a while. The engine revved up to high pitch, and then its noise diminished into the winter night.

Ten terrible minutes later the doorbell rang. It was the police. They had tried to phone, they said. They had come too late. The rest of Christmas Eve was spent with questions asked by the officers and Mathilda giving her sobbing answers. Ferdinand described the pick-up truck. While he talked, he felt a strange hesitation. Was he talking about his own father? Talking to those who wanted him back behind bars?

One of the officers rolled the Don Jail uniform he had found on the bedroom floor, into a bundle. Then they left.

The radio choir sang jubilantly:

"Deck the Hall with Bows and Holly,

Trala lala la, lala lala,

'Tis the Season to be Jolly,

Trala lala la, lala lala."

Ferdinand turned it off. "Good night, Mom," he said, going up to his room. Tender warmth came through his breaking teenage voice.

"Good night, my boy. The lamp is beautiful."

Between Christmas and New Year, the Star was screaming out the news of the two convicts' escape. The other two dailies joined in the journalistic feast. Mathilda's description of the clothes taken from her house was prominently reported. The get-away truck had been found in Hamilton, but there the trail stopped and speculation took over. Maybe they had crossed the border. It was thought the convicts might be armed, and caution was urged. Then followed an attack on the prison authorities under whose noses the escape had occurred. An editorial urged that Christmas celebrations in jail be abolished.

This time, Ferdinand did not miss school. He faced the class bravely. No paper clippings were brought to school by anyone.

Ferdinand had established himself as a conscientious and hard-working student, and he had the sympathy of his school mates. Above all, he was admired for his work with pigeons. He had brought honors to the school when the Star had printed his and Tom's picture and an article about their breeding experiments. Mr. Malcolm had asked the reporter to interview the boys. Ferdinand had discovered that hard work in school was the best cure for the unhappiness his father had caused in the home. He plunged into it with determination. In mathematics, he rivalled Tom, and he moved ahead in other subjects as well, so that in June his report card listed him second in his class. The office had stamped "Transferred to Humber Collegiate" under it, and the Principal wrote in his old-fashioned, utterly correct handwriting beside his signature, "Congratulations, Ferdinand."

9

Mother Theresa sent a note home with Jenny, asking her mother to see her, if possible, Monday morning at ten in her office. Would she please confirm this appointment through Geneviève. The school continued to use the name of the Parisian saint that Joe and Anna had chosen for their first-born.

Anna was lucky. There was no timetable for completion of the blouses and skirts and tunics she was sewing for Teitelbaum. Time was money to her. Yet she felt cheerful. She had no apprehension about Jenny or any aspect of her work. Her daughter had even improved her mark in Brother Felix's Catechism class up to sixty per cent. It was still the lowest mark on her report card. Only the twins had some marks lower than that.

When Anna entered the Principal's office she was astonished to find Father Domenico sitting there. His hair was now white but otherwise he hadn't changed much since the day she had addressed him in Italian at Union Station, freshly imported from Calabria for marriage and almost crushed under all the new impressions of a foreign country. The priest gave her his usual kindly smile. "Hello, Anna," he said warmly.

"Have a seat, Mrs. Fabrini," said Mother Theresa. If she had changed in the seven years that Anna knew her, that change was not discernible. Her grey eyes surveyed the visitor with benign authority.

"Father Domenico has kindly consented to take part in our conversation," said the Principal.

"How are you getting along with your five children?" asked the priest. "Are you still working for Teitelbaum's?"

"Yes, thank you. Everything is going well, Father. The three girls are helping a lot in the house."

"That's good. You're doing a fine job, Anna."

"Mrs. Fabrini, we would like to talk to you about Geneviève," said the Principal. The Fabrinis had never learned to pronounce that name properly. Mother Theresa said it in painfully correct French.

"I gather she's doing fine," said Anna.

"More than that, Mrs. Fabrini. We feel Geneviève should go to high school next year."

"But Jenny is only in Grade seven."

"Well, you may have noticed she has taken the whole Grade eight program in Arithmetic and English during the last semester."

Anna had not noticed it. She felt a little guilty.

"All her teachers have recommended that she be promoted to Grade nine, rather than Grade eight. We are convinced she'll have no difficulty skipping one Grade now." The Principal was obviously pleased to report her school's success with this student.

"That's amazing. Remember, you rejected her in Grade one? You thought she should wait another year before going to school."

Mother Theresa threw an uncomfortable glance at the priest.

"Children often develop in jumps," said Father Domenico.

"Now she can catch up," the nun added. "She'll be of average age when she enters Grade nine."

"Well, that's something I didn't expect. Jenny has not mentioned the possibility to me either. But she was talking about the Humber Collegiate and the science laboratories there. She wants to study science, she told me."

"You're not considering sending Geneviève to a collegiate, Mrs. Fabrini, are you?"

"Humber Collegiate is a good school, don't you think?"

Mother Theresa sat up when the name of the collegiate was mentioned. "It is not a Catholic school, Mrs. Fabrini."

Now the priest seemed ill at ease. "Anna," he said, "you are the mother, and you have every right to send your children to any school you like. Certainly there's nothing wrong with the collegiate. But. . ."

Mother Theresa interrupted him. "We owe it to the Lord to inculcate an understanding of His word throughout school. That is not done in the other schools. The nourishment of the soul is missing. We don't have to tell you, Mrs. Fabrini, that we want Geneviève to be happy in the Lord. You yourself have been raised in the lap of the Church. You have been faithful all your life. . ." She looked to the priest again.

"Joe would have wanted Jenny to go to the Abbey," said Father Domenico.

"The Abbey?" said Anna. "Joe would have sent her to a good school where she can learn important things. Jenny wants to go into science, and Joe would have let her do that. He always said that he hoped his children would learn a lot more about sciences than he ever did. He said he felt left out in the modern world. That's what he said. I remember it so well."

"Oh, but Mrs. Fabrini, the Abbey teaches the sciences. We know how important science has become. But more important than any subject is the basic philosophy of a school. There is no basic philosophy at the collegiate, none whatsoever. The Church provides a central philosophy at the Abbey. You want your children to be raised in the riches that the Lord provides, don't you?"

"Yes, I do. But. . ."

"And in the certainty of the life hereafter?"

"Yes, of course. . ."

"Now then, the Abbey is the school for your family," said the Principal. How could one not agree with that kind of argument?

"Joe would have chosen the Abbey," said the priest.

"But Jenny told me the Abbey has no laboratories."

"There's a lot of science work you can do without laboratories," said Mother Theresa.

"They never dissect a rabbit or a frog," said Anna.

"Oh my God!" The Principal leant back in her chair and closed her eyes in disgust. "I thought that was all in the past by now." An embarrassed silence crept into the room. Father Domenico cleared his throat. "Does Jenny still see this. . .what's his name?"

"The Bauers boy," Mother Theresa said resignedly, her eyes still closed as if suffering from a headache.

"Oh, Ferdinand? No, she doesn't. I told her not to." She didn't say that Ferdinand had avoided Jenny. She was really quite satisfied that the contact had discontinued. She said, "By the way, did you read the article about his breeding experiments with pigeons? He goes to Humber Collegiate too. Jenny says he's an excellent science student."

"No, I didn't read the article," said Mother Theresa irritably, "and I don't know whether I care after what happened in the Dudston Tavern."

Her daughter had given her nothing but joy. Anna wouldn't want to hurt her. She was fourteen now, and when mother and daughter walked downtown, Anna noticed young men looking at Jenny more than casually. Jenny was not aware of that, but her mother saw it with a mixture of pleasure and worry.

Jenny was now a little taller than her mother. Her slender neck carried an intelligent and feminine head with grace and simple nobility. Her dark hair still framed her face in loose ringlets. Her lips were full and fresh. Her large dark eyes looked innocently out from under long lashes at the world. She wore a skirt and a blouse as she always did. Her tight little breasts and her unconsciously feminine gait made her attractive to passers-by.

Oh, Anna would protect her innocence with everything she had at her disposal.

Did she now have to protect her from the study of science?

Anna left St. Boniface with mixed feelings. She loved her Church and she loved Jenny. Why should her two loves be incompatible?

"Who told you about the laboratories at Humber Collegiate?" she asked Jenny after school.

"The Grade eights are talking about it. Some have already enrolled there. I'm going there too, am I not, next year?"

"Mother Theresa says you will skip Grade eight. So you can go to high school this year."

"Oh boy!" Jenny jumped up and down. She was still the little elementary school girl. "I'm skipping a whole class? You know what they are doing in Grade nine? They're breeding mice to show Mendel's ratios."

"Show what?"

"Wait a minute Mom." She ran into her bedroom and came

back with a book on popular genetics. "See here," she said with enthusiasm, leafing through it.

"Where did you get that book?"

"I borrowed it from the library." Then she told her mother about the Austrian monk Brother Gregor Mendel who had discovered such miraculous ways in which plants and animals receive their traits from father and mother.

"Oh, Jenny, Jenny," Anna exclaimed, "have you talked about it with your teachers?"

"They don't know about Mendel. I asked them. I had to go to the public library to learn about him."

"Why did you want to learn about the monk?"

"When Ferdinand had his picture in the Star, the article said he was studying Mendelian inheritance. I told you about his blue-and-white pigeon that died. Well, I think there's nothing more interesting than genetics." She ran back to her room. Anna was deflated. How could that happen right under her eyes? Was she too busy with her sewing machine and with all the decisions she had to make every day in a household with six people? Had she neglected her children?

Jenny came back with more books under her arm. "They don't have books on genetics at St. Boniface," she complained. There was an X-ray picture of a human fetus on the cover of one of them. "Look here, Mom," she said. "This is how I looked when I was in your womb. I'm the fruit of your womb."

Anna was shocked and embarrassed. "You take those books back to the library," she said, "and see Father Domenico about it. When is the next confession?"

"It's not a sin to read about Nature, Mom, is it?"

"I don't know, ask the priest."

"It can't be a sin, Mom. God made Nature and everything in

it."

"Maybe you're right, but promise me to take those books back and see Father Domenico."

"Okay, Mom."

It was getting dark when Mrs. Pavarone emerged from St. Boniface Separate School. She had an expression of grim determination on her broad face. She heaved her corpulent body with some difficulty into her green Austin, slammed the door and drove the short distance to the Fabrinis' bungalow. She had visited Anna on and off over the years. After Joe died she often brought little gifts for the children, ten-cent Woolworth toys and such. They all called her Signora Pavarone. In a way she felt at least partly responsible for Anna's well-being. She had been a widow for a long time and her children were grown up. Collecting the weekly rent from her roomers and supervising the cleaning woman and the occasional repairman left her time for daily early mass and some parish work such as visiting old folks. She had been called to the school by Mother Theresa.

"Buona sera, Anna," she said warmly as the bungalow door opened.

"Oh, Signora Pavarone, comme va?" Anna motioned her in, offering her the favorite seat on the sofa in the large kitchen. Anna had all her sewing things in the kitchen too. Here she often worked to midnight. Italians live mostly in the kitchen. The children slept in their own rooms. Only the twins shared a room downstairs, the first bedroom their father had built.

"I won't stay long," said the matron. "You have work to do."

"What brings you to us, Signora?"

"I think you're lucky, Anna, with Jenny doing so well in

school."

"I know I am. Jenny is going to high school this year."

"So I hear. The Abbey is a fine school."

"You heard about her skipping one grade?"

"Mother Theresa is so proud of her."

"Oh, I see," said Anna. "You talked with her."

"The Abbey is an excellent school, Anna."

"I don't know yet whether she goes to the Abbey. I haven't decided."

"Of course she goes to the Abbey. It's our school."

"It has no laboratories."

"Laboratories? Mamma mia! Jenny is a girl, isn't she?" The matron's hands pierced the air in theatrical gesticulations reinforcing the words.

"She loves science."

"Don't make me laugh, Anna. Girls don't love science."

"Things are changing, Signora."

"I know they are, and that's the trouble. The world is falling apart, and we must be on guard. We owe it to our children to keep them away from the evil things happening all around us."

Anna watched the matron giving her a lecture. There was a wart on her chin near the left corner of her mouth. Three black hairs protruded from it, dancing to the rhythm of her words. She had never noticed the wart before. Anna found herself watching the bristles and not listening to the words. She had heard all that in the Principal's office, and there it had been much more eloquently expressed, without the passionate handwaving.

"Jenny is the brightest student in her class. She has to set an example," insisted Signora Pavarone.

"She's not leaving the Church, Mrs. Pavarone. If she goes to a collegiate, she still remains a good Catholic."

"But it looks bad. And what will her influence be on Maria when she graduates from Grade eight next year? And Sofia the year after? Can you imagine the disaster if the whole Fabrini family ends up in a school like Humber Collegiate? This could spread like cancer, says Mother Th. . ."

"Oh, Mother Theresa said so."

"She's right, Anna. You've got to listen to her and to Father Domenico."

"I haven't made up my mind. Give me some time."

"Thanks, Anna." She rose, supporting herself on the armrest. "You have the fate of your children in your hands. Don't make a mistake. I'll come and see you again soon. Tell Jenny I'm proud of her. Ciao, Anna."

"Arrivederci, Signora."

Anna sat down at her sewing machine. She finished the navy blue tunic which, together with one of the white blouses, would make a uniform for the Abbey. Teitelbaum counted the Abbey among his customers. The synagogue's schools did not wear uniforms, and Teitelbaum didn't care who bought his products. The Abbey couldn't find a Catholic Teitelbaum.

Just when the newspapers and the radio were celebrating the end of the war and a sigh of relief went through the tortured world, Anna was called to the school again. Mother Theresa was all smiles. "Isn't it a good time to be alive?" she said. "The forces of evil have been overcome. But we mustn't forget our personal matters, must we? Mrs. Fabrini, we didn't touch on what I thought to be essential in all our considerations. You see, the school is not set up to give the children all the detailed specific tools they need to manage in the world. The school must develop the strength of character and the determination to acquire those skills for life when they leave school. No school can prepare a boy for a specific job or a girl for the actual upbringing of a baby in the home. But a school must bring out the strength of character in our youngsters to keep them going in the right direction when they are on their own. The adversities of life come storming on to them the moment they leave school."

Anna was listening but she wasn't quite sure what the Principal implied.

"We were talking about science the last time you were here. Science can wait, Mrs. Fabrini. It has no value in character building. Science is always asking questions, never giving the reassuring answers our young impressionable students need."

Now Anna sat up straight. "Mother Theresa, do you remember the first time I came to see you in this office? I was worried about Jenny asking me a thousand questions, questions, questions, and I had often no answer for her. You said at the time, the question is the beginning of serious study."

Mother Theresa leaned forward, folding her hands in front of Anna. "My dear Mrs. Fabrini, you misunderstood what I said. If you ask the right question you get a valid answer. There is no hollow question in the Catechism. God has given the answers, and those answers are as solid as a rock. Untold millions of faithful people all over the world have asked questions and have received the answers that lead to their salvation. Scientists never made anyone happy by their scepticism. Their answers change every year. Somebody discovers something and the old answer is thrown out. So, what I'm saying is, if you want to go into science, you should do that after your spiritual life is settled."

"Have you talked with Jenny about this?"

"With Geneviève? Why?"

"Jenny is reading books from the public library about genetics."

"From a public library, you say? About genetics?" Mother Theresa raised her eyebrows, so that the narrow ridge of forehead showing under her veil was creased in grooves.

"Yes, about an Augustine monk who made experiments in heredity." Anna smiled apologetically. "I saw those books, and I told her to take them back. But I couldn't help looking at them closer when she was in school. You know what this monk did? He had white and red pea flowers in his garden, you see. . ."

"Please, Mrs. Fabrini, please. Not you too !"

"Jenny took them back that night."

Mother Theresa didn't listen.

"The books," said Anna, "Jenny took them back to the library. They are out of the house now."

From far away the nun said, "You see what happens when you choose the wrong friends." She sounded defeated.

"It isn't the Bauers boy any more, Mother Theresa. It comes from Jenny herself now. It worries me because she seems determined to study science."

The Principal collected herself. "But you are the mother. You make the decisions. That's why I talk to you, not to Geneviève. You can't expect your children to know the right way. Children need guidance. They will follow if the home and the school provide leadership they so richly deserve. They will be grateful to us in later years."

"Jenny gets that guidance, Mother Theresa. But she's growing up, and she has her own mind. Right now she wants to go to Humber Collegiate. Don't you think we should listen to her too?"

"I can only repeat, Mrs. Fabrini, it's you and I who are responsible for her education. She's only fourteen, a child really, and she has to obey."

"There is one other matter. My work for Teitelbaum is barely enough to keep six of us in food and clothing. The fees for the Holy Cross Abbey are three hundred dollars, aren't they?"

"Yes, but that may go up this year."

"I just can't afford to pay three hundred dollars."

"For your next child it will be only two hundred."

Anna sighed. "I can't pay three hundred dollars, and even if I could, Mary and Sophie and the boys will never be able to go to a Catholic high school. It's just out of the question."

"We'll cross that bridge when we come to it. Leave it to me. I'll talk to Mother Monica at the Abbey."

"Maybe you shouldn't. Humber Collegiate costs nothing, you know."

"But look what you are getting for three hundred dollars. Nothing less than the salvation of your child, Mrs. Fabrini."

Father Domenico had been in the Fabrinis' bungalow only once. That was after Joe had died. He had been a real comfort to the family then. Now he came to see Anna again while the children were at school.

Anna stopped her sewing machine and, while she made him a cup of tea, he watched the outlandish angelfish sailing through the weeds in the aquarium on the kitchen counter. Anna handed him the cup.

"Thank you." He put it down beside him. "I have good news for you, Anna," he said, pulling an envelope from a pocket in his robe. He opened it, put on his glasses and read with a smile on his face:

"Dear Mrs. Fabrini,

It is with great pleasure that we accept your application for admission of your daughter Geneviève to Grade nine at Holy Cross Abbey. On the recommendation of the Principal of St. Boniface Separate School your daughter has been granted a full scholarship for entry into Holy Cross Abbey. We congratulate you and your daughter on this fine achievement. We are looking forward to seeing your other daughters at the Abbey in the years to come.

The Lord bless you.

Mother Monica, Principal.

The priest took a sip from the tea cup. He was happy with this development, and it was obvious that he was proud of being the one to convey the generosity of the Church to such a deserving member.

Anna didn't know what to say. She had not made an application to the Abbey. It was probably taken for granted that she would. And she was honored that Jenny received the scholarship. It was a blessing to have a child of such merit in the family. How she wished Joe were here now ! Jenny would be proud too. And Holy Cross Abbey had a fine reputation throughout the country and even beyond. From South America, from France and Spain, parents sent their daughters to this Canadian school. Yes, good things were happening to Anna. The Lord had given her His blessing. But she still wanted to talk it over with Jenny.

The priest took a pen from his pocket.

"Mother Monica wants you to put your name on the dotted line here."

Anna read, "I hereby accept the Full Scholarship. . ."

Father Domenico gave her the pen. "I'm glad for you,

Anna," he said.
Anna signed.

10

Humber Collegiate was a modern school, quite progressive and willing to experiment. Ferdinand was one of its best students. He was allowed to take two Grade ten subjects while he was in Grade nine. Now in Grade ten he took three Grade eleven subjects. The guidance counsellor had worked out a plan for him to compress his five years of high school into four, with a little extra work each year. The future looked good for Ferdinand. His trouble began on a Friday afternoon.

Ferdinand was a good athlete. He was well built and strong, and he was quick and skilful as well. But he couldn't stand any team sport. He found it ridiculous to run after a ball and then throw it away. He couldn't remember the rules and he had no idea which Canadian or American football or baseball team was on top of the heap at the moment. This attitude was quite abnormal, inexcusable and almost insane. Ferdinand had openly expressed in class that he thought mountain climbing was more exciting than whacking a piece of rubber with a crooked stick. And he mused that there was no reason to make the nets on the ice rink that small just to increase the difficulty of knocking the puck in.

He ridiculed the beer-drinking masses in the stands and the frenzy when a team shot the puck into one net and not into the other. His anti-sport attitude aroused hostility in his school mates. But far from being annoyed by it, he was amused by their reaction.

By his looks and the way he moved, and also by his leadership qualities, Ferdinand seemed destined to become a quarterback on the school's football team. But he laughed when he saw Tom Dudston in his new uniform in orange and green Viking colors. "You look like a gorilla," he said. "Your neck is gone and you're all shoulders."

Tom was proud to have been offered a place on the school's junior team. The Humber Vikings had reached the semi-finals last year. Their glory had spilled over on the Juniors. And the Juniors had beaten Scarborough fourteen to ten.

The coach of the Vikings was Warren McLenny. McLenny taught Physical Education at Humber Collegiate. All his energy and enthusiasm was directed towards winning the championship. He would have no difficulty securing a department headship in any high school if he succeeded.

When he saw Ferdinand in the work-outs he recognized an exceptional potential in him and he planned to recruit him at the next opportunity.

Like every student in the school, Ferdinand enjoyed getting a half day off. The school closed at twelve noon on Fridays to allow the students to attend the football game. Ferdinand had gone to the stadium once. The bleachers were crowded with high school students from all over town. They were sitting and screaming and smoking, chewing gum and drinking Coca Cola. The cheerleaders were the only non-combatants who got some physical exercise swinging their pretty limbs about and yelling their special kind of poetry:

"Give me an H
Give me a U
Give me an M

> Give me a B
> Give me an E
> Give me an R
> Humber Collegiate
> Rah, rah, rah !"

And they were all there, thousands of them, in the name of Physical Education.

Rah, rah, rah !

It didn't appeal to Ferdinand. There must have been a few more who skipped the Friday afternoon games because Mr. McLenny tacked a notice on bulletin boards throughout the school:

"It has been brought to our attention that a few students do not attend the football games. You have been given Friday afternoons off so that you can support our team. Starting tomorrow the athletic society will sell tickets to the Friday games. The price is ten cents. Students who choose not to buy a ticket will attend school instead. The Vice-Principal will organize a class for those who do not support our team. Warren McLenny, Coach."

Ferdinand didn't buy a ticket. He went hiking on Friday afternoon. Not a big trip but a walk along Linden Street and the riverbank, his favorite hunting ground. He scrambled down the embankment to the river and jumped from boulder to boulder. Fallen leaves were dancing on the gurgling water. Then he climbed back up, brushing through the goldenrod.

There was the solitary linden tree. He picked up a pebble and threw it at the trunk. When he hit it smack in the middle, he smiled. He sat down among the shrubs and dreamed about nothing. It was a perfect Indian summer day to dream about nothing and everything. He lay down, folded his hands under his head and watched the cumulus clouds floating in the postcard blue sky. Then he heard the familiar honking of Canada geese pushing the letter V southwards. He closed his eyes and noticed with astonishment that he was crying. Tears trickled down his cheeks.

Why would he cry? The geese and the linden tree made him cry. He was seventeen and crying, crying about nothing.

Here at the river one couldn't hear the Rah, rah, rah from the stadium. He would never wear a baseball cap or a football helmet, never drink beer on the bleachers in the hockey arena. He wouldn't ever sit in Dudston's Tavern and play cards there. He wouldn't want to learn how to play cards. Suddenly he wished Mr. Wong were alive. He would do all his shopping at Wong's, now and always. And he would like to meet Mr. Fabrini. He would go to Mr. and Mrs. Fabrini and ask them whether he could take Jenny out to the school dance that was coming up. Jenny was fourteen. She must be a big girl now. He once saw her, or so he thought, in a crowd on Yonge Street, entering the Eaton's store. But he wasn't quite sure. She looked different, taller and very beautiful. His heart had started to pump wildly. Maybe it hadn't been Jenny. Thinking of measly little Jenny made him cry too. Yes, it was Jenny who made him cry. Her house was only a five minute walk from here.

On Monday, Mr. McLenny told Ferdinand he wanted to see him after school in the Phys. Ed. office next to the shower room. It smelled of steam in here and of sweaty socks. The coach was in a bad mood. His red curls flopped like flames around his pink face. "What do you have to say for yourself?" he demanded.

The Vikings had lost to the Harbord Collegiate team and it sounded as if the coach was blaming Ferdinand for the shame of it.

Ferdinand said sullenly, "Nothing, sir."

The coach pulled up his socks and tied his shoe laces. "The Vice-Principal will give you a detention because you didn't show up in school Friday afternoon. But I want to talk to you because I think you could be a fine football player. Your bad example won't help our efforts. The least you can do is go to the games and show some school spirit in the stadium. I can't understand why you don't volunteer for the team."

"I don't want to sit on the bleachers for hours," said Ferdinand. "I have other interests, sir."

"If you think a man can live by books alone, you're wrong. There's much more to life than books, and sports is more than a pastime. It's part of our national life." He pointed to a poster he had tacked to the upper left corner of his bulletin board.

"Mens sana in corpore sano. You know what that means?"

"I don't take Latin, sir."

"I didn't learn Latin either, but I sure know what it means: a healthy mind in a healthy body."

"I like that," said Ferdinand.

"So you see the relationship between the mind and the body?"

"Sir, you're talking about the team, not the spectators. They don't get anything for their body in the stadium."

Now the coach came directly to the point, "I want you to play on the team, Ferdinand."

"But there are thousands of howling spectators and just a handful of people getting any exercise."

The coach didn't like the argument. He changed the subject. "Well, then, what about the school spirit?"

"I don't understand."

"Don't you think that rooting for our team and even the curses hurled at the opposing team are sure signs of a good school spirit?"

"I don't know, sir. I think school spirit is more than yelling at football games".

"I'm surprised to hear you say that. I thought you had a better understanding of the psychology behind sports. Don't you see how hockey binds Canada together?"

"Mr. McLenny, I've just read a book about Banting and Best. . ."

"The insulin people? What have they got to do with this?"

"I felt proud to be a Canadian when I read about their discovery."

"Okay. But thousands of people get a kick out of watching their team win, millions of people. And a school needs school spirit. National pride begins with school spirit. You won't jeopardize our efforts to build school spirit. I won't let you, Bauers." The coach stood up. "You will buy your tickets from now on and support our school team."

Ferdinand turned around and walked to the door.

The coach shouted after him, "Is that clear?"

"It is clear, sir, but it doesn't make sense." He left.

Ferdinand entered the detention room with the daily delinquents, the ones that had been caught smoking in the toilet, the ones who had not done their homework three times, the signature artists who wrote their own parental excuse letters, and Warren Potomac from Grade eleven who had grabbed Tina under her skirt and was considered a sex maniac by some and a Don Juan by others. Tina was voluptuous, but that was no reason for the boys to leave decency behind. The Vice-Principal didn't know how to keep Tina from being the way she was, so he punished the boys who periodically made passes at her in the hall or in the cafeteria. Ferdinand had felt the lure of Tina's big eyes himself when she walked down the hall, shifting her hips rhythmically left and right.

There was now in this classroom a new category of culprits, those who sabotaged the school spirit, represented by four boys and two girls. The boys had been caught playing soccer in their backyard the previous Friday afternoon when they were supposed to have been sitting on the bleachers, and the two girls who were disciples of Tina, had been seen on Yonge Street that same afternoon. The spirit spoilers stated it wasn't worth it. From now on they would buy themselves out of detention for ten cents. Ferdinand kept mum.

The teacher in charge entered, took attendance and made sure there was no conversation in the room. Ferdinand looked out the window. He decided to go to the prom. He had never taken a girl out. The Commencement Exercises were going to be held in the school auditorium in two weeks, and the Students' Council had made preparations for the formal ball afterwards.

The science teacher had told him confidentially that he was eligible for the Proficiency Award in Science because he had the highest mark, a phenomenal ninety-eight per cent. Ferdinand was very proud of his achievement. He had also been invited to represent the school at the Ontario Science Fair with his demonstration of Mendel's Laws in his pigeons. All this was to be celebrated on Commencement Day. His mother was going to sit in the audience when the engraved plaque was presented to her son on the stage. For his mother's sake, too, Ferdinand was very happy. He had not told her about his plan to take Jenny to the prom. Every time he thought about Jenny, he felt a little stab in the chest. He couldn't talk about Jenny with his mother. He couldn't imagine at this moment how he would go about getting the invitation to the girl. She must have changed a lot. He knew she went to Holy Cross Abbey. The only other thing he knew was that she was worth a thousand Tinas.

Next Friday the Humber Vikings were to play the all-important game against the Etobicoke Lions. Ferdinand didn't buy himself a ticket nor did he go to the class for those who lacked school spirit.

It was a cool, damp day. Low clouds were sweeping across a grey sky. Ferdinand wore his windbreaker and a woollen ski cap with a tassel. His mother had knitted it just in time for the first nasty fall day. He was thinking about the Commencement and the prom, walking aimlessly through the streets, his hands in his warm pockets.

He had no choice if he wanted to be honest about it. He had to break the school rules. Nobody would force him to do something that didn't make sense to him. He was going to stick to his conviction and he would pay the price if he had to.

The cloud ceiling was so low, he couldn't make out any migrating birds except for some small flocks of starlings settling on empty lots and feeding among the weeds. They seemed to be in a hurry, walking in little zigzags, picking all the time. Next Friday they might be in Ohio and the Friday after that in Kentucky. Who knows?

He stopped at a wrought iron gate which was part of a heavy fence surrounding the park. A gravel driveway led from the gate to a portal with a broad flight of stairs. The windows were surrounded by stone masonry with pointed arches on top. The whole structure looked like a medieval cathedral, in fact like the ones in Ferdinand's history textbook. The building couldn't be that old, not in Canada. There was no medieval Canada. Whenever Ferdinand had walked past this building, he had thought it must be an imitation. But the ivy, covering much of the façade, gave it dignity and tranquillity.

The complex was deserted except for a lone gardener trying to rake up leaves from the stately lawn. He competed with the wind. On a granite pillar beside the gate a polished brass plate said in gothic letters:

HOLY CROSS ABBEY

A small bell started to peal from the turret on one corner of the edifice. Through the pointed arch hole one could see the bell swinging to and fro. A nun emerged from the main door. Her gown was caught by the wind. She turned around and faced the girls coming down the stairs in their navy blue tunics over white, long-sleeved blouses. They walked slowly in single file. The silent procession, with the nun leading, moved along the front of the building to another door under the turret where the bell kept tolling.

Looking into their faces, Ferdinand saw at least a dozen of the girls who could have been Jenny. Now, from the rear they all looked the same. Under the turret the girls lined up in three columns, taller girls on the left, medium ones in the middle and short ones on the right. They were still absolutely silent. Didn't they feel cold? None of them hopped up and down or swung her arms in the frigid air. They looked like wooden dolls.

Jenny would probably be in the right column. Maybe she was tall enough to be in the center. Now they filed into the door in the same sequence in which they had emerged from the portal. The bell stopped swinging. One more little ding. Then it was silent except for the rustling of the wind making waves on the ivied walls. Ferdinand remained for a while. The gardener had packed his tools into the wheel barrow in frustration. The wind kept scattering leaves over the lawn.

Somewhere in the building was Jenny, probably talking to God.

If he, Ferdinand Bauers, could find a way to believe in God the way Jenny and all the girls in their tunics did, he wouldn't mind becoming a monk. He would be known as the pigeon-breeding monk, Brother Ferdinand. He would devote all his time to the pursuit of his genetic studies. Brother Gregor had done it. Mendelism was old hat now, but a hundred years ago it seemed weird and outlandish to the world. No one took it seriously for thirty years. What an exciting life Mendel had lived! There's still so much more to know and to discover. One didn't need to become a monk though. Research is not done by monks any more, not in science. One doesn't have to be a Catholic to study biology.

Monks don't marry, that's a drawback. Ferdinand wanted a family. But celibacy leaves a lot of time for studies. Ferdinand wanted to study all the time, but if he became a monk he couldn't marry. That eliminated the monk's career.

As he walked away from the Holy Cross Abbey, he imagined himself married to measly Jenny. He would have time enough for both, Jenny and science. The thought gave him a feeling of contentment. He went home, climbed up to the attic and fed the pigeons. Tomorrow he would go to the Fabrinis. Did they still have the aquarium?

On Saturday morning it was pouring. Ferdinand started an essay he had to do for his English class, but his mind wasn't on it.

Jenny had almost choked him when he carried her piggy-back up to the attic. He smiled. And the way she had forced herself into the door, that skinny little kid! She was a lousy fisherman. Not once did she catch anything. But then he himself caught more debris than fish. How she had giggled when he pulled a rusty bicycle wheel from the water! And how she turned away when he pierced a squirming bait worm with the hook. The worm didn't like the steel going through its intestines and out its side. At first, he had laughed but then he had begun to feel sorry for the worm too. Funny little kid! She had the cutest dimples when she smiled. But she was fourteen now. She'd probably lost the dimples.

Why did she have to go to Holy Cross? If she had gone to Humber, he could have seen her every day. Maybe she would have become a cheerleader. No, she was too skinny. Ridiculous, throwing those measly bones through the air!

But no, she was fourteen, probably had real breasts now. And she would be a contributor to the school spirit, dammit! Would be on the girls' basketball team. The least she would do would be to go to the stadium on Friday afternoons and help the Vikings win.

Oh, dammit all!

The raindrops on the window ran diagonally down the pane in fits and starts, accelerating when they joined other drops. Some drops seemed to linger forever. The larger they were the sooner they reached the bottom. When the wind swept a whole sheet of water on the pane, it became blurred and the house across the street wiggled its contours for some time. It rained and rained. The day was long and dreary.

On Sunday it finally cleared. Ferdinand finished his essay and left the house. He made his way round to the Fabrinis' bungalow, but he passed it on the opposite side. He walked aimlessly with his heart beating heavily. Should he go home? No, he wasn't a coward. He turned around, determined to knock at the Fabrinis' door now. He hadn't realized it would be such a hard decision to make. There was the neatly trimmed privet hedge again. It must be over five feet high now. It had only just been planted when he and Jenny had set up the aquarium in the kitchen. Would the guppies still be alive? No, they must be dead by now, but their offspring would occupy the tank. They are so proliferous. Freddy and Frankie should be old enough to look after the fish.

It was Freddy who opened the door. Maybe it was Frankie.

"Can I talk to Mrs. Fabrini?"

The boy turned around. "Mom," he shouted, "someone to see you."

Anna came from the kitchen.

"Hello, Mrs. Fabrini, remember me?"

"Oh, Ferdinand, sure I remember you. Come in. How have you been?"

"It's Ferdinand," announced Freddy, maybe Frankie into the bungalow. They all assembled in the hall - Mary, Sophie, Frankie and Freddy, all with smiles on their faces.

"I'm fine," said Ferdinand. He took off his cap. "I just wanted to. . .I mean. . .How are the fish?"

They all stepped into the kitchen. One of the twins felt he had been addressed. "We have two aquariums now. This one is Frankie's, 'n this one is mine. He's got the guppies and I have the angelfish. We had to separate them. The angels ate the guppies as soon as they were born."

Frankie said with the air of an expert, "They all eat smaller fish, even their own babies if you don't separate them."

"But the angels are the worst. They're cannibals," said Freddy. Mary added shyly, "They shouldn't be called angels."

"So how are you doing, Ferdinand," said Anna. Did she guess why he had come?

"Fine, just fine, thank you."

"Do you still have your pigeons?" asked Sophie. Ferdinand saw the likeness between the three sisters, even if Jenny had been much younger when he went fishing with her. "Yes, I do," said Ferdinand. "They're fine too." Then they looked silently at the aquariums. The silence had just started to become uncomfortable when Frankie said, "Can you show us how to breed worms, Ferdinand?"

"Shush," said Anna, "I want no worms in the kitchen."

"Fish should get live worms to eat, please, Mom."

"We'll talk about it some other time," said Anna. Turning to Ferdinand she said, "Can I get you a piece of pie?"

"It's a really good pumpkin pie. Mom makes good pumpkin pie," said Mary.

"No thanks, I've got to be going. I just happened to go by your house, and I remembered the aquarium. I'm very much interested in plants and animals and things."

"I know," said Anna. She accompanied him to the door. Ferdinand pulled his wool cap over his ears. "Well, it was nice seeing you again." He held the door knob in his hand. He hesitated. Should he talk about the prom? Where was Jenny? Her sisters and brothers stood in a semi-circle around the door, looking at him with their modest smile.

"Good luck to you," said Anna.

"Goodbye then," said Ferdinand, closing the door. When he had taken a few steps down the walkway he heard the door opening again. Anna came out and said, "Too bad Jenny wasn't here. She's at St. Cecilia in Buffalo."

"St. Cecilia?"

"Yes. She might come home for Christmas."

"But it's only October now," said Ferdinand. He regretted having said that. "Tell her I once saw her going to Eatons on Yonge Street."

"I will."

Ferdinand stomped home through the puddles and went right up to the attic.

11

The English teacher was collecting the essays. She was interrupted by a knock on the door. The girl nearest the door opened it. "Miss Madrigal, please," she said turning around. The teacher went to the door and out into the hall, leaving the door ajar. Then the door closed.

"Who was that?" someone asked.

"Mr. Bulnik," said the girl near the door.

"Oh, oh," mumbled the class.

Ferdinand had an uneasy premonition. Something dark and heavy was looming. Mr. Bulnik was the Vice-Principal. When Miss Madrigal returned she went on collecting papers. Then she started teaching. None of her questions was directed to Ferdinand. Did she ignore him, or was it only his bad conscience that made him imagine it?

When the lesson ended and the class filed out, she said to Ferdinand, "Mr. Bulnik wants to see you."

"When?"

"Right now."

Ferdinand sat down in the office where half a dozen delinquents waited at the Vice-Principal's door. It would probably take the whole period waiting for Mr. Bulnik, and Mr. Smith in the physics lab would wonder where his top student was. Ferdinand loved the experiments on Archimedes' Principle. Why waste time sitting here in line for a tongue lashing, when he could weigh solid objects under water? So he went to his physics class. He was the leader of a team and they finished the experiment and all the cleaning up in time to enter their data in the lab report. Ferdinand handed his paper to the teacher.

There was a knock on the door, hard and threatening. Without waiting for anyone to open it, Mr. Bulnik came in. "Bauers," he said ominously through his beard. "Excuse me," he added more softly to the teacher. "Bauers, to my office!"

Ferdinand followed the Vice-Principal who strode back to his office. There Mr. Bulnik slumped into his armchair. "Get your act together, Bauers!" Ferdinand knew he had lost the battle before it started.

"Number one," Mr. Bulnik continued while searching for his cigarettes, "Miss Madrigal sent you to me. Why didn't you obey?"

"My mistake, sir, I should have."

"Number two." He finally found his pack, shook out a cigarette and lit it. "You have refused to attend a school function at least three times." He sucked the smoke into his lungs and blew it up towards the ceiling. "Friday afternoon is not a holiday. The game is a school function." He seemed to relish the phrase 'school function'. He pronounced it with convincing finality. It radiated authority and order and, yes, a touch of sanctity.

"Yes, sir," said Ferdinand, standing five foot ten tall in front of the enormous desk and watching the Vice-Principal go through the ritual of a smoker. The ash tray already contained six or seven stubs and it was only ten o'clock.

"I take it you know you broke the rules three times. You stayed away from the stadium and you didn't even buy a ticket."

"I didn't have the money, sir."

"What! You didn't have a dime for the ticket?"

My mother gives me money for things I need, not for football games."

Bulnik got irritated. "Who determines what you need? Here in school we determine what you need, " he thundered. "We, that is the Principal and I."

"Yes, sir."

"You also had to take a detention. That detention was designed to bring you to your senses. Mr. Smith tells me you have some sense. You took the detention, but you didn't learn the lesson. You did not attend the game, you didn't buy the ticket and you didn't show up in class on Friday afternoon."

"I am sorry, sir, I truly am."

The Vice-Principal stubbed his cigarette in the ashtray, "Does that mean you will now buy your ticket and go to the games?"

"No, I won't do that, sir. I explained my reasons to Mr. McLenny."

Bulnik jumped from his chair. He leaned forward. Pointing his finger at Ferdinand's chest, he screamed at the top of his lungs:

"In a word, Bauers, you are anti-social."

Ferdinand watched the words coming through the beard. He saw the yellow stains on the man's fingers. He kept cool under the onslaught of this educator's indictments. At the same time it was clear that he had thrown a wrench into the school system. But the system was wrong. It shouldn't be so rigid. His motives had been good ones. Good motives should be acknowledged in a good system.

"What do you mean by anti-social, sir?" said Ferdinand.

"Come on, if there's anybody in this school who would know all about anti-social behavior, it should be you."

"I'm sorry, sir, I still don't get it, sir."

"Is your mother divorced now?"

"Yes, she is."

"That's good."

Suddenly Ferdinand saw the implication of these remarks. His face turned deep red. The ghost of his father had returned. For three years he had been allowed to be himself, the intelligent late-bloomer, highly gifted in mathematics and scientific reasoning, recognized by his schoolmates, a solid friend to Tom Dudston, a hardworking student with pride in his successes. Now, in the smoke-filled office of the Vice-Principal he was reduced to the son of his father, offspring of a convicted killer, a crude drinker, a cardplaying baseball fan who deserted his family, an outcast and now a fugitive from justice. How could he have forgotten!

The Vice-Principal sat down and lit another cigarette. His fingers were trembling in bottled-up anger. Ferdinand stood with stooped shoulders waiting for the verdict.

"I tell you what I'll do," said Bulnik, "I'll give you one more chance. You will serve a double detention today and tomorrow, and you will promise not to break any more rules from now on. You have to be more careful than any other student, because you carry the load of your background with you."

Ferdinand was in a daze. He had turned around during the last words. He silently walked out of the office, down to the catacombs. The catacombs were low-ceilinged halls in the basement, lined with lockers. He opened his locker and put on his windbreaker and boots. As he pulled his wool cap over his ears he felt a hand touching his shoulder.

It was Tina.

"You going to the prom?" she asked. Her lips were parted. She smiled at him. Ferdinand took his books out of his locker.

"I was," he said.

"So was I."

"Now you're not going?"

"I don't want to go with a jerk."

"So. . ."

"Wanna go with me?" she said, her hands on her hips, her head tilted sideways.

"Hold it. I don't even know you."

"Everybody knows me," said Tina, tilting her head the other way, smiling impishly.

"That's your trouble, Tina."

"Everybody has troubles."

"Damn right," Ferdinand said bitterly.

"Take me to the prom, Ferdinand."

"I'm not in the mood for anything."

"Cheer up. If you wanna wait for a good mood, it might take a year."

"You're a philosopher. Who would've thought. . .Tina a philosopher?"

"Don't be sarcastic."

"Sorry, I'm in a bad mood."

"I know about your trouble with McLenny and Bulnik. Let's have some fun at the dance. Forget about McLenny and Bulnik."

"What about the jerk?"

"Oh, him!" She pouted her lips. "I wanna go with you."

"Girls don't ask boys to go to the prom with them. It's not done."

"Nothing I do is done," pronounced Tina. Ferdinand had to admit to himself she was very attractive.

"Funny you should say that. Whatever I do isn't done either," he said.

They were facing each other. Her perfume rose into his nostrils. This girl had a soothing effect on him, but at the same time he felt a tingling sensation running through his body.

"What d'you say?" she flipped her eyelashes.

"I'll think about it." He turned and began to walk to the staircase.

"Here are the tickets," she said, catching up with him.

"You bought the tickets to the prom? That's not done either."

"That way I get the choice, see?"

"You are a philosopher."

She stuffed the tickets into Ferdinand's pockets. Then she rose to her tip-toes and gave him a kiss, smack on the lips. It stunned him. No girl had ever touched his lips. He felt a shiver creeping from his neck down into his toes.

The bell rang and he climbed the stairs. Tina said after him, "You buy the corsage."

Ferdinand walked straight home and up to the attic. At four o'clock he left the house and went to the Dudstons' place. Tom wasn't in.

"Go right up, Ferdinand," said Mrs. Dudston. "Tommy should be home any minute. He'll come up and join you."

Ferdinand mustered the pigeons. Nothing exciting genetically had happened in Tom's breeding. Maybe the blue-and-white was in his own stock, rather than in Tom's. More breeding was needed. But his mind wasn't on the pigeons for long. He went over the Bulnik episode with all the painful details. What a lousy day! And then Tina. Of all the nice girls in school, why Tina? Better no girl than Tina! He heard Tom coming up.

"Hi, Ferdinand. Heard about you. The whole school is talking about you." He had brought two Cokes up with him. He uncapped them and handed one to Ferdinand.

"Thanks." They had a sip.

"Don't take it too hard, Ferdinand. It will all be forgotten soon."

"Not this one."

"Look, you're bitter right now. Just plunge back into your work. Work is a tremendous healer. You've done it before, with astounding success. You can do it again."

"I'm back with the old inferiority complex. When I was cross-eyed and wore those wire glasses, I was too young to know that unconsciously I had a chip on my shoulder, blaming God or my parents or fate or something for my troubles. I'll never forget the Dudston family for giving me the operation. I was a different person when I came out of the hospital. But right now I am worse than ever before. The eyes are straight, but something is very crooked."

"Nonsense, Ferdinand. You're a good-looking boy. And now the girls are crazy about you, haven't you noticed?"

"You're kidding."

"I hear much more about that kind of thing than you would."

"What d'you think, Tommy, how will I make out with girls?"

"Oh, well, you're old enough and good looking, how can you miss?"

"Tommy, have you ever. . .?"

"You mean all the way. . .? No, I haven't. . .but almost."

"Why almost?"

"I was too young, I guess. And it was all the girl's fault."

"You see, Tommy, I think I'm a complete dud when it comes to girls. I have never been near one. I haven't even kissed a girl." One had kissed him in the catacombs that day. But he had been on the receiving end, the victim so to speak. He couldn't count that.

"There's lots of time," said Tom.

"Tell me what happened when you came near. . .you know what I mean."

"Oh, I think we were only six years old."

"That's young all right."

"She told me to take my pants off. It was in the summer among the bushes at the Humber River."

"Oh, there," said Ferdinand, "where the goldenrod bloom."

"They weren't golden yet, but they were tall enough to hide us. I don't think anybody could have seen us unless they'd stumbled on us."

"And you took them off."

"The pants? Yes. And then I told her to take hers off too."

"In retaliation."

"Exactly. Not more than that. And now I'm going to tell you a secret, Ferdinand." He took a drink from his Coke bottle. "On that day my future was fixed."

"You're going to marry her because she took her pants off."

"Don't be silly."

"What happened next? Did she take them off?"

"She had them half off before I told her."

"Quite a girl. How old was she, six?"

"About that. But she was years ahead of me in handling the situation."

"If you don't want to marry her, what did that do for your future?"

"I'm coming to that. There she lay in the grass, saying peekaboo, flipping her skirt over her face. Then I saw her bellybutton. I took a little stick and poked it into her navel. She resisted saying, 'You're tickling me,' but I persisted. I wanted to see whether her bellybutton was like mine. I had studied it with care trying to get the soap out of it in the bath tub. Hers was like mine. It now became clear to me that the rest of her body was different from mine, and I intended to study that too. But then I decided to first turn her over and try to explore with my wooden stick what there was on the backside.

"That didn't do much good because she squeaked like a piggy at feeding time. Somebody could have heard us. Then she turned around and tried to grab me. 'It's my turn now,' she said. But I'd had enough sex for one day, pulled up my pants and climbed up the slope. 'Catch me,' I said. But she never did. She stayed in the ravine. She must have been disappointed."

"Is that all?"

"That's all. And that's why I now want to be a doctor."

They both burst into liberating laughter which made some pigeons flutter. Downstairs, it also made Mrs. Dudston smile. When two boys between childhood and manhood roll in laughter until the tears are flowing, it can only be good.

"Who was she?" said Ferdinand when the laughter subsided. "Is she still around?"

"I can't tell you."

"So I know her?"

"No, I don't think you do. But there's some sort of chivalry that keeps me from telling anyone. You're the only person I told the story, the only one I could possibly tell it to. But I don't want you to look at the girl and say, 'Wow, that's the one!' "

"I have no such story," said Ferdinand. The only girl I went with was just a thing. I didn't know then that she was a girl. We usually talked about pigeons. I haven't seen her for years. By now she must be somebody too."

"Jenny Fabrini."

"Yes, remember her? She had the funniest dimples when she smiled. She was just a thing, you know what I mean?. . .No, I take that back. I've come to like her. I wanted to take her to the prom. But she's out of town."

"That's too bad. Maybe you can get her to come home for the prom."

"I don't even know whether she wants to. She's at St. Cecilia's. Maybe they don't let her go anyway. They're very strict in these Catholic boarding schools."

"Why don't you ask another girl to go to the prom with you? I bet you have your pick if you want to."

"I've been picked, Tom. I'm going with Tina."

"No, you're not," said Tom. "You're not taking Tina. You're joking, aren't you?"

"It's not that funny, is it?"

Tom looked rather disturbed. "You didn't ask her, she asked you, didn't she?"

"How d'you know?"

"You said you've been picked, and I know how Tina works. Did she offer you the tickets?"

"Don't tell me you know that too. She didn't go with a jerk that had asked her to go with him."

"I'm the jerk, Ferdinand."

"What? You asked Tina to go with you to the prom, and you didn't want _me_ to ask her?"

"No," said Tom, "I didn't ask her, she asked <u>me</u> and I turned her down because I'm going with Lizzie Brown."

"And now you're a jerk."

"Don't worry about me, worry about yourself. She will likely tell you to take off your pants. She told me that when she was six."

12

Mathilda Bauers had her hair done for the occasion. Her straight blond hair was now fluffed up and her bun was converted into a stately structure on top of her head. She wore her best dress and tugged at it in front of the mirror in the hall.

Ferdinand had asked her what a corsage was, and she had offered to buy it for him. It lay in a box on the table under the mirror. Ferdinand wore his navy blue blazer with the white shirt that his mother had given him on that memorable Christmas Eve when Tim Bauers escaped from prison. She had moved the collar button as far as it would go to accommodate Ferdinand's growing neck. The sleeves of the shirt and blazer were a little short now too, but his mother said he looked fine and manly. Ferdinand still had difficulty knotting his tie. There weren't many occasions to wear one.

Mother and son were in a festive mood. Ferdinand had put aside his disappointment about Jenny, his trouble with Mr. Bulnik and the thoughts about the punishment he expected for his latest truancy. He was about to receive the award they owed him, and then he was going to celebrate the event with beautiful Tina. He was in for something exciting with Tina. With all his mess in school, Tina was perhaps just what he needed. The more he thought about Tina the more he looked forward to the dance.

The Proficiency Award in Science was something to be proud of. Neither Mathilda nor her ex-husband had ever reached a mark of ninety-eight per cent in any subject. Ferdinand had designated the wall space over his chest of drawers in his room for the plaque. It used to be occupied by a photograph of Tim Bauers wearing a baseball uniform, before his conviction. This memento now lay upside down in the bottom drawer.

"Listen, Mom, I'll take the corsage to Tina's place after the Commencement Exercises, when I pick her up. She's not going to the Commencement. Her folks won't show up either because Tina's not going to be on the stage for anything. She's not even a cheerleader. No awards for Tina. She scrapes through, though. Has never failed a year, unlike your son."

"That was in Grade one and two. You shouldn't mention it. Let's forget it," said Mathilda.

"But she's a terrific dancer. She will teach me a step or two."

"I hope she's a nice girl."

"She's very pretty."

"My son is not bad looking either." She looked proudly at Ferdinand. "I hope she's the kind of girl you'd like to remember. It's your first prom, Ferdinand. You will always remember your first prom."

"Do you remember your first prom, Mom?"

"Yes, I do," she said, wiping a tear from the corner of her eye.

The auditorium was already half filled when they arrived. An usher led them to their places. On stage the choir boys and girls in their purple, rented gowns were still chatting with each other. In front of them a double row of empty chairs waited for the administrative staff and prominent guests. On the left, near the six steps that led up to the stage stood the huge black piano.

The Tech. teacher said "one, two, three, testing" into the microphone at the lectern, then he tapped his finger at the gadget, noticed with a smile the amplified sound from the rear speakers and walked off into the wings.

Ferdinand saw Mr. Dudston's bald pate three or four rows farther forward. Mrs. Dudston was sitting between him and her son. Tom would probably get the History Award and the English Award. Then he would get the Best All-round Student Award because he was also a member of the Junior Team. The Dudstons were used to seeing Tom on stage every year. He would make an excellent doctor.

"What are you smiling about?" said Mathilda.

"I was just thinking about something."

"About what?"

Ferdinand chuckled. "Something Tommy said."

"What did Tommy say?"

"Oh, he was talking about the medical profession."

Mrs. Bauers was about to find out more about Tom's funny remarks, but Miss Madrigal, who had taken her seat at the piano, raised her hand and the mass of purple robes rose as one. Standing up was contagious, so the audience rose too. The teacher played an introductory chord and now, at a nod of her head, the choir sang "Pomp and Circumstance" for which Miss Madrigal had written words that dealt with happy days and hard work in school, ending in graduation and general bliss. She accompanied on the piano with flair and enthusiasm. While some of the audience craned their necks, the procession of graduates entered the auditorium from the rear and solemnly walked forward through the centre aisle, in front the Principal and the

Vice-Principal in academic gowns with their colorful hoods, the Chairman of the Board in a tuxedo, and then the department heads in the regalia of their alma mater, then the junior graduates and finally the seniors.

The woman beside Ferdinand said to her husband, "It's his own tuxedo. He bought it for the occasion. I saw him buying it at Eaton's." She was obviously referring to the Chairman of the Board who just then took his place on the stage.

The choir sang tirelessly. There was only one stanza, but they repeated it, varying it between singing the words loud, not so loud, whispered, and finally humming with closed lips, and then starting with the loud version again. It was a long procession and the audience was moved. The only trouble with the music was that Miss Madrigal was unable to prevent the choir from going a little faster with each stanza. By the time the dignitaries were all standing in front of their chairs and the graduates had filed into their rows, there was a rhythm to the music that made some of the audience want to dance. Miss Madrigal was head of the English department and she only volunteered to coach the choir, an offer which was gratefully accepted by the administration. You don't look a gift horse in the mouth. Teachers were not only evaluated in their classroom work but also by their contribution to school spirit.

Yes, this was a school function designed to create school spirit.

"Remain standing, please, for God Save the King," said the Principal into the microphone. Miss Madrigal seemed to enjoy it. She had opened the piano lid as high as possible and now she thundered away with élan, and the Principal sang with patriotic gusto. One could single out his voice from the huge chorus of the audience. Humber Collegiate had its greatest day of the school year, not counting the Athletic Dinner held when the Vikings almost won the championship.

Everybody sat down. The Principal apologized for not getting the printed programs out in time for the Commencement Exercises. Then he welcomed everybody. Introducing the dignitaries on stage, he pointed to the man in his own tuxedo. "Ladies and gentlemen, this is Mr. Teitelbaum, Chairman of the Board. Mr. Teitelbaum needs no introduction." Then he introduced him nevertheless. "Mr. Teitelbaum has always taken an active interest in community affairs. As Chairman of the School Board, he has been responsible for developing a sound business posture this year. We are the only Board in the area to lower school taxes. Our mill-rate is one of the lowest in the Province."

The audience clapped enthusiastically. It was their money he was talking about. "Mr. Teitelbaum has now created the Nathan Teitelbaum Award," continued the Principal, nodding to the Vice-Principal. Mr. Bulnik, who in anticipation had walked to the left side of the stage behind the piano, held something up, but the audience couldn't see it because of the piano lid. Miss Madrigal lowered it hastily. Her fingers slipped and the lid came down with a bang. The Principal and the Chairman smiled politely. A few choir girls snickered, but then held their hands over their mouths.

Now the trophy was clearly seen. It was a twenty inch skyscraper on top of which a helmeted football player was about to kick a ball into the yonder. The whole thing was mounted on a maple wood socket on which Miss Madrigal from her piano stool was able to detect a brass plate with an engraved name. The audience roared in appreciation and Mr. Teitelbaum had to stand up and acknowledge the ovation, which he did with a modest smile.

"It's all tax-exempt," said the woman beside Ferdinand to her husband. Ferdinand wasn't sure whether there was derision in what the woman said. "Do you know the Chairman?" he asked her.

"He's my boss," she said. "I sewed some of those choir gowns he rented to the school."

Mathilda pushed her elbow into Ferdinand's side.

"All right, Mom," he whispered apologetically.

"Did I mention what the trophy is for?" asked the Principal into the mike. "The Nathan Teitelbaum Award goes to the best football player of the season." His words were greeted with more applause.

"Mens sana in corpore sano," said Ferdinand to his mother.

"What does that mean?" whispered Mrs. Bauers.

"It's a long story, Mom."

It sounded Latin to Mathilda. Neither she nor her son had ever taken Latin. Now Mr. Bulnik took to the microphone. He introduced Miss Madrigal. The Proficiency Awards were the first items on the agenda. Miss Madrigal approached the lectern looking very dignified in her black gown with the white fur trim of her hood.

"Ladies and Gentlemen," she began, "I'm proud today to give proper recognition to one of the finest students I have had the privilege of teaching over the years." For humor, she added jovially, "And that has been more years than I care to admit." She paused a little but no one laughed.

Ferdinand watched the Dudstons. Mrs. Dudston sat up high in her chair and Mr. Dudston's neck swelled over his collar.

"The Proficiency Award for the highest mark in English goes to Tom Dudston," said the teacher. Tom got up, his father patted him on the behind. Mr. Bulnik handed the plaque to Miss Madrigal who passed it to Tom. As the audience applauded she shook hands with him, so did Mr. Bulnik, and Tom walked back to his parents.

The Mathematics Award went to Lizzie Brown who emerged from the choir. Two gowns met at the lectern, one black and one purple. Someone kneeling in the aisle popped a flash bulb. Ferdinand noticed the frantic applause from the lady next to him. She looked around with moist eyes and said to Ferdinand, "That's my girl."

"Congratulations," whispered Ferdinand. Then Mr. Brown came back with his camera, smiling happily.

Now it was Tom's turn again. He received the History Award. Ferdinand applauded vigorously while watching Mr. and Mrs. Dudston. One could almost feel the pride as Tom returned with the plaque in his hand. His mother would be just as proud when it was Ferdinand's turn. Now Mr. Smith, who wore a dark suit, came out of the audience, climbed up the six steps and walked past the piano to the lectern.

"Is that your science teacher?" said Mathilda, laying her hand on Ferdinand's arm.

"Yes, Mom." The great moment had come.

Mr. Bulnik handed the plaque to Mr. Smith who held it up for all to see. "The Proficiency Award in science this year goes to one of the finest students we've ever had. He is an all round top student and I am just one of the teachers who are proud of him. Will you please come forward, Tom Dudston."

Tom didn't rise. His mother looked at her husband. Tom shook his head. Now he stood up. He looked around in the auditorium. Where was Ferdinand? The audience started applauding.

"Come forward, please," said Mr. Smith. The Vice-Principal looked down, studying his feet.

Tom worked his way past all those knees again to the centre aisle and slowly forward to the stage. He took the plaque, ignored the hand that Mr. Smith stretched out, grabbed the microphone, bent it towards his mouth and said, "I don't deserve the Science Award. The best student in Science is Ferdinand Bauers."

The audience was first shocked by the extraordinary course this event had taken, but then they applauded wildly. Mr. Smith didn't seem to know how to deal with the unexpected and Mr. Bulnik kept studying his feet as Tom placed the plaque on the lectern and returned to his seat. The Principal, sitting beside the Chairman, had a worried look on his face. The audience was still clapping as Mr. Smith left the stage and sat down in the audience.

Now the Vice-Principal collected himself. He would deal with the insubordination at the proper time. The task at hand was to save the situation. He nodded to Miss Madrigal, and the choir rose to sing the next number on their program, an Irish folksong. Lizzie Brown held her mathematics plaque under her song book.

Mathilda and Ferdinand sat silently staring into their laps. They had no explanation, although Ferdinand connected the turn of events with the man near the lectern who, in his black gown and crimson hood, peered like the devil through his beard. But Mr. Smith, what about Mr. Smith?

The audience applauded the choir.

Now Mr. Bulnik announced the issuance of the coveted Award for the Best All-Round Student.

Mr. McNelly was not yet a department head either and so he wore no gown. He had tamed his red curls with pomade. His movements, as he rushed from the audience, were springy and spry. One could see the athlete in him.

"Ladies and Gentlemen," he began. His voice was that of an umpire, decisive and sure of himself. "The motto under which we will present the next award may well be the one on the bulletin board in my office, 'Mens sana in corpore sano.' "

Mathilda gave Ferdinand a glance as if she wanted to ask him something.

"That's the only Latin I know," continued Mr. McNelly.

The audience chuckled.

After Tom had received the award, Ferdinand took his mother's hand and led her out, apologizing to Mr. and Mrs. Brown who pulled in their knees.

They didn't wait for the presentation of the awards for the most successful fundraisers. One was to go to a boy who sold chocolate bars door to door and another to a girl who had persuaded a hundred and fourteen citizens to subscribe to Better Life Magazine. Their names had been on the bulletin board for a month. The Principal had praised their selfless contribution to school spirit at the last assembly and had promised the appropriate recognition at the Commencement Exercises. The money was for the Athletic Dinner.

Neither were mother and son in the mood to see the Nathan Teitelbaum Award go to Chuck Wilson. Chuck was twenty-one. He had done Grades twelve and thirteen twice each, and had at last been accepted with a scholarship to an American university.

He was six feet four and weighed two hundred and twenty-five pounds. Some people said he had a glandular problem.

None of the awards was a surprise. The school had known who would get what for quite some time. Ferdinand's science plaque had been no secret either. Now it was a mystery.

13

"Why is it that so many bad things happen all at once?" Ferdinand said to his mother as they entered their home.

"Some people are lucky, others are not," said Mathilda. They sat down in the livingroom.

"Maybe I should be more of a conformist. I didn't have to buck the school rules. But I did, again and again."

"You have to do what you have to do," said Mathilda. She looked worn out. Her expensive hairdo was incongruous with her limp posture as she sat slouched on the sofa. She had taken so many beatings in life, this was only one more. But she suffered for her son who clearly didn't deserve such treatment.

"You better eat a little before you go," she said.

"Maybe I shouldn't go. I don't feel like dancing."

"You can't leave the girl now, Ferdinand. A girl doesn't want to be left out in the cold."

Ferdinand sighed. "I want to talk to Tommy."

"Not now. He's picking up Lizzie Brown. You'll meet him at the prom anyway. So eat a sandwich and go."

Tina lived a ten minute walk away in a little house near the collegiate.

THE HUTTINGS' PLACE was carved on a piece of rustic plank hanging from a wrought iron stand on the lawn in front of a splendid blue spruce. Tina Huttings sounds nice, thought

Ferdinand. He held the cardboard box with the corsage in his hand as he rang the bell. He wasn't half as excited as he was when he knocked at the Fabrinis' house. No, this was a cinch compared with when he went to Jenny's. It took a long time until someone opened. It was almost dark in the house but there stood Tina in a long velvet house coat, her brunette hair falling on her shoulders. He saw her eyes glowing in the semi-darkness.

"Come on in," she said. Her alto voice was not that of a school girl. In fact, she looked and sounded awfully adult, thought Ferdinand. She took the box out of his hand. "Oh, thanks for the corsage. Take off your. . ." She wanted to say 'coat' but she said 'windbreaker'. Ferdinand had felt a jolt going through his chest. Thank heavens, the sentence ended harmlessly.

"It's time to go, I think," objected Ferdinand, "I'll keep my coat on. I'll wait for you to get ready."

"I'm going to put the flower on your lapel," she said opening the box. Ferdinand didn't know there was also a flower for the escort in the box. He hung his coat on a hanger in the closet.

"The Huttings are out of town," she said. "Oh, this is beautiful. I love carnations. Smell !" She held the single flower under his nose. Then she pinned it to his lapel. "You look smart." He liked the way she tilted her head when she complimented him. "And dashing," she added, tilting her head to the other side.

"Thank you. But you'd better get ready now."

She was in no hurry. She pinned the corsage to the breast of her house coat, looked into the hall mirror and said, "How do you like this?"

"Don't you want to get dressed now? I bet the flowers will look nice on your dress, too."

She took his arm and led him into the livingroom which was barely lit by a table lamp in a corner. "Sit down."

Ferdinand sank into the sofa. "I'll wait for you," he said. But she sat down on a big arm chair, crossed her legs and spread her arms over the broad armrests. Her coat had parted a little and her white leg was showing. "There's no hurry," she said.

Ferdinand thought of Tom's warning. She had asked embarrassing questions at the age of six. What would she ask now? She made no attempt to cover her knee and Ferdinand visualized Tommy with his wooden stick poking in her navel.

"Your parents have gone out?" he said almost fearfully.

"The Huttings are spending the weekend in Muskoka. We have a cottage there. It's probably their last opportunity before the snow comes."

"Do they know you're going to the prom?"

"The Huttings let me pretty well do what I want to do, and they don't care much what I do. Sometimes they do what I suggest they should do. The Muskoka trip was my idea." Was she hinting something? He meant to ask why she had sent them away. But he knew the answer. Something ran down his spine. Then he asked, "Why do you call them the Huttings?"

"They're not my parents."

"Oh, I'm sorry."

"What d'you mean, you're sorry. There's nothing to be sorry about. They're okay." She got up and took a box of chocolates from the buffet. "You've got to try these, they're fantastic." She stood in front of him, taking the lid from the chocolate box. Her knee touched Ferdinand's but she didn't adjust her position. "Take this one," she said, "it's got mocha."

Ferdinand took it. Her hair fell forward, framing her radiant face. She certainly had the longest eyelashes he had ever seen, even longer than Jenny's. Yes, little Jenny had eyes like that. Why had he never noticed it? He moved his knee out of the way but then he thought, he could have left it where it was.

"Mmmm," he said, "good chocolate."

"Aren't they."

"Shall we get ready then?"

"Do you really want to go to the prom?" said Tina, now taking her place on the sofa, in the opposite corner.

"Of course, and you wanted to go too, didn't you? You bought the tickets."

"Don't you think it's cozy here, just you and me? If we want, we can even dance. We got a big kitchen with a tile floor."

"To tell you the truth, I don't feel like dancing at all."

"Why did you buy the corsage?"

"Because you told me to."

Tina giggled. "You know something, you're very nice and I appreciate your corsage. I always liked pink carnations. What kind of music do you want?" She went to the phonograph.

"Anything you like, Tina."

"Okay, I'll play the record I like best. It's an old one, Glen Miller plays In The Mood."

"Will do," said Ferdinand. He was no expert in musical matters. He began to feel more comfortable now. "You know, I almost didn't come to pick you up. I was sick of everything about Humber Collegiate."

"I've been sick of school for a long time, but I keep going."

"Why?"

"I don't know. One does, I guess."

"You mean it's a habit?"

"A necessary evil. And you know, one day it's bound to be over. That's a comforting thought, don't you think?" Tina now sat on her crossed legs like a Buddha. She didn't look so adult, so lady-like that way.

"There were times when I liked to go to school," said Ferdinand. "Some classes are really interesting. But now I think the people in the school are more important than the subjects. People can make your life enjoyable or really miserable, either way."

"You mustn't let them make you miserable, Ferdinand. . .Have another chocolate." She moved closer, holding the box before her escort.

"I have too many things against me," said Ferdinand, "things I can't do anything about." He munched the mocha chocolate. "They're really delicious, Tina."

"Have another." She moved further towards Ferdinand. This time she shoved the chocolate into Ferdinand's mouth. "There's nothing nicer for a girl than to see her friend enjoying what she gives him."

"You are a philosopher, Tina."

"Yes, you said that in the catacombs," she smiled.

"Maybe Bulnik was right. He said I carry a burden with me that I can't get rid of. He called me anti-social, not doing a thing for school spirit and all that. Do you think one can inherit anti-social behaviour?"

"Do you mean, we're going to be like our parents? I don't know, Ferdinand. You're certainly not like your father."

"Sometimes I think I have a streak of cruelty in me."

"You wouldn't kill anybody. I know you wouldn't."

"I could have killed Bulnik. Given the right circumstances, I could have. There wasn't much missing. I've always been aware of the power of the genes. Maybe the Bauers are given to violence."

"The whole town has been talking about your father, but everybody I know said if your father hadn't been drinking, he would've been all right. Mr. Huttings knew him. He says Tim Bauers was a fine young man before he took to the bottle."

"Tina, that's the nicest thing I've heard in a long time."

"You still love your father?"

"No, I don't, but I sure would like to. Everybody deserves a father."

"Where is he?"

"We have no idea."

"Maybe he's off the bottle now, wherever he is."

"Once an alcoholic, always an alcoholic. I read that somewhere. And I also read there may be something inheritable about it."

"Do you feel you want to drink alcohol?"

"No, I don't, and I would fight it with all my strength if I ever got the urge."

"You know something, Ferdinand?"

"What?"

"You're nice." She moved right beside him and kissed him on the cheek. Ferdinand stood up. It's like with alcohol, he thought. Once you start kissing you get hooked. He was scared by his own desire to return the kiss. He would love to feel her lips on his again as he had in the catacombs. No, he had to hold himself together. Now the picture of a little girl saying peekaboo among the goldenrod flashed through his mind. He pressed his lips together. Dammit, who's in control here?

"Let's play another record," he said walking to the record player. "What else have you got?"

"Let me see," said Tina, who had followed him. She picked a record.

"Here's Chatanooga Choo Choo." Ferdinand placed the record on the turntable. When he turned around she grabbed him and dragged him to the kitchen. They started dancing and found their steps easily co-ordinating. Yes, she was a good dancer, light as a feather, and she let Ferdinand do the leading. He felt her breasts moving to the rhythm of the fox trot. He worried about the corsage. If there had been no corsage, he could have drawn her closer. He wouldn't want to ruin the beautiful flowers his mother had bought. Maybe he should ask her to take them off. No, it would look suspicious. And then, the corsage was a kind of safeguard keeping him from holding her too tight. Maybe that was one of the functions of a corsage at a formal dance. His own lapel flower was not in the way because he was taller than Tina. She's just the right size for me, he thought. My gosh, she's the right girl for me!

She looked up at him with her dark eyes. The Tina fragrance rose from her again. It had lingered in his nostrils and in his memory long after the meeting in the catacombs. He would have found Tina in a crowd of a thousand if he had been blindfolded. She smelled like no one he had met before. But nobody could ever begin to describe it. Can one fall in love with someone's scent? Was he in love with the whole Tina? Curiously her eyes spoke the same language as her scent. And how she responded to his movements! Her left arm rested on his shoulder and her right hand held his left, pressing with varying intensity to the rhythmic movements of their bodies. Words were neither possible nor necessary.

When the record stopped, they kept holding each other. Ferdinand kissed her gently, closing his eyes. When he opened them, Tina's lashes were still covering her eyes. Did she love him? Did peekaboo Tina love him, Ferdinand Bauers? Or did she consider him a substitute for Tommy Dudston who had turned her down?

She slipped away from him. "I'll make some coffee," she said. "We'll have coffee and cake."

"I wonder how Tommy Dudston is doing at the prom," shouted Ferdinand from the livingroom. He was sitting down in his corner of the sofa.

"I'm glad we're not at the prom," said Tina working in the kitchen.

"You bought the tickets. You wanted to go."

She had stuck her corsage in a vase. It stood on the tray beside the coffee pot. "Give me your lapel flower, too," she said. "Now, doesn't that look nice?" It looked pretty in the centre of the coffee table.

"You wanted to go, Tina, didn't you?"

"Not just with anybody." Tina poured the coffee gracefully and placed a slice of the layered cake on each of the plates. "No," she said, looking into his blue eyes, "not just with anybody."

"The cake is terrific," said Ferdinand.

"I made it this morning while you were getting ready for the Commencement. The recipe is from an Italian lady. Her cooking is out of this world. Some day I'll tell you more about her. I've made this cake often, and the Huttings like it too."

"Mmmm, just terrific."

"I'm terrific all over," she giggled.

Ferdinand put his cup down. "When you say that, it sounds perfectly normal, not exaggerated and not even vain."

"And you are terrific too."

"Now, that's exaggerated," said Ferdinand. They laughed. Then she put her arm around his neck, touched his nose with hers and said, "I'm so glad we didn't go to the prom." Ferdinand kissed her until he forgot the world around him. They sank into the sofa. "Oh, Tina," he whispered, and they said a lot of other things that didn't make sense.

Ferdinand woke up hearing voices in the street. He held Tina in his arms. He looked at his wristwatch. "It's almost one o'clock," he said. The voices came nearer. They were singing Miss Madrigal's version of Pomp and Circumstance.

"They're coming home from the prom," said Tina, sitting up.

"I should go home now, Tina. My mother's waiting up for me."

"Stay a little longer, please."

"I've never been out so long. I don't want my mother to worry. She knows when the prom is over."

He put on his windbreaker and Tina closed the buttons. At that moment, they heard something like a small pebble thrown at the door. Only now did they notice that the voices outside had fallen silent. They held each other.

Another stone was thrown at the door.

"Who would do a thing like that?"

"The same guys that pinch me between classes in the hall."

Now they heard a bass voice close to the door. "Hey, Tina !" Suppressed sniggering from other boys followed.

Another pebble.

"I'll go out and see," said Ferdinand.

"No, don't. That won't do me any good. Let's sit down. They'll go away."

"Did you tell anyone your parents are out of town?"

"I told Lizzie."

"Why?"

"I thought we could have a little snack after the prom. But then I phoned her and told her I had changed my mind, I wasn't going to the prom."

"I feel trapped, Tina."

"Don't. I love you."

"I love you too," he said. But now he wasn't sure whether he really meant it. When does one know whether one is in love or not?

A big stone bounced off the door.

"That's enough now," said Tina, "you stay here." With determined strides, she walked to the door and opened it. The street lamp lit the front lawn. She knew they were hiding behind the blue spruce.

"Come out, you cowards," she shouted. Two figures came around the tree. One of them was giant Chuck Wilson with his Nathan Teitelbaum Award under his arm. Ferdinand watched the scene from the dark hall through the open front door. "Hey, Tina, where've you been?" said the other boy. Ferdinand recognized him as Warren Potomac from Grade eleven who had served a detention with him for grabbing Tina under her skirt.

"What are you creeps doing here? Why don't you mind your own business and go home?" said Tina. She was a cool cookie, thought Ferdinand.

"Oh, Tina," said the football hero coming closer, "be a good girl now."

"One step closer and I call the police," said Tina. Did she mean it?

From behind the spruce, a boy said, "Chuck, let's go."

"Yes, come on, let's get outa here," said another.

Then the experienced skirt grabber jumped forward and pounced on Tina, clutching her around the waist. It took Ferdinand only a fraction of a second to dart out through the door and wrestle the attacker to the ground. Kneeling on him, he punched him in the mouth. He was blind with fury. He didn't notice the big footballer towering over him with his trophy raised, waiting for the right position to come up for the strike.

"Watch out!" he heard Tina. Turning around he saw Chuck Wilson holding the skyscraper, using the sculpture on the top as a handle, poised to smash it down on him. His reaction must have been the right one because a second later, there was Chuck Wilson lying in the grass, knocked out cold, and the three other intruders were scrambling away as fast as they could. Their clattering feet were still heard a block away.

Tina picked up the Nathan Teitelbaum Award, saying breathlessly, "I'm proud of you, Ferdinand."

"What did I do?"

"You knocked him on the chin."

"No kidding."

She studied the trophy. On the skyscraper, she read: " 'Mens sana in corpore'. . .What's that mean?"

Ferdinand was still surprised at the result of his lightning reaction to Tina's warning.

"And here," Tina continued: " 'For outstanding contribution to school spirit.' " She put the award on Chuck's belly, like one places a helmet on the casket of a dead soldier. Just then, he opened his eyes. They were kind of glassy.

"He'll be all right," said Tina.

Mrs. Bauers was glad Ferdinand came home before she had to worry about him. "Did you have a good time?"

"Yes, Mom."

"How was the music?"

"The music was fine."

"Did you dance a lot?"

"Yes, we danced."

"Is Tina a good dancer?"

"Yes, she is. We had a good time."

"As I said, you will never forget your first prom."

"You can say that again, Mom."

"Want something to eat?"

"No, Mom, I'm going right up. Good night."

"Good night, son."

Monday morning the school day began as it always did. But after lunch, Ferdinand was called to Mr. Bulnik's office.

"I want you to know that no charges have been laid against you. Nothing has been reported to the police, thank goodness."

"I don't understand. . ." Ferdinand hated to stand again in front of this executive desk, with the bearded man hurling unfounded accusations at him.

"You're piling one misdeed upon another, Bauers, and now you have the nerve to suggest you didn't knock two front teeth out of Warren Potomac's mouth?"

"I don't know whether I did, sir. But if I did, I'm not sorry."

"You're not sorry !" shouted the Vice-Principal. "You knelt on the boy who was lying helpless on the ground, you punched him repeatedly in the face, and you are not sorry !" With automatic ritual he lit a cigarette. "Mrs. Potomac was very upset on the phone. She kept her son home. They are seeing a dentist today. We don't want publicity about the fracas. Once the newspapers get hold of it, God help us ! The prom was a great success. We're not going to ruin it. Mrs. Potomac wants your assurance that you will pay the dentist's bill, otherwise she will lay charges."

"Mr. Bulnik, the reason why I punched him was such that I had to punch him." He had to keep Tina out of this at all cost.

"Oh, I know the reasons, Bauers. You don't have to tell me. It was plain jealousy. For your own good, Bauers, let's not get into the fishy circumstances. If you want to avoid legal action you'd better pay."

"I'm not going to pay one cent to that sex maniac !"

"Look who's talking. You were spending the night with a girl whose looseness has brought trouble to several of our boys, and you're calling Warren Potomac a sex maniac !"

"There were witnesses who can tell you I did the right thing."

"Yes, I know. One of them is Chuck Wilson. He gave me the details this morning."

"Now there. . ."

"If he hadn't pulled you off Warren Potomac, you might have killed him. Oh, Bauers, you carry a formidable burden. I warned you before but you didn't listen."

"Wilson is lying."

"You ridiculed the Nathan Teitelbaum Award and tried to get it out of his hands. We know you didn't get an award at the Commencement, Bauers, but that is no reason for envy."

"Lies, lies," Ferdinand cried.

"You were also incredibly stupid trying to tackle a Viking Quarterback. Of course, he knocked you out cold."

Ferdinand stormed out of the office, down into the catacombs, and straight home.

Without taking off his windbreaker or his wool cap, he threw his school books into a corner of his room and climbed up to the pigeons. He shut the exit to the landing platform and then counted the birds. They were all home, thank God, all sixteen of them. He grabbed one and put it into a wicker basket, closing the lid again. He did the same with the others. Most of them were tame enough, a few were hard to catch. Now he shut the lid and bolted it. He stuffed the basket into a jute bag and carried it downstairs. He took his old bicycle out of the shed in the backyard and mounted it, holding the sack with the basket in it on the back carrier with one hand and steering with the other. He had forgotten his gloves and it was bitterly cold. He knew a petshop on Queen Street. It took him ten minutes to get there. He parked his bike in front of the window. He loved petshops. Rows and rows of fish tanks, weird birds in dozens of cages making strange noises, puppies yelping and a little monkey staring out of large, fearful eyes.

Today he didn't see or hear any animals. He flapped his arms around his windbreaker, then blew into his hands.

"It's a cold day," said the owner.

"I've got sixteen pigeons. Will you buy them?"

"How much?" asked the friendly man in charge.

"A dollar fifty each," said Ferdinand. It sounded more like a question than a statement. He kept rubbing his hands.

"Too much," the man said.

"This stock contains a very interesting recessive gene. If you breed them and get a homozygous bird, you have a pigeon with a blue body and snow-white wings," said Ferdinand. Why did he tell him that? He won't understand. Maybe it wasn't even true. Maybe Tommy has the elusive gene.

"Ever seen one like that?" asked the petshop owner.

"Yes, I had one, a male. It died."

"Ninety cents," said the man. "That's all a pigeon is worth to me."

"Okay."

The man took the basket out of the bag, carried it to a backroom and returned with the empty basket. He took the money out of the till and counted fourteen dollars and forty cents on the counter. Ferdinand pocketed it and stuffed the bag into the basket.

"Thanks, bye."

"Come again when you have more pigeons."

Ferdinand jumped on his bicycle and raced away, again steering with one hand and pressing the basket on the carrier with the other. Was it the wind that made his eyes water? Tears were running profusely down his cheeks. Maybe it was the pigeons. He had never loved them so much as he did now, pedalling furiously on his rattling bicycle through the windy city.

He stopped in front of a Royal Bank branch that looked like a Greek temple. He put his bicycle against one of the majestic pillars and entered, wiping his face with cold hands.

"I want to withdraw my money," he said to the teller.

"How much?"

"All of it. How much do I have?"

She looked it up. "A hundred and ten dollars and twenty cents."

"Fine." He filled out the withdrawal slip, took the money and left.

At home he went to the phone.

"Greyhound? When does the next bus go to Buffalo? Four thirty? Thank you."

Then he took an old knapsack from the shelf in his bedroom closet and stuffed it with socks, underwear and sneakers. From the bathroom, he took his toothbrush, his shaver and a comb. He sat down at his little desk and wrote on a sheet of paper:

"Dearest Mom,

I'm going away. You were right, Mom, you have to do what you have to do. Don't worry, everything will be fine. I want you to know I'm in perfect control. I know what I'm doing. I'm sorry to have to hurt you. I'll be in touch.

Your loving son, Ferdinand."

14

St. Cecilia's Academy was a secondary school with a reputation for being highly successful in straightening out girls who had a problem. Not that such a goal was printed in their catalogue or that any official of church or school would publicly mention the word 'problem' but it was no secret among the boarders who lived closely with each other that there were problems looming in most of their backgrounds. Parents in New York State and in Ontario knew about its special nature. Some of the girls came from as far away as San Francisco and Vancouver.

Such problems were not so much in academic work, but in flaws of personality and open clashes with the authority of the Church. No, academically the girls were bright and responded well to high level instruction. Most of them received what was called a good Catholic education. The measurable results in the graduating class were consistently above average, and the universities' admissions officers were aware of that fact.

The school fees were exorbitant, but most of the parents were more than well off. Some philanthropists' names were written on the bottom of the stained glass windows in the school's chapel.

For Geneviève Fabrini, a scholarship had been provided by the Church at the ardent request of Mother Theresa. Anna had given in after much soul searching and initial resistance.

She had taken the day off from her work for Teitelbaum to take Jenny to Buffalo on the bus. On her way back she thought of her own arrival at the Union Station in Toronto. She knew from experience how hard it was for a young girl to be transplanted from her home to a totally strange environment. But Jenny was still a child, and her mother's heart bled when she placed her daughter's suitcase on the bed that the nun had assigned to Jenny out of the twenty in the dormitory.

All the way back to the terminal she regretted having brought Jenny to this strange place. While she looked out the bus window at endless orchards rushing by, she couldn't help thinking there was not the slightest hint of anything cozy or attractive in that dormitory, with the beds in perfect military order and the walls bare and whitewashed. The only interruption in the monotony of the whiteness was provided by the crucifix which could be seen from every bed. Anna Fabrini found consolation in that, but her heart was heavy on this memorable ride home without her first-born child.

Tomorrow was the twenty-second of November, the name day of St. Cecilia, the saint of music. Soon after its founding ninety years ago St. Cecilia Academy had abandoned its musical ambitions. Now Mother Veronica kept the choir going and old, old Brother Vincent played the organ. The girls said he was over a hundred, but that was probably an exaggeration. The rumor had perhaps arisen from his constant talk about the heavenly music he played at the inauguration of the Academy. Now, in spite of a slight tremor in his hands, he was still a master at the organ. Mother Veronica and Brother Vincent had prepared the music for the special mass to be celebrated on St. Cecilia day.

Jenny had finished her prayer and slipped under her blanket. Within a few minutes all the girls had spoken their last prayer of the day, kneeling at their bedside, and now it was quiet in the dormitory. Jenny counted the nine strokes of the little bell on top of the chapel. Each chime sounded twice because of an echo from the post office building across the street. The nun on duty switched out the light.

"Hey, Jenny," whispered the girl next to her, breaking the firm rule not to make any more conversation after lights-out.

"What?"

"Who's Ferdinand?"

"What?"

"Shhhh, not so loud. You were mentioning Ferdinand in your prayer."

"You were listening to my prayer, that's not fair, Barbara," said Jenny, keeping her voice down.

Barbara giggled into her bed cover. "Tell me about him."

"Just a guy."

Barbara giggled again. "I see."

"No, you don't see. He's just a guy I used to go fishing with."

"Fishing, eh?"

"Yeah, fishing and such."

"And such, eh? Is he important enough to pray for?"

"Mind your own business, Barbara." She turned around and pulled the blanket over her shoulders.

The nun on duty must have slipped into the dormitory. "No more conversation, please," she said reproachfully in the dark.

Jenny lay awake thinking about Barbara Kalinski. Barbara had nothing but boys on her mind. She had told someone - it was hard to believe - but she had actually told another girl that she had once spent a whole week with a young man in a summer cottage. But Barbara was very lucky. Her parents had given her singing lessons in California. She had been discovered by Mother Veronica to have a beautiful soprano. Joannie Bommelstring was another of Mother Veronica's discoveries. She hadn't had any formal training, but she had a warm, natural mezzo soprano. It might eventually develop into an alto, said Mother Veroncia.

How lucky those two girls were to have been chosen as soloists in all the more important church events.

It was dark in the dorm. Heavy curtains were drawn over the two large windows. Jenny couldn't see the crucifix. But she looked in its direction. She imagined the pain when huge rusty nails were hammered through a man's hands and feet, and she cried herself to sleep. All day long she had felt like crying. Now she had a reason.

Barbara Kalinski was not asleep when the bell rang ten times. She slipped out of bed and walked over to Joan Bommelstring's bed which was close to one of the windows. She touched her arm. Joan must have anticipated this because she immediately got out of bed and followed Barbara. The girls parted the heavy drapes and looked out of the window, carefully closing the curtain behind them. Below the window, man-high junipers concealed the foundation. In the soft half-light of a streetlamp they saw the pebbled driveway leading to the wrought iron fence. Beyond the leafless maples lining the street, they saw the old post office building. The street was deserted.

"There he comes," said Barbara. "Do you have the string?" Joan pulled a skein of thread from under her nightie.

"Did you stick the safety pin on it?" whispered Barbara.

"Yes, here it is."

They watched someone climb up on to a low maple branch and work himself over the wrought iron fence.

"Those spikes are sharp," said Joan.

"He's been clearing them every time," replied Barbara, piercing the corners of four envelopes with a safety pin. Now they both raised the window and stuck a ruler in the gap to support it. Cold air rushed in. Barbara lowered the letters on the line while Joan held the end of it wound around her hand.

"Hi," they whispered down.

"Hi," said the young man. "Cold night." He took the letters off the pin and stuck some others on it. The girls pulled up the thread. "Thanks again," said Barbara. Brrrr, it was cold. They gently lowered the window, laying the ruler on the sill. They watched the young man climb the fence and drop from the maple branch on to the sidewalk. Then they emerged from behind the drapes, Joan with the letters and the thread in her hand. They groped their way back to bed.

Suddenly the light went on and the nun said, "Give me that!"

The girls froze. Jenny woke up and looked with squinting eyes.

"Go to bed now," said the nun on duty, taking the corpus delicti out of Joan's hand. "We'll talk about it tomorrow." She switched off the light and left.

Barbara pulled her blanket over her face. "Dammit, dammit, dammit!" she muttered.

Jenny heard the muffled curses. "Pray a Hail Mary," she said. "No, better say three Hail Marys, Barbara." Why these terrible curses? What had happened?

"Hail Mary, full of grace, the Lord is with thee. . ." Barbara spoke so softly, only Jenny could hear it.

At seven o'clock, when the day was still grey and uncertain, the girls got up. They made their beds.

"What was it Joan had in her hand last night?" asked Jenny.

"Letters from outside."

"Letters from whom?"

"From anybody, friends, fathers, mothers."

"To whom?"

"To some girls in here."

"I get my mother's and my sisters' letters from Mother Elizabeth."

"But your letters are open, aren't they?" Barbara gave her bedding a finishing pat.

"Aren't yours?"

"Not when I get them directly from the post office."

"You mean your letters haven't been read by the Principal?"

"Nope."

"What good is that?"

"Don't you think I feel better when I'm the first to open my letters? It's like virginity. Most people appreciate virginity."

"But the school rules, Barbara, what about the school rules?"

"A little sin here and there won't do any harm." Barbara laughed. Then she added as if on second thoughts, "In severe cases there's always the confession booth."

"Barb, you're terrible. And now you and Joannie are in trouble."

The girls were dressed in white flannel tunics, appropriate for this day of celebration. No classes were scheduled on St. Cecilia day.

The organ reverberated through the arches of the nave in a glorious affirmation of faith. Shafts of golden light fell obliquely through the stained glass windows on the altar and on Brother Vincent's bald head at the organ keyboard.

Jenny loved the celebration of mass. She sang in the chorus:

"Sanctus, sanctus, sanctus
Dominus Deus Sabaoth !
Pleni sunt Coeli
et terra gloria tua.
Hosanna in excelsis."

But her heart began rejoicing in the Agnus Dei when the heavenly voices of Barbara, the soprano, and Joannie, the mezzo-soprano rose like celestial ornaments above the chorus:

"Agnus Dei
qui tollis peccata mundi
dona eis requiem sempiternam.
Lamb of God,
that takest away the sins of the world,
grant them Thine eternal rest."

Oh, to be able to sing like that ! Singers must be favorite children of God. Jenny loved to sing too, but she wouldn't qualify for a solo part. Her special gift was her keen power of reasoning which showed in her mathematics class. Too bad there was no science to speak of going on at St. Cecilia. She would pursue the study of science at a university when she graduated from the Academy in a short two years. There was no Grade thirteen in the United States. Too bad scientists are not children of God, at least not favorite children.

If Barbara is a favorite child of God, how could she do such terrible things as smuggling letters and using foul language? There she sang like an angel in the balcony, thinking that she had cleansed herself by saying three Hail Marys. Maybe God had forgiven her at least for her cursing. How else could she now sing like that, moving the hearts of the faithful?

But tomorrow she and Joannie would have to face Mother Elizabeth for last night's misdeeds. They couldn't escape that.

Joannie of course was only a hanger-on. She would get away with maybe a dozen Hail Marys. But Barbara had probably exhausted the Principal's patience by now. She had been the enfant terrible at St. Cecilia from Grade nine on.

But nothing happened the next day, except that the nun on duty removed the ruler from the window sill and the girls discovered in the evening that padlocks had been installed on both windows.

Barbara said, "We've got to think of some other way." She was incorrigible. But neither she nor Joan was ever called to the office.

The girls were now looking forward to the Christmas holidays. They would disperse over the continent for two weeks to be with their relatives. They were quite excited about the prospect, except Barbara who said she would probably 'hang around'.

On the twenty-ninth of November Jenny received a puzzling letter from her mother.

"Dear Jenny,

We are all glad to see you soon at home. I hope you are all right.

Be strong, Jenny, when the temptation comes. We thought you were safe across the border. I know you, darling, and I know you will not follow the lure of the evil because you have a good Catholic upbringing. Father Domenico and Mother Theresa both phoned and sounded concerned. You know what I mean. Don't let your mother down.

Frankie and Freddy want me to tell you Tom Dudston will give them a pair of pigeons. He's coming over next week to build a bird house with them. Tom Dudston is the son of the Tavern owner.

We miss you.

Love Mom."

Jenny read the letter once more, and then again before going to bed. It didn't disturb her that the letter had been opened. Why should it? She had nothing to hide. If she could only understand what her mother was talking about!

The light was switched out in the dorm but Jenny had a lot to think about. She didn't want to let her mother down. Let her down on what? She didn't feel the lure of evil. She thought of Barbara Kalinski, but the thought made her smile. Barb's antics were not evil. It would be easy not to follow Barbara. Basically, Barbara was an artist. Artists are beyond good and evil, so to speak. A touch of spice, that's what distinguishes them from ordinary people. It makes them exciting. You forgive artists. God does. Some actors get divorced, says Joannie Bommelstring. She knows because she comes from Los Angeles. Her own father is either divorced or separated, says Barbara. He's a movie star.

Kurt Bommelstring left his wife in Germany and he now lives in sin, or so they say. He's still a star in Hollywood making lots of money. Johanna Bommelstring, now called Joan, didn't have the slightest talent for acting, so she was sent to St. Cecilia. Joannie isn't a sinner either. So where's the lure Mom is talking about?

Why should Father Domenico and Mother Theresa give Mom a phone call and tell her they were concerned? Had they not succeeded in persuading Mom to send her to the Abbey and then to St. Cecilia? Humber Collegiate had been their concern. Humber Collegiate was far away now. So was Ferdinand.

Ferdinand !

Was it a sin to think about Ferdinand? It couldn't be. She had recently had a beautiful dream. She dreamt about Jesus and a great sweetness had come over her. She had the feeling the Lord was right here with her. If she had stretched out her hand she could have touched his beautiful face. The love for Jesus had run through her whole body. Then the sweetness grew and grew and as it engulfed her totally and heaven seemed to pour down on to earth, the face changed and the features became slowly those of Ferdinand.

She woke up clutching her pillow.

No, it was no sin to think about Ferdinand. She included him in her prayers as a matter of routine. But she whispered her prayers so softly now, Barb couldn't listen in any more, no matter how much she strained her ears.

She would ask her mother about the meaning of that letter when school closed for the Christmas season and she was home again.

She could hardly wait.

15

"Hey, Dennis, why don't I get an answer to my letter?" Ferdinand was sitting on a chair in the modest room he had rented on Denver Road. He wore a handsome blue uniform with the logo of McDolly's fast food store on the chest.

"It takes some time for a girl to make up her mind to write a letter to a boy, especially if she has never written to him before," said Dennis, a bright young man about Ferdinand's age. Dennis was making tea near the sink. The kettle was just beginning to boil on the gas stove. Ferdinand placed two hamburgers and two large tomatoes on paper napkins with McDolly's two dolls, holding hands, printed on them.

"When are you going again?"

"Not tonight," said Dennis. "The ruler isn't up at the window. If the girls haven't put the ruler against the glass tomorrow, we're in trouble."

"Is there any mail for the two girls?"

"I went through the pile of mail in the box for St. Cecilia. Nothing for Barb and Joannie. And they obviously have no mail to send out either. No ruler, no mail."

"Maybe tomorrow."

"Maybe tomorrow," echoed Dennis. He poured the water into two mugs with tea bags, put the sugar on the table and sat down. "Say, how do you know your girl is in there? You have no proof that she is."

"Don't call her my girl...she's just an acquaintance, a neighbor's girl."

"Then why do you want to use me and my connection to contact her?"

"Because I can't just go to the Principal of that school and ask to see a certain Jenny Fabrini."

"Why not?"

"Oh, Dennis, that is really a long story. I just can't. They don't want me to see Jenny."

"You're lucky your roommate works at the post office."

"And is in love with a singer at the Academy," said Ferdinand.

"How does that sound, 'Singer at the Academy'?" Dennis grinned.

"Sounds fine," said Ferdinand. They were eating the tomatoes like apples.

"Vitamin A." said Dennis approvingly, sucking the juice noisily.

"We make a good pair, the McDolly-Post-Office team."

Then they cleared the table, washed the mugs under the tap, put them in the drainer and threw the serviettes into the waste can. Dennis withdrew to a small table near the window while Ferdinand folded his legs into an old armchair and started reading a book from the Buffalo Public Library. He had talked about that book for some time. Dennis had listened politely but genetics wasn't of any interest to him. He was doing his homework for a course in History of Art that he took two evenings a week at the Lincoln Community College.

"You know, they can now actually see genes," said Ferdinand. "They have photographed them in salivary glands of fruit flies."

"You don't say."

"Hold your sarcasm, Dennis. Don't you realize everything we are has been laid down in the fertilized egg, and there isn't a thing you can do about it to improve the darn thing? All your characteristics, physical and mental, are fixed as genes from conception on. Well, doesn't one want to see those mysterious blobs? Up to now nobody had actually seen a gene."

"If the genes fix everything, we don't need education," said Dennis more seriously.

"Education can only make the genes work and bring out those characteristics," said Ferdinand. "If you haven't got good genes from your parents, education is for the birds."

"So you need both, parents and teachers."

"And I haven't been lucky in either of these," said Ferdinand with resignation.

"I think you are all right. All you need is some more education."

"I don't fit into a school," said Ferdinand. Every time he talked about school, the face of Vice-Principal Bulnik appeared before him through a cloud of cigarette smoke.

"I didn't say you need more school, I said you need education. I got fed up with schooling myself long ago. Now I'm using my night school courses only as an aid to my education. Nobody can give you an education; you have to take it. And you can take it anywhere. You don't have to go to school for it."

"But if you want to go to university you need a diploma from a high school."

"There are universities that give you a chance without that diploma. If you make it, all right. If you don't, you can always become a postal worker."

"Or a hamburger dispenser."

"No, Ferdinand, we'll make it."

Then it was quiet in the room except for the occasional leaf turned over and a shifting of legs.

At nine o'clock they heard the distant ringing of the bell from the Academy, varying in loudness in the gusting wind. The two young men looked up from their books.

"Nine o'clock," said Ferdinand.

"They're down on their knees now. . ." After a while Dennis said, "Now they're going to bed."

"A little early for young ladies."

"They've had a long day."

"How did you meet Barbara?"

"She stabbed me."

"She did what?" laughed Ferdinand.

"She stabbed me with her eyes. I took the mail for St. Cecilia out of the pigeonhole in the post office every day, stuffed it in my leather bag and delivered it to the school office. I usually walked through their gate at about three o'clock. At that time they seemed to have a kind of recess. Groups of girls in their white tunics were standing or walking about. All very dignified, no running, no screaming, no ball throwing.

"At first I felt uneasy, like running the gauntlet. But after some time I got used to it. Girls in uniform are not quite real. I wasn't even sure whether they took notice of me. If they had any interest in me at all, it was because of my leather bag which contained their mail. Until one day. . ."

"Barbara stabbed you."

"I had just placed my bundle of letters on the office counter and left through the main door on my way to the gate, when I heard a plop against my satchel. I had the distinct impression somebody had thrown a stone at me. I turned around and saw fiery green eyes in a face smiling with a mixture of innocence and mischief, but at the same time with something that hit me like a dagger in the chest."

"I can understand that," said Ferdinand. "It's love at first sight. I've never fallen in love on first sight myself. Love kind of creeps up on me. But I know what you mean."

"By throwing that kind of dart at me she became a person, the one in hundreds of white-robed creatures that dared to do what one surely doesn't do at St. Cecilia. Now she stuck out of the masses. I don't know how long I stood there looking into those green, luminous eyes."

"Yeah, I can understand that," Ferdinand said again.

"From then on I saw her every day on my tour of duty. Her eyes threw lightning bolts when I passed her. We never were close, always surrounded by dozens of impersonal white tunics.

"That went on for three months, until one day she dropped a crumpled piece of paper into my path. I scanned the faces of the crowd around us. None of the girls had noticed it. I picked it up and stuffed it into my pocket. I uncrumpled that paper when I got home. Here it is." Dennis opened the drawer under his table and produced a sheet of paper that still showed the creases. Ferdinand deciphered the handwriting:

"Dear Postman,
   At ten o'clock sharp tonight please come. . ." And then she developed the detailed strategy of her rope trick, ending, "We will be eternally grateful to you, the dashingest postman I have ever seen.
   Barbara Kalinski."

"Wow," said Ferdinand, handing back the letter.

"That night, at ten sharp," continued Dennis, "I had my first adventure among those junipers under the dorm window. I felt like Romeo. The day after that the weather turned raw, and when I delivered the mail, the yard was empty. No Barbara. They probably cancelled recess. She explained the trick with the ruler in the next letter which dangled from the rope. She also told me she wanted to become an opera singer. This time she signed 'Yours Barbara' and the next time it was 'Love Barbara.' I have written her several notes too. In her last letter, only a week ago, she said she would look me up on December twenty-third when school closes for the holidays."

"Lucky duck !"

"Well, I don't know. I'm a little scared. But I tell you, Ferdinand, she's the one that can make things happen in life. If there's a Jenny Fabrini at the Academy, Barbara will get your letter to her."

When Barbara designed the complicated plan she probably didn't know that the janitor locked the gate every night at nine o'clock. So Dennis had to climb the fence with those sharp spikes twice each trip.

When Dennis described the sparks flying from Barbara's green eyes, Ferdinand knew the postman was under a spell.

But the ruler was not seen leaning against the window pane again, and Dennis didn't get the chance to risk his record as a reliable postal worker any more.

16

The manager of McDolly's gave Ferdinand a week off at Christmas. On his last workday he ate his fish and chips at one of the plastic tables in the noisy establishment. Plastic Christmas trees, plastic angels and a big plastic Santa Claus adorned the fast food restaurant. His heart wasn't at McDolly's, but he had been lucky to find a job only one day after his arrival in Buffalo. And it was at McDolly's where he met Dennis, the postman who came in for a hamburger from time to time. Dennis suggested he move in with him on Denver Road so Ferdinand had to stay only two nights in a hotel. He was able to save most of his wages from then on. His finances were in better shape now than when he left Toronto.

He sat on a bench in the Greyhound terminal, his knapsack beside him. He had packed everything he owned. He opened a side pocket in the canvas bag and took out two little boxes and a brown envelope. Then he looked at the clock on the wall. He had another half hour. A ragged man lay stretched out on the bench occupying the whole rest of it. His sweaty hat rested on his stomach. It reminded Ferdinand of Chuck Wilson with the Nathan Teitelbaum skyscraper on his belly on Tina's front lawn.

Maybe Jenny was in this crowd milling about in the hall. He studied the faces for a while. It reeked of people in here and it was a dismal place altogether. But the tall Christmas tree opposite the entrance was real and it filled the bustling hall with anticipation of the joyous festival coming up. Maybe Jenny was already home. Ferdinand wrote on the Christmas card he had taken out of the envelope,

> To the dearest Mom on earth
> With love
> Ferdinand.

And on the other card he wrote,

> To Jenny
> From Ferdinand.

He wanted to write so much more, and he had his pen poised for endless minutes. But the words didn't come.

Oh, he was going home! He said it loud: "Home!" He wanted to scream it into the hall full of people: Home! Never had he sensed so much sweetness in that word. The man beside him had put his hat over his face. He probably had no home.

When the bus reached the outskirts of Hamilton, it started to snow, and by the time they had crossed the city and turned around Lake Ontario, the windshield wipers could hardly keep up with the massive cloud of snowflakes threatening to block the driver's vision. He slowed down. The traffic was dense on the road to Toronto. Everybody seemed to go home for Christmas.

Ferdinand started to get worried. He should have phoned home and announced his coming. He hadn't written all these weeks either. He shouldn't have done this to his mother. And not to Tommy Dudston. Maybe he should have written even to Tina. But all the time in Buffalo he hadn't thought about Tina at all. Jenny had been on his mind, Jenny only. He was going to see Jenny. Mrs. Fabrini said she expected her daughter home for

Christmas. After what had happened between him and Tina, why did he never think of Tina? She had told him that she loved him and he had almost said as much to her. He hadn't touched Jenny at all. He didn't even know what she looked like now, going on sixteen. She must be a very attractive young lady in her white tunic. She used to show her lovely dimples when she smiled.

The bus rolled on through heavy slush. The windshield wipers were furiously kicking left and right. Do dimples disappear when you get older? He was smiling in a half-doze. Now his fantasy focused on one dimple, zooming closer. Suddenly he became aware that he was looking at a bellybutton. That's what it was, a bellybutton, not a dimple. Now Tommy's grinning face appeared. "I wanna be a doctor," he said.

But then Tommy's features became blurred, growing a fuzzy beard. There were two vertical furrows over the nose, and the face was surrounded by a flaming red hood. The voice sounded hollow with a menacing echo, "You carry a terrible burden, Bauers!"

Someone touched his shoulder. Ferdinand woke up, still frightened. Why was it so dark outside? It took some time to realize that the bus had stopped in the Toronto terminal. He was the only rider left in the bus.

"Let's go," said the driver smiling. Ferdinand shouldered his knapsack and stepped from the bus.

"Merry Christmas," said the Greyhound man.

"Merry Christmas, sir."

"Hi, Mom."

Mother and son flew into each other's arms. "I knew you would come home," said Mathilda over and over, "I knew it, I knew it. I had no doubts at any time, my son would come home."

"It's good to be home, Mom."

Mathilda had put up a small Christmas tree on an end table beside the chesterfield. All the familiar glass balls and snowflakes and gold chains were on it, and a five-pronged star topped it. The electric candles made the tinsel glitter.

"I knew you would come for Christmas," she said again. "That's why I have the lights on." Then she led him to the kitchen, opened the freezer and pointed to a goose. "Twelve pounds," she said, "just for you and me."

"How have you been, Mom?"

"Waiting."

"I should have written you."

"Now you're here, Ferdinand. What have you been doing all this time?"

"I've been working at McDolly's."

"McDolly's, the fast food restaurant on King Street?"

"McDolly's in Buffalo. They're everywhere."

"I knew you were in Buffalo."

"You did? How did you know?"

"Listen, you're hungry, aren't you? What would you like, a sandwich? I've got liverwurst, cheese, salami? Shall I make you ham and eggs? Would you like tea? Or a glass of nice cool buttermilk?"

"I'm not hungry, Mom, thank you."

"I've got all your favorites."

"You did know I was coming."

"Just a hunch, Ferdinand. A mother's hunch. It's as good as knowing for a fact."

"You said you knew I was in Buffalo."

"Let's talk about that tomorrow. Things like that should be left for tomorrow."

"Okay, Mom. Jeeze, it's nice to be home," he said looking around the room.

"Tommy will be glad you came home too. He's been here several times. Once he brought two little boys with him. Fabrini's twins, you know. He asked whether he could go up to the attic with them to show them how you had built the cages and nests and all that."

"What for?"

"He was going to teach the boys how to breed pigeons, he said."

"Makes me feel like a grandfather."

"What do you mean?"

"I taught Tom, and now he teaches other boys. Dad was the great-grandfather. He taught me all he knew about pigeons. His father had shown him how to do it in Germany."

"But you're the one who talked about genes for the first time. Tommy thinks you will one day be a geneticist."

"One day, perhaps."

"And you know what he said? He said he might drop his plan to become a doctor and study biology like you. He said he wasn't interested in bellybuttons any more."

Ferdinand burst into laughter.

"I found that funny too," said Mathilda. But she thought Ferdinand's boisterous glee was overdoing it.

"The Vice-Principal of Humber Collegiate phoned me the day after you left," said Mathilda at the breakfast table.

"Oh, Bulnik. What did he say?"

"You have been expelled from high school, Ferdinand."

"Expelled? That's a joke. I quit."

"You didn't tell them that you would leave. They expelled you for repeated insubordination. That's how they put it in the letter they sent me. I didn't believe everything Mr. Bulnik told me. I know my son, and he isn't like that, I said to him."

"Like what, Mom?"

"You're not a violent person, I told him. You wouldn't kneel on a small boy and pummel him in the face with one fist and strangle him with the other. I told him you were a gentle boy and you would never do a thing like that."

"I did, Mom. He was no small boy though. Yes, I did punch him in the face."

"Oh, no, you did? Oh, my God."

"Sorry, Mom, he deserved it."

"Mr. Bulnik told me the boy lost two teeth."

"We'll have to take his word for it. I didn't notice it."

"His mother sent me the bill, Ferdinand, five hundred dollars. I paid it."

"Five hundred dollars? That's three months' salary?"

"If I hadn't paid, they would have sued us. Mr. Bulnik said it wouldn't look good in The Toronto Star. The name Bauers had seen enough publicity."

"Five hundred dollars, oh, Mom !"

"It's water under the bridge. Let's forget it. But it got me thinking Ferdinand. Now, I'm sure you had a good reason. I don't mind if you don't tell me why you did it. But. . .how shall I say it? Could it be possible. . . now, please don't feel bad about what I'm going to say. Do you sometimes feel you have to hurt a person?"

"Oh, Mom, you listen too much to Bulnik."

"He did say something like 'pattern in the family'. And, you know, we have to be honest about it, he was your father."

This hit Ferdinand hard, coming from his mother. He sat quietly for a while. Then he said, "Tina told me her father knew Dad before he started drinking. Mr. Huttings said Dad was a fine fellow."

Mathilda blew her nose with a kleenex. Then she said gently, "He was that, Ferdinand. He was intelligent and considerate and he was a good-looking man, just like you. But maybe deep inside he was what we now remember him for. Alcohol brings out the real man, they say."

"Mom, I'll pay you back the five hundred. So help me God, I will."

"Don't worry about that, it's only money."

"Three months at Austen and Blimp for nothing !"

"It's all right, Ferdinand. Now you're home. It was hard to be alone. First my husband, then my son. All I had left was Austen and Blimp. If I hadn't had my work, I don't know what I would have done."

"Work is a great healer."

"That's true."

"Tommy said that to me when Bulnik made school miserable for me. But I couldn't have worked at Humber Collegiate any more. I had to get out of here. The work in Buffalo was good for me."

"Do you know Mrs. Pavarone?" said Mathilda out of the blue sky.

"Pavarone? The name rings a bell. Maybe I do."

"She came to see me last week. She introduced herself at the door as a concerned neighbor. She said she wanted to talk to me about you. So I asked her in. I made her a cup of tea. Anyone wanting to talk about my son deserves a cup of tea.

" 'Your son is in Buffalo,' Mrs. Pavarone said point-blank.

" 'How do you know?' I said.

" 'He contacted a friend of mine at St. Cecilia's Academy.'

"I suddenly sensed she was speaking the truth. Didn't you tell me Jenny Fabrini had been transferred to St. Cecilia in Buffalo?"

"Yes," said Ferdinand, "and it's true, I tried to contact her."

"Well, this woman told me she would appreciate it if I would tell you not to contact Miss Fabrini any more. Miss Fabrini is preparing to be a nun, and, of course, nuns don't have anything to do with men."

"How does Mrs. Pavarone know all that?"

"She's working for the Church. She said Mother Theresa says Jenny was the best student at St. Boniface, and she wants nothing to interfere with her education."

"So Jenny must have written home about me."

"It's all over now, Ferdinand. You're home, that's all that matters. Forget about Jenny Fabrini. If you don't want to go to school, that's fine with me. Why don't you work for McDolly's on King Street?"

"I don't know yet, Mom."

"Don't leave me again."

"All sons leave their mothers eventually."

"Not so soon, and not for so long, Ferdinand."

"Okay, Mom."

"Oh, and one other thing. Did you climb over a fence with sharp spikes on it to get to St. Cecilia?"

"No, I didn't. That was Dennis." Ferdinand smiled.

"It's very dangerous, you know. It makes me shudder when I think of it. . .Dennis? Who's Dennis?"

Now Ferdinand told his mother the whole story.

One day before Christmas Eve the sky opened and the town had not been cleared of snow by noon when Ferdinand stalked through the streets to the Fabrini bungalow. Two boys were shoveling snow, piling it up neatly on both sides of the driveway.

"Hi Frankie," said Ferdinand. The boys looked up, leaning on their shovels.

"Hi, Ferdinand," one of them said, obviously pleased to see him.

"Ferdinand," said the other, "Tommy said you've gone away for good."

"Here he is," said the first. "So he's not gone for good." They stuck their shovels into the snow and grabbed Ferdinand each by one arm. "We made a pigeon cage just like yours."

"Which one of you is Freddy?"

"My scarf is red, I'm Freddy."

"And mine is blue, I'm Frankie."

"That's good," said Ferdinand. "Now I know."

"Wanna see Jenny? She's home for Christmas," said Freddy.

"Go right inside," said Frankie. "We'll finish the driveway first. The fish are still on the kitchen counter."

Ferdinand stood at the door. A holly wreath with a red bow adorned it. His boots were heavy as if filled with lead.

"Go right in," repeated Frankie.

Ferdinand stamped off the snow, climbed out of his boots and walked in, closing the door behind him. He heard someone moving things in the kitchen. "Hello," he said. And then Jenny emerged. Ferdinand stood transfixed. She smiled and said, "Ferdinand, it's nice to see you."

"Same here," said Ferdinand. What a stilted way of saying things. He wanted to say so much, but he couldn't bring it out. She certainly had changed. She wore a grey turtle-neck and skirt as she often did, but she was tall and well-proportioned now. He had never seen breasts on skinny Jenny. The light from the kitchen emphasized her young womanhood, and her smile was as radiant as ever. She was a delight to look at.

"Can I take your coat?" she asked.

Ferdinand took the box with his present out of his pocket and gave it to her. "For you," he said, still groping for words, always looking at her. She hung his coat in the closet.

"Come in," she said, leading him into the livingroom. "Mom and the girls were picked up by Mrs. Pavarone for some last-minute shopping. We have no car...You shouldn't have done that." She unpacked the box, opened it and said, blushing, "Is that for me?" She held a chain with a gold cross on it in her hands. "It's beautiful !"

Ferdinand was still not relaxed. He heard himself saying, "Your dimples are. . .as they always were."

She blushed again. Now she put the chain around her neck. "It's lovely. What made you think of a cross?"

"That's what you would like, isn't it?"

"Yes, it is."

"I thought dimples go away when you grow up."

"I'm not grown up yet."

"Oh, but you are." Now Ferdinand blushed.

"I have nothing to give you," said Jenny. "If I had known you were coming. . ."

"I wrote you about that."

"When? I never got a letter from you."

"You didn't? And I've been waiting for an answer so long."

"I would have liked to get a letter from you, Ferdinand."

"It must have got lost. It went by your rope mail."

"Oh, that! I always thought Barbara was a fool. She's the one who operated the rope mail. The nun on duty confiscated the last letters. Your letter was probably caught too."

"Then you never complained about me to your mother?"

"I wouldn't complain about you to anybody, Ferdinand," she said with so much simplicity and sweetness, it made Ferdinand warm and comfortable.

"Barbara has green eyes, doesn't she?" he said impishly.

"You know Barbara?"

"I can visualize her. She's beautiful and capricious, just like an opera singer should be."

"You're teasing me." Jenny looked puzzled.

Now Ferdinand told her about Dennis, the postman, his infatuation with Barbara and the whole Buffalo adventure. When he was finished and they had laughed together heartily, Jenny said, "You have changed a lot too, Ferdinand."

"Yes, I didn't know if you would recognize me with my eyes straightened out."

"What do you mean, your eyes straightened out?"

"It looks better this way, don't you think?"

"What looks better this way?"

"Well, cross-eyes are ugly. That's a fact. Not that it bothered me. But Mrs. Dudston thought so, and she was right."

"You mean you were cross-eyed?"

"Don't you remember?"

"I never saw it."

"And I wore glasses too."

"I never saw glasses on you either, Ferdinand. I only remember your eyes were blue." Jenny blushed deeply.

"I always remembered your eyelashes and your dimples," Ferdinand said softly.

Jenny fingered her new pendant.

"The cross looks good on you too," he said. A long silence crackled with electricity.

They heard the engine of a car on the driveway.

"Here they are. Mrs. Pavarone drives an Austin. We thought at first there was too much snow, but she made it."

"Mrs. Pavarone? She's the one who told my mother to make sure I never see you again. She said nuns don't have anything to do with men."

"I'm not a nun." She rose and Ferdinand followed. While he put on his coat he heard the boys telling their mother, "Ferdinand is inside. He came to see the fish." Then he heard a hurried goodbye from Mrs. Pavarone.

"Will I see you again, Jenny?" said Ferdinand. They were facing each other.

"I'll give you a call."

The door opened and the boys came in. "They're home now," they said, and to Ferdinand, "What do you think of my angels?" "And my guppies?"

"Ferdinand is just leaving," said Anna Fabrini to her boys. To the visitor she said, "Hello, Ferdinand. Merry Christmas." Sophie and Mary walked by, smiling and loaded with parcels.

"Merry Christmas, Mrs. Fabrini," said Ferdinand. "I have to go. Goodbye."

"Bye, Ferdinand," shouted the boys.

Jenny stood in the background. Their eyes met once more.

She would give him a call.

Ferdinand stalked through the snow, hands in his pockets. People were shoveling everywhere. A monster of a machine pushed the snow on to the curbs. But Ferdinand didn't see any of that. He was bursting with happiness. She will call, she volunteered to say she will call.

He had felt in Buffalo that she was near him in that school. Buffalo had not been in vain, even if he had never met her there. He now knew he loved Jenny more than anything in this world. No, Mrs. Pavarone couldn't do anything about it, neither could Mother Theresa or the priest. And Barbara Kalinski wouldn't get a chance again to louse things up. He walked briskly and was refreshed by the wintry air. On a wooden plank before a tall blue spruce, he read 'The Huttings' Place'. How did he get here? He turned around and traced his steps back. Did he lose his way in his home town where he thought he knew every nook and cranny?

Tina was history, passé, fini. Oh, well, she was attractive, very much so really, in fact she was seductive, he certainly could attest to that. He wouldn't think of Tina and Jenny at the same time. It would be offensive to think that Jenny had a bellybutton too. You don't think of Jenny's bellybutton. You can't compare the two girls. Nobody would dare pinch Jenny in the you-know-what. There's no chance of that in a girl's school anyway. But let's assume Jenny had entered Humber Collegiate. Would anybody ever make a pass at a girl like Jenny? Maybe they would. She had lovely breasts now and her Italian eyes gave him the shivers. If anyone ever made a rude remark about Jenny, Ferdinand wouldn't stand for that, even if the guy was two hundred and twenty-five pounds and collar size seventeen. He knew how to deal with giants like that. Tina was witness. Tina was a good girl. She had consoled him in his most troubled days. She baked a terrific layer cake too with a recipe from an Italian lady. She didn't get around to telling him more about the lady. And she had a sense of style when she poured and served coffee.

Tina's propensity for making you feel at home was obvious. Well, she's just experienced. She surely must be experienced. She wouldn't admit it, but she had had her adventures. Ferdinand wasn't her first. It had never occurred to him to ask Tina about her past. It would have ruined the evening if he had. But maybe not. Tina was straightforward. She might well have told him about her previous adventures. Why was he thinking of Tina? There was the plank again 'The Huttings' Place'. He must have walked in circles. Now he was angry with himself. He concentrated on the road and got home before Mathilda. Austen and Blimp closed for the season two hours earlier today.

The phone rang. Ferdinand almost fell over the rug as he ran to it.

"Ferdinand?"

"Oh, hello, Tommy, it's you. . .it's good to hear your voice."

"You sound manly, Ferdinand. Growing up, eh?"

"Don't we all."

"Ferdinand, my parents want you and your mother to come over for dinner tomorrow."

"That's very nice of you. Mother would like that, I'm sure. But I'm expecting a phone call, Tommy. I'm afraid I can't leave the house right now."

"Not now. What about tomorrow?"

"If I get the call today, we can come tomorrow. But I don't know, maybe the call will come tomorrow. If we're not home and the phone rings and rings with nobody home, that would be awful. I know I can't leave you hanging like that, so I'd better say no. But tell your parents thanks for the invitation."

"We have so much to talk about."

"Tell you what, Tommy. You just come over here."

"When?"

"Any time."

"Be right over, Ferdinand."

"See you."

Half an hour later Tom Dudston and Ferdinand shook hands.

"Welcome home," said Tom.

"Good to see you, Tom."

"Hello, Mrs. Bauers," shouted Tom.

"Mom isn't home. She's getting red cabbage from a European shop downtown. Red cabbage goes with goose, you know. Make yourself comfortable, Tommy."

"You're looking at the President of the Students' Council of Humber Collegiate," said Tom with artificial bombast. "I want you to know that right away."

"No kidding. Congratulations !"

"The Vice-President and I have decided to ask you to leave Buffalo and come back to Humber Collegiate," he said with a grin.

Ferdinand laughed. "The President has decided that Humber is better than Buffalo?"

"Absolutely. All things considered you would be better off here than there."

"How did you know I was in Buffalo?"

"We all know at Humber that you fled to Buffalo. Seriously, give me one good reason why you should not come back to school."

"Jenny Fabrini," said Ferdinand without hesitation.

"You are really hooked, aren't you?"

"You asked me to give you one reason. There are a dozen more."

"I know, Ferdinand. There's the school's pre-occupation with sports."

"I have nothing against sports, only against forcing people to sit in the stadium if they have something better to do."

"And you didn't like Bulnik's attitude with the Proficiency Award," said Tom.

"I didn't get a chance to thank you for your courage on the stage that day in the auditorium. But if anyone deserved the plaque, you did, Tommy."

"No, you did. I had only ninety-five per cent in science. I want you to know that the Vice-President and I, at our last meeting, have been delegated by the whole Council to see the Principal on your behalf. The plaque is now in the Principal's office. The engraving has been changed. Ferdinand Bauers is the recipient."

Ferdinand was moved. He cleared his throat. "Bulnik changed his mind. Who would have guessed!"

"No, he didn't. He's not the kind of guy who can admit his mistake. The Principal overruled him."

"You must have been very persuasive, Tom. It's good to have a friend like you."

"I'm not so good at persuasion, but I'm pretty good at objective reasoning, if I have the facts. Most of the credit actually goes to the Vice-President of the Students' Council. The Principal will have the expulsion revoked, if you come back."

"Who's the Vice-President of the Students' Council?

"Tina Huttings." Tom squeezed his lips together into a broad grin. He watched the effect of his statement on Ferdinand. "We both were elected by a large majority," he said still grinning and enjoying his friend's surprise.

Ferdinand was lost for words. "Tina Huttings!" he finally gasped.

"She's the one that stood up for you at the students' assembly. She informed the student body that you were in Buffalo."

"How did she know?"

"Did you not tell her on the prom night?"

"No, I told nobody."

"Then her mother must have told her. She seems to be informed about affairs in the community."

"Her mother was in Muskoka that weekend."

"I'm not talking about her foster mother. Her real mother is a certain Mrs. Pavarone."

"Wait a minute, Tom, not so fast...I know of a Mrs. Pavarone. She's Italian. If Mrs. Pavarone is her mother, why doesn't she live with her?"

"If she did, Mrs. Pavarone wouldn't have peace in the house because of her legitimate children."

"Tina is her illegitimate child?"

"Yes, she was adopted by the Huttings. At least she lives with them."

"Have you ever eaten her layer cake?"

"What's that got to do with it?"

"Never mind. Sorry. Mrs. Pavarone works for the Church," said Ferdinand. "She tried to drive a wedge between me and Jenny."

"Maybe she has sinned enough in her life, and this now is atonement for her sins."

"Quite possible, because she was sent by Mother Theresa, the Principal of St. Boniface."

"You are a non-believing pigeon breeder and your father is a criminal who escaped from jail. Some people even said you had joined him in the United States. But worst of all, they cannot tolerate the loss of an innocent follower to an agnostic."

"I don't know whether I'm an agnostic. I think it takes a lot more years to find out what I believe in."

"You're a threat to them with your biology. You and your pigeons and their genes and Mendel and Darwin, it's all a threat. I don't blame them for that, it's their honest conviction. No conviction is stronger than the one that comes from faith."

"But why are they not open about it? Why do they send Mrs. Pavarone to my mother?"

"They are willing to try anything, because they want to save Jenny."

"Sometimes I wish I had a strong loyalty to something like a religion. No doubts, no problems, no harassment. If I were a Catholic I could marry Jenny, and the Church would be happy, Jenny would be happy, Mrs. Fabrini would be happy, and the rest of the world doesn't care. My mother would be happy either way."

"You have to do what you have to do."

"Funny, that's what my mother says."

"It's very vague."

"That's why it fits all the time."

"What about coming back to school, Ferdinand? Pick up where you left off and get your diploma."

The phone rang.

Ferdinand jumped up. "That's the call. Excuse me." He ran to the telephone in the hall.

"Hello. . .you have the wrong number."

He slowly came back and sat down again.

"You're expecting a call?"

"From Jenny. She said she would give me a shout."

"Oh, I see, the call you were talking about. Well, if you stay in Toronto, there's no hurry with our getting together for dinner. We'll talk with your mother about that."

"Everything depends on Jenny," said Ferdinand resignedly, and Tom didn't dig deeper.

"Frankie and Freddy seem to follow in your footsteps," said Tom. "They were talking about you all the time. They didn't see your pigeons flying out of your gable any more. So they went to your mother, and she told them to see me. They're nice boys."

"The Fabrinis are a nice family, don't you think?"

"The girls are very pretty. Of course I haven't seen Jenny."

"No, you haven't. . ."

Tom saw a gleam in Ferdinand's eyes. Goodwill welled up in him for his friend. Ferdinand stood up and turned on the Christmas tree lights.

"You are a hero at Humber Collegiate now. Anybody who can knock out a football quarterback with one blow deserves to be celebrated. Tina bristled with pride when she told the Principal about the brawl on her lawn. And you didn't punch out Warren Potomac's teeth. Tina testified she had seen Potomac stumbling on the concrete steps at her home when he attacked her and you came to her rescue. She actually saw him spitting out his teeth after he fell."

"And she said that to the Principal?"

"She said if you hadn't been so gallant, the two intruders would have raped her that night. And she said they reeked of alcohol."

"Good old Tina. Mother will be pleased to hear I didn't kick out somebody's teeth."

"So why not enjoy the glamor of a real hero and come back to Humber?"

"Did you say the school will revoke the expulsion?"

"The Principal, on recommendation of the Students' Council, will bring the matter before the School Board. Expulsions are the responsibility of the Board. Tina says there's no problem; she was talking to her father, her biological father about that."

"Who's her biological father?"

"The Chairman of the Board, Nathan Teitelbaum."

17

Jenny didn't phone that day. The next day, on Christmas Eve, Ferdinand stayed home all day. Jenny didn't call. Mathilda was working in the kitchen. She sang happy little songs while cutting the cabbage and testing the goose in the oven. She sang as any mother would whose son had come home after a long absence. A woman needs someone to care for. There's bliss in serving.

"Mom, I'm going to take a shower now," said Ferdinand.

"Go ahead."

"I can't hear the telephone in the shower."

"Do you expect a call?"

"You never know. People call a lot around Christmas."

"I'll watch, Ferdinand. Take your shower."

But Jenny didn't call.

Ferdinand tried to show his appreciation for the delicious dinner, the white damask table cloth with matching serviettes, the two candles casting a mild and festive light over the table.

"How's the goose?" said Mathilda.

"Utterly yum yum."

"Is the cabbage right? I cut two large apples into it."

"I love your red cabbage, Mom. You know that."

"Maybe there's a little too much salt in the gravy."

"No, I think it's just right."

The phone was silent.

Sometimes phones are out of order. Maybe the Fabrinis' phone doesn't work. Or this one right here is conked out. Maybe Jenny won't talk with all her brothers and sisters listening. One needs privacy to say really important things. She could go to a phone booth. If it was important to her she could go to a pay phone. How important was it to her?

"What are you thinking, Ferdinand?"

"Oh, nothing."

"I can see your mind is on something else."

Ferdinand sighed. Then he said, "Tommy wants me to go back to Humber Collegiate."

Mathilda's face lit up. "Can you? What about the expulsion?"

"Tom says they'll let me back in."

"You do that, Ferdinand, you do that. Oh, my God, that's the best news we could get on Christmas Eve."

After dinner they opened the gifts under the Christmas tree.

"You shouldn't have done that," said Mathilda holding a silver chain with a blue pendant against her chest.

"It's an aquamarine," said Ferdinand proudly.

"How can you afford a beautiful gift like this?"

"I'm a working man, Mom."

"Listen, Ferdinand, I love this chain but if you go back to school you don't have to give me any more gifts."

Ferdinand helped his mother carry the dishes into the kitchen. Then he sneaked to the phone and lifted the receiver. It sounded perfectly regular, disgustingly normal.

Maybe it was out of order in the Fabrinis' home... He could dial the number and see whether anyone answered. Then he could hang up. He wouldn't initiate the call to Jenny. When he left the Fabrinis, the situation had been rather embarrassing.

Mrs. Fabrini had been decidedly icy and Mary and Sophie had not exactly sounded friendly either. The boys, of course, were too young to know what was going on. The only thing he was sure of was his own love for Jenny. He thought he had noticed her shy response to his feelings. Did she like him a little, just a teeny little bit?

The phone didn't ring. Tomorrow was Christmas Day.

Ferdinand tossed about in bed. He tried counting sheep for a while, knowing it wouldn't work. It never had. Finally he went down to the phone. He dialed the Dudstons' number.

"Hello, Mrs. Dudston, this is Ferdinand. Remember me?"

"Don't be funny, Ferdinand, of course I remember you. Too bad you and your mother can't come over."

"Thank you, maybe after Christmas some time. . .Is Tommy in?"

"Just a moment." Ferdinand heard her calling her son to the phone.

"Merry Christmas, Mrs. Dudston," said Ferdinand.

"Merry Christmas, Ferdinand. . .Here's Tommy."

"Hi, Ferdinand."

"Listen, Tommy. When do Catholics go to church on Christmas Day?"

"I thought you were going to tell me you're coming back to school."

"I've something else on my mind right now."

"What's on your mind at midnight on Christmas Eve?"

"Sorry, did I get you out of bed?"

"No, it's all right. But what makes you think I know what Catholics do on Christmas Day? You have more connections with Catholics than I have. Can't you phone the Fabrinis?"

"I would if I could."

"Phone Mrs. Pavarone."

"Don't make jokes like that. I'm serious."

"Okay, phone Tina."

"She's not Catholic. The Huttings are Baptist, I think."

"The Huttings are only her foster parents."

"Maybe she's Jewish," said Ferdinand.

"You can't go by looks. If you'd go by looks, Tina's Catholic."

"Do Catholics look different?"

"Can't you recognize an Italian when you see one?"

"You're talking about nationality, not religion."

"I'm getting confused. Where were we?"

"Tina might be the person to ask. She's got a Jewish father, a Catholic mother and Baptist foster parents. Tina is a religious melting pot. But will she know what Catholics do on Christmas Day? What I would like to know is why that should concern you, an agnostic?"

"We're back to where we started."

"Is it really so important?"

"I guess not. Thanks anyway and Merry Christmas again, Tommy."

"Merry Christmas, Ferdinand."

Ferdinand hung up. Then he leafed through the yellow pages. He dialed the number for the rectory of the Church of the Holy Virgin.

A man's drowsy voice said, "Hello."

"Hello, sir. When is mass tomorrow?"

The voice sounded annoyed. "It's after midnight. You probably mean today."

"Yes, sir, sorry."

"At seven. . ."

"Thank you." Ferdinand hung up.

"What is all this phoning about?" Mathilda asked from her bedroom.

"I'm getting up early, Mom. I'm setting the alarm clock at six."

"What for?"

"I'm going to church."

"So early?"

"The early bird gets the worm."

"We haven't been to church for quite some time. Why go now on Christmas Day?"

"Maybe I'll find something I'm looking for in church."

"Some people do, I know. I have given up looking."

He went up to his room. His mother had hung a calendar on the wall where he had taken down his father's photograph. She probably found the spot bare when Ferdinand didn't get his Proficiency Award. The plaque would have looked great over the chest of drawers. It would be nice to tell Jenny he had won the award. She would appreciate it. Maybe she would advise him to go back to school. He should have a good long talk with her about what he should do with himself. He would certainly like to hear her advice. He would love to be near Jenny and to listen to her voice, giving advice or saying just anything.

Was she going to be a nun? She didn't say she intended to take the vows. Oh, Jenny, don't take the vows. It's like death or going to prison.

Why didn't she phone?

Christmas Day was bright and cold. The snow sparkled in the early morning light. People were streaming up the stairs to the Gothic door of the Church of the Blessed Virgin.

Ferdinand stood inside the door in the darkest corner of the vestibule, watching the steaming breath coming out of the mouths of the faithful as they entered.

Yes, Catholics look different from Protestants. Many were short and dark-haired. He could practically tell who came from Italy or Portugal. And the French Canadians came to Christmas mass too. The taller ones, particularly the ones with red hair, were Irish whose ancestors had escaped the famine in their home country. The Polish people and half the Germans went to church too, at least on this day, the Birthday of Christ.

If Tina was a melting pot of religions, this church was a melting pot of races. How lucky these people were to find fellowship in the belief in one God, regardless of their racial and cultural differences. Nobody forced them to get up early, dress in their Sunday best, and face the bitter cold. Their faith had made them go. Why did he, Ferdinand, not have such an affiliation? Not that he suffered or felt deprived, but he wondered whether his life would be richer if he were one of them. And, of course, Jenny is a member of this church. He would like to be with Jenny.

Where was Jenny?

Hundreds had walked through the door, but not Jenny. Nor Mrs. Fabrini nor any of her children. This was Christmas mass. They wouldn't miss it.

If she came through the door right now, would he emerge from his dark corner, approach her and say, "Hi, Jenny, Merry Christmas"? He knew he would freeze and not do any such thing.

Mrs. Pavarone could have entered the church, but he wouldn't recognize her, never having seen her, and she didn't know him either. She must have been beautiful when she was young. Tina certainly was. What nerve this woman had to interfere with his personal life! And she was Tina's mother! Did she get absolution for her affair with Mr. Teitelbaum? Maybe Tina looks more like Mr. Teitelbaum, not that he could see Tina's eyes in those of the donor of the Nathan Teitelbaum Award. Mr. Teitelbaum of course would never come through this door. The synagogue was only two blocks from here. Jews and Christians are clearly separated in their beliefs. They don't marry each other. If there has to be a Tina, she is predestined to be born out of wedlock, to be conceived in sin, as her mother must clearly know.

While all this went through Ferdinand's head, the flow of people diminished to a trickle. Now massive organ music poured from the nave.

Ferdinand was dejected.

The helpers closed the doors. As he stood and listened to the jubilant cascades from the organ, a smiling old man opened the door to the nave again to let him in. Ferdinand saw the last men and women file into the pews and kneel down. The altar was bathed in the morning sun's rays streaming through the stained glass windows. Hundreds of candles shed warmth over the festive congregation.

Ferdinand walked out of the church, wondering why he wasn't one of them. He felt like crying.

"That was a short service," said Mathilda when Ferdinand sat down at the breakfast table.

"I didn't stay to the end."

"Which church did you go to?"

"Blessed Virgin."

"That's a Catholic church."

"It doesn't make any difference to me. Since we don't go to church, it doesn't matter which church we don't go to."

"But you went."

"It doesn't make any difference to you, Mom, does it?"

"No, it doesn't. But why didn't you choose a later mass?"

"You mean they have another mass today?"

"The Church of the Blessed Virgin has four masses each Sunday, maybe five on Christmas Day."

"I was told it starts at seven."

"That's only the first mass."

"I should've asked you about that."

An hour later, Ferdinand was standing in the dark corner of the vestibule again, scanning the next flock of believers pouring steadily through the door. When some of his former classmates and their parents came in, Ferdinand sank deeper into the background.

And now there was Mrs. Fabrini, wearing a black hat and looking festive. Her similarity to Jenny was striking. None of her children was with her.

When the doors were closed, Ferdinand entered the nave and sat down in the last row beside a sandstone pillar that soared up and joined in a bold arch with other pillars high up on the ceiling. The upward striving pillars and arches and their supporting ornaments seemed to flow up to God, in a strange unison with the organ music.

Suddenly, Ferdinand recognized Frankie and Freddy in black and white robes walking solemnly to the altar, holding flickering candles in their hands. Their sleeves were wide and hanging down to their knees. Identical twins with angelic Italian faces, they were now part of the Church, officiating in the venerable institution that had come down to them through the centuries, two ordinary boys whom he had seen shoveling snow in their driveway, breeding guppies and angelfish, hammering a pigeon stable together, laboring in school and doing everything else that boys do. Here they were one of the focal points of the celebration of the Birthday of the Son of God.

Ferdinand was unable to see Mrs. Fabrini in the multitude of worshippers. But she must be a proud mother at this moment, he thought. If he could have watched her now he would have noticed the tears in her eyes. Joe, her late husband, never saw Frankie and Freddy as Altar Boys, neither did he ever hear the fresh and devoted voices of Mary and Sophie singing in the choir. Nor did he see the excellent report card Jenny had brought home from St. Cecilia. It was a day of rejoicing for Anna, but when she thought of Jenny, an extra tear rolled down her cheek.

"There was a phone call for you," said Mathilda when Ferdinand entered the house.

"Who was it?" he said anxiously.

"I don't know, it was a long distance call."

"But who was it, Mom, who was it?"

"I don't know. It was person to person. I only talked to the operator. I said you weren't home."

"What did she say?"

"The operator said. . ."

"I mean Jenny, what did she say?"

"It wasn't Jenny, it was long distance."

"That's right. Jenny wouldn't call long distance. She's in

Toronto."

"It was a man on the other end."

"From where?"

"He didn't say, Ferdinand."

"Didn't you ask who called and from where?"

"No. I didn't."

"Oh, Mom. . ."

"The operator said to the person on the other end that you weren't in. Then the man said he would call later."

"Strange."

"Do you know anyone out of town who would call you?"

"No, I don't." Then he added, "It couldn't have been important, it wasn't Jenny."

At five o'clock the phone rang in the hall. Ferdinand picked it up. Mathilda heard her son say, "Hello. . .This is Ferdinand Bauers. . .Dennis?. . .What a surprise. . .Merry Christmas to you too. . .You don't say!. . .." Now Ferdinand was listening for a long time. Then he said, "Yes, I will. . .I'll phone Greyhound right away. See you, Dennis."

Mathilda stood beside him, pale and trembling. "Don't leave me again, Ferdinand," she said.

"I have to, Mom," he said leafing through the phone book. "Buffalo is only a bus trip away."

"What about going back to Humber Collegiate, getting an education?" said Mathilda with a quivering voice.

"I'll get an education, Mom. I'll even get a diploma."

"And Tommy and all your friends?"

"I have friends in Buffalo. And I'll see Tom when I visit you."

"When?"

"Soon, Mom, don't worry. I have to do what I have to do."

"Oh, I wish I hadn't said that," muttered Mathilda.

"Greyhound told me the next bus would go at seven fifty."

"Can't you wait till tomorrow? What's the big hurry?"

But Ferdinand was already up the stairs and in his room, packing his stuff into the knapsack.

"Don't cry, Mom," he said at the door. "I'll write you, and I'll be back soon."

On the bus he started to sort things out. He hadn't phoned Tom. There was no time. Mom would tell him. He should have phoned Tina and thanked her for her efforts to defend him. What were Tina's motives to fight so hard on his behalf? She was just a good solid citizen who couldn't stand injustice, that's what it was. Good old Tina. He wondered where all his affection for her had gone. He wasn't fair to Tina. She deserved better.

Oh, but Jenny! He felt a physical jolt every time he remembered her facing him only one foot away in the hall of the Fabrinis' bungalow, when she said, I'll call you. He should have kissed her then. But he distinctly remembered having felt paralyzed. Was it the sweetness of her face, the warmth of her smile, her tender blushing that immobilized him? There was no way to analyze his feeling. He loved Jenny with everything he had. And now he was going to see her. How did all that come about?

The bus arrived at the Buffalo terminal at eleven thirty. It was a twenty minute walk to Denver Road. He walked faster and faster. A good work-out with the knapsack on his back! Most windows in the rooming house were still lit. Somebody played Silent Night on an accordion. Ferdinand unlocked the front door and climbed the stairs to the room where he had lived and struggled for the past few months. He was still panting from the brisk walk. Now he felt he was home.

Voices came from his room. He opened the door.

"Hello, Ferdinand," said Dennis who had jumped up to shake his hand. "Good to have you back. This is Barbara. Come here, show Ferdinand your green eyes."

Ferdinand didn't see Barbara. He saw Jenny sitting in the armchair. He went to her and said gently, "I've been waiting for your call."

"He doesn't want to see my green eyes," said Barbara with mock disappointment.

"Oh, I'm sorry," said Ferdinand. "I'm pleased to meet you, Barbara. I know about your eyes. In fact it seems I know you very well. Dennis has described you in living color."

"What about a midnight snack?" said Dennis.

"Oh, let's," said Barbara enthusiastically.

"The hamburgers are still hot. I picked them up half an hour ago. Guess where I got them?"

"McDolly's," said Ferdinand, "good old McDolly's."

So they sat around the little table and had hamburgers and potato salad and Coke. Ferdinand was bursting with questions, but he decided to wait till the hamburgers were gone. They all sensed heavy questions hovering in the air. But for the time being four young people were hungry and thirsty, and they were happy together. Eating is the very foundation of the universe.

It turned out that Mrs. Pavarone had taken Jenny back to St. Cecilia the same day she had learned that Ferdinand had been with her in the house. Mother Theresa and Father Domenico had both come to see Anna Fabrini and suggested to her that under the circumstances the best way to proceed was to let Jenny spend the latter part of the holidays at the Academy among those few students who for one reason or another couldn't go home. Jenny had resisted, but the combined strength of the priest, the Principal, Mrs. Pavarone and even her mother had made her go with the chaperone. It had been a hurried departure, almost a flight. There was no time to phone Ferdinand. She had wanted to, she said.

"Now you wonder how she got here, eating hamburgers with us," said Dennis. "Remember, Barbara can make things happen."

But Barbara let that question hang for the time being.

"We rented the room next door," she said, "for Jenny and you."

Ferdinand blushed, and when he looked at Jenny, she had her eyes cast down and had blushed too. She held her hands folded in her lap, and she seemed to press them together in embarrassment.

"It's a comfortable room," continued Barbara. "There are no problems, the landlord lives out of town."

Neither Ferdinand nor Jenny offered a comment. After a tense silence Dennis said, "That arrangement suits you, we thought."

Another pause. "Well," pressed Dennis, "what do you think, folks?"

Ferdinand pulled himself together. "Is it a nice room?" he said.

"Almost identical to this one, two comfortable beds, the sofa is new, and it has a corner window."

"Why don't the girls sleep there? I'd really prefer to be back in my room," said Ferdinand.

All of a sudden the tension was gone. They all talked at once. "Of course, excellent idea, why didn't I think of it before? A new sofa? And a corner window! The girls have lots to talk about. So have the boys."

"All right," said Barbara. Did she have a little frown on her forehead? "Let's go then, Jenny, the gentlemen want to be on their own."

She pulled the sheets off one of the beds and led the way to the neighboring room. They all followed, Jenny with her suitcase. After they had looked around and approved of the room, Dennis said, "I turned the heater up. If it gets too warm, open the window. There are no locks on these windows."

Barbara giggled. She gave Dennis a fleeting kiss.

"Good night then."

"Good night everybody."

"Good night," said Jenny. She was so grateful to Ferdinand.

"Oh, I almost forgot," said Barbara. She pulled the linen from one of the beds and dumped it on Ferdinand. "Here, sleep well !"

Everybody smiled. Ferdinand threw a glance at Jenny.

She was smiling too, and Ferdinand loved her dimples.

"So, that's your Ferdinand," Barbara said between brushing her teeth and gargling. She was standing in her nightie in front of the sink. Jenny had just knelt down beside her bed and begun to say a silent evening prayer.

"Oh that," said Barbara when she saw Jenny in the mirror. She waited for Jenny's Amen. Then she gargled once more and spat out. "We don't have a crucifix in here," she said, crawling into bed.

"You can pray anywhere," said Jenny.

"To tell you the truth, Jenny, I haven't prayed for a whole week."

"I didn't think you had."

"What's that mean?"

"How can you talk to Jesus when you live in sin?"

"You know, there comes a point beyond which I don't care."

Jenny sat up in bed. "Don't say that, Barbara. You care and I care."

"All right, I care. But I love Dennis."

"Maybe you shouldn't have taken me with you. I'm in your way."

"Everything would be fine if your Ferdinand had co-operated."

Jenny laid down again. "I like the way he arranged it," she said.

"You like him very much, don't you?"

"Oh yes, I do, Barbara, I do. . .I do."

"He's a dashing guy."

"Oh yes, and he's smart."

"But he's not Catholic?"

"Is Dennis Catholic?"

"I don't know. I haven't asked him, and he hasn't brought it up. I don't care about it."

"Don't say such things, Barbara. You do care, don't you?"

"If I wanted to marry him, I probably would care."

"You've got it all wrong, Barbara. If you don't want to marry someone, you can't. . .you shouldn't. . ."

"I don't want to discuss it," said Barbara abruptly.

Now there was a long pause.

"Jenny, are you still awake?"

"Yes."

"I admire you."

"What for?"

"You have principles."

"If I had principles I would now be asleep in the dormitory at St. Cecilia."

"I shouldn't have persuaded you to move in here with us. I shouldn't have sneaked you out of there after your chaperone had gone home."

"Oh, but I love him so."

Early in the morning they had breakfast together in the boys' room.

"How was your first night on Denver Road, Jenny?" asked Dennis.

All eyes converged on Jenny. Ferdinand thought she was as lovely and fresh as the morning dew on the goldenrod growing up the banks of the Humber. Why did he suddenly think of Sunday mornings with Jenny at the Humber?

"I did a lot of thinking," said Jenny. "I think I'll turn myself in today."

"Go back to St. Cecilia?" Barbara was disappointed. "Turn yourself in? Sounds like a criminal going to the police and confessing his misdeeds. Your adventure is just beginning."

"I feel like a criminal. I've let my mother down. The school may have contacted her by now. I have to go back."

"Jenny is right," said Ferdinand. "Let's make a plan for the future."

"Why worry about the future?" said Barbara. "Let's live now. The future comes all by itself, without our doing."

"What do you say, Ferdinand?" asked Dennis.

"Here's what I think we should do. Dennis works for the post office and I distribute hamburgers as before. That leaves us time to study for entrance to university."

"It's a long grind," said Dennis.

"But we want to do it, don't we, Dennis?"

Dennis looked at Barbara, "What about the girls?"

"I have no idea what to do next," said Barbara. "I want to be a singer, but I can't get the training at St. Cecilia. Mother Veronica is a nice old nun, but she can't teach me much."

"It costs a lot of money too," said Ferdinand.

Barbara shrugged. "Money is no problem for my parents, they've got too much of it."

"I suggest you ask your parents to give you lessons at the Conservatory."

"What about St. Cecilia?" objected Barbara.

"Music comes first, with or without St. Cecilia," said Ferdinand.

"Come back to St. Cecilia, Barbara. I'd miss you if you didn't. But no more rope mail and other weird things." Jenny looked at Dennis.

"No more this, no more that. I hate that. I'm almost seventeen, and I want to go my own way."

"As long as we are going forward, it doesn't matter which way we are going," said Ferdinand.

"Who's going to say what's forward?" Barbara was collecting the dishes and Jenny joined her. "Your forward may be my backward."

"We have to leave that decision to each individual," said Ferdinand. "As long as you don't step on anyone's toes, you can go in any direction you like."

"I agree with that," said Dennis. "Tomorrow I'll start the middle shift at the post office. At about three I'll be in the school office with your mail, as always."

Barbara seemed reconciled. "I'll stay home and cook your

dinner. School starts next Monday. I'll be there. See what they've got to offer. And I'll write Dad for lessons. Not a bad idea, Ferdinand."

"I'll go and pack my stuff," said Jenny, drying her hands.

"What's the rush, Jenny?" said Dennis. "We'll have lunch at McDolly's and then we'll all take you to St. Cecilia's. We'll carry your little suitcase."

Somebody knocked at the door.

"Who could that be?" said Dennis. "No one has ever knocked at the door except the landlord, and he's out of town." He went to open the door.

Two men in dark-blue trenchcoats entered. "Police," they said.

They were broad-chested, calm and polite, symbols of order and authority. They flashed their identification cards.

The boys and girls stood in silence, baffled.

"Sorry to interrupt," said one of them. He wore a moustache and seemed to be the spokesman.

"We understand this room is occupied by Mr. Dennis Neelson and Mr. Ferdinand Bauer?"

"Yes, sir," said Dennis. The younger policeman made notes.

"You are Mr. Neelson, I take it?"

"Yes, sir."

"And you must be Mr. Ferdinand Bauer."

"Bauers, with an s," said Ferdinand.

"It says Bauer here on this warrant." He took a piece of paper out of his pocket.

"It's Bauers, sir, with an s."

"What's your name, miss?" he asked Barbara.

"Would you mind telling me what this is all about?" she said. She had spunk. Her green eyes pierced the moustached policemen. Ferdinand remembered Dennis telling him he had been stabbed by Barbara's flashing glance. He saw Jenny shaking like an aspen leaf. She was frightened to death. He felt like putting his arm around her shoulder. But he didn't dare.

"Keeping a bawdy house, involving juveniles." The policeman stroked his moustache. "Your name, please."

"Barbara Kalinski."

"How old are you?"

"I'll be seventeen next week."

"And you, miss?" he addressed Jenny. "How old are you?" He sounded almost fatherly.

Jenny swallowed. Then she whispered "Fifteen."

"Who slept here?" He pointed to one of the beds.

"This is my bed," said Dennis.

"And this is my bed," said Ferdinand.

"Where did you sleep, miss?"

"The girls slept in their own room next door," Dennis cut in before the girls could speak.

"Where's that room?" said the questioner.

"Next door."

"Can we see it?"

Dennis led the policemen to the girls' room.

"So the ladies slept in this room here?"

"Yes, sir."

They went back to the boys' room.

"Whose slippers are these?" The officer pulled a pair of blue plush slippers with tassels on top from under Dennis's bed. As he lifted them up, something pink came with one of the slippers and fell on the floor in front of him. It was a pair of ladies' panties. The junior officer made notes.

The air in the room was suddenly thick and choking.

"Are you a student at St. Cecilia's Academy?" he continued with Jenny's interrogation.

"Yes."

"A boarding student?"

"Yes." Jenny's teeth were chattering. She tried to bite them together, but she didn't succeed. Everybody in the room heard it. Ferdinand suffered for her.

"Look, officer," he said, "Why don't we make it short? What's in the warrant?"

"You're all arrested. Put on your coats and let's go."

"Where to?" asked Dennis.

"Precinct Five."

As they went down the stairs, they saw the landlord disappear into a room. When they came out into the street and were just about to climb into the unmarked cruiser, Ferdinand caught a glimpse of two nuns scurrying around the corner.

18

It had happened several times at St. Cecilia's Academy. The police were aware of the special kind of students who had congregated at this school throughout its history. They had always worked closely with the administration. Only plainclothes officers were assigned on cases concerning St. Cecilia's.

There had been girls caught shoplifting at the department stores, and about once a year a girl disappeared, leaving her bed empty in the dorm for some time. In all these cases publicity had been avoided. The reputation of the institution had never suffered through such digressions of some of its students. And when graduation time came, the newspapers reported in full on the academic excellence of the school. After all, that's what counts, that's what impresses parents, and that's what attracts students from all over the world.

It was the fifth of June, and Barbara Kalinski was rehearsing for the musical offerings at the graduation exercises. Nothing much had changed for Barbara. Her father, after learning that his daughter had been released by the police and was safely back at the Academy, had immediately cabled five thousand dollars to the Church, with no strings attached. The Principal of the Academy had of course hoped for such generosity. In her report to Mr. Kalinski about the escapades of his daughter, she had gently hinted that much unnecessary expense and effort had been spent on Barbara's behalf, and that these were difficult times to keep the ship afloat in the name of the Lord. In her thank-you letter to Mr. Kalinski the Principal promised to have his name inscribed on one of the stained glass windows in the chapel that had not yet been assigned to any specific donor.

Barbara had not been given so much as a tongue lashing for having been found in a bawdyhouse. Since she was no longer a juvenile, she received no admonition from the police either. They had not gone into enough detail to establish whose panties were found under Dennis's bed.

Barbara and Joan Bommelstring were now taking lessons from Signor Mascagni at the Conservatory. Signor Mascagni was past his prime as an opera singer, but he had established himself as one of the finest teachers in the State of New York. His method of developing the chest for proper breathing had made him famous.

The two girls had been given permission to leave the school every Thursday at four o'clock to walk to the Conservatory. When they auditioned, Signor Mascagni admitted Barbara without hesitation. He told Joan to come back after some more preparation. But Barbara insisted that she wouldn't be able to come unless Joan were taken too. She told the teacher that her father's monthly check covered the tuition for both girls. She also told him, more or less truthfully, that the Academy wouldn't allow her to go alone to the Conservatory. Joannie served as a chaperone.

Jenny, of course, was an entirely different case.

Her mother would never have her name painted on a window in the chapel. She did not contribute at all to the cost of her daughter's education, let alone make a substantial donation to the establishment. Jenny obviously had been the victim of two unprincipled young men who had taken advantage of her innocence. She was crushed by the experience. In the precinct she had been a helpless bundle of remorse who evoked the pity of the investigators of this case. Before any more of the circumstances that led to the arrest were divulged or explained during the hearing, she had been released together with Barbara into the hands of the two nuns who had been attending the proceedings.

She had wondered what Mother Theresa of St. Boniface Separate School of Toronto had to do with all this. But she was sitting in the Principal's office when Jenny was told that she was on probation from now on. One more offensive action of any kind, and the scholarship would be revoked, she was told.

When she left the office and walked down the corridor, still in a daze and not sure about the magnitude of her sin, Mother Theresa came after her.

"Geneviève," she said, "You have been very lucky. It is by no means the end of your road. In a way it is fortunate that it has come to this. Now the case is out in the open, and you have been saved by the Grace of God through the vigilance of the Church."

"Mother," said Jenny, turning around and facing the nun squarely, "Saved from what?" For the first time in her life she felt resistance welling up in her. She was now as tall as the nun and could look firmly into her grey eyes. And for the first time in her life she saw the Principal's eyes shying away. Jenny resented this woman coming all the way from Canada to meddle in her personal life. She suddenly felt she was growing up, stepping over a threshold. The nun's eyes were shifting and avoiding her former pupil's stern face.

"Saved from what, Mother Theresa?" Jenny insisted.

"Saved from evil, my child."

The hall had filled with students who were silently rushing in single file to another classroom.

"What evil, Mother?"

"Evil influences from the past that don't seem to go away."

"I have just turned sixteen, Mother Theresa. I am grateful to my mother for bringing me up the way she did. I am even grateful to the Church for the scholarship to go to St. Cecilia. I don't see any evil influence."

Now the nun regained her authoritative confidence. She came down harshly: "The influence of Ferdinand Bauers."

"How can you say that?" said Jenny under her breath, "You don't even know him."

"Don't you see, Geneviève? He comes from a crime-ridden background, has been expelled from school for cruelty to fellow students, is characterized as anti-social by his school, and has persistently pursued you with his insanity even into another country. He's wicked and totally godless, don't you see that?"

Jenny smiled. "I love him," she said simply, more to herself than to the Principal. There was serenity in her face that was downright disarming. Mother Theresa was shocked and alarmed. Her lips were moving in a silent prayer, while she clutched her rosary and thumbed the beads.

Then Jenny said something that was quite inappropriate for the occasion.

"Have you never loved, Mother Theresa?" At no time had she talked like that to an adult, let alone a nun, the Principal of her former school. She regretted it as soon as the words were spoken. The effect on the nun was surprising. Her face lost all its harshness. Her eyes filled with tears. She dropped her rosary and left it dangling from her gown. Then she laid her hand on Jenny's arm.

"Yes, I have," she said softly.

Jenny realized there was a woman in that stern black convent's habit. The human being in that robe had just spoken.

She grasped Jenny's arms with both hands, swallowed and said, "Now I love Jesus, Geneviève." Her face radiated utter happiness. "And He loves me !"

Dennis and Ferdinand were the real culprits in the eyes of the police, but they were magnanimous with Dennis. They let him go, telling him to keep out of trouble if he wanted to work at the postal service. They kept Ferdinand locked up overnight in a tiny cell because they had to obtain information on him from Toronto. After a tormented, sleepless night behind bars Ferdinand was led to the hearing room again.

"Why were you expelled from school?" they asked him.

"I was accused of insubordination."

"And of beating up fellow students?"

"I only helped a lady who was attacked by a fellow."

"Oh yeah?" said the officer. He then leafed through a large book that looked like a photo album. Shoving it under Ferdinand's nose he pointed to two photographs, one en face and another in profile. "Do you know this man?"

Ferdinand recognized his father. With the stubble on his chin, the cropped hair, the desperately hollow eyes and the five-digit number on his chest he looked like many other criminals in the book. 'Tim Bauer' it said underneath, Bauer without an 's'. Ferdinand remembered the arresting officer spelling his name without the 's' too. They must have known all along that Ferdinand was the son of the fugitive. For him the bottom fell out. He buried his face in his hands.

"My father," he said in a choked voice.

"Where is he?" said the interrogator, sharp and commanding.

"I don't know."

"Come on now, don't give us that. Why did you come to the United States?"

"Not because of my father."

"I didn't ask you why you did not come. Why did you cross the border? And why to Buffalo?"

"I'm working at McDolly's." He couldn't tell them he was following Jenny. He had caused enough trouble for Jenny.

"Couldn't you work at McDolly's in Toronto?"

"Maybe."

"Did you try?"

"No."

"Don't play with us, Mr. Bauer. You met your father here, didn't you?"

"My name is Bauers, not Bauer. The name is misspelled here." He tapped on the album. "No, I didn't meet my father here. I didn't know he's in the States."

"You have been seen with your father at the Greyhound terminal here in Buffalo on December the twenty-third."

"That's a lie," shouted Ferdinand.

The officer kept calm. "Would you say that a servant of the Church lies?"

"Your servant of the Church either lied or was in error."

"Were you at the Greyhound terminal on December twenty-third?"

"Yes, I was."

"You see, nuns don't lie. What were you doing there?"

"I was going home for Christmas."

"Who was the man lying beside you on the bench?"

Somebody must have watched him really closely that afternoon. He remembered the vagabond snoring beside him on that bench, and he remembered the old hat heaving up and down on his stomach like the trophy on Chuck Wilson. He hadn't studied the man's face. His mind had been on going home and writing cards for Mom and Jenny.

"I have no idea who he was."

"You admit there was a man lying beside you?"

"Yes, I vaguely remember."

"See, nuns don't lie," the officer said again triumphantly.

"It wasn't my father."

"There are two witnesses who identified the picture in the book. It definitely was the fugitive beside you. When we got there you both had gone."

"I took the bus to Toronto."

"Was your father on that bus?"

"No, he wasn't." Ferdinand didn't say that with much conviction. Maybe they were right. It could have been his father lying there on the bench. He didn't see his face. If it was Tim Bauers, where was he now? Maybe he was in Toronto. He didn't see him on the bus. He hadn't been in the mood for studying faces in the bus, and he had dozed much of the time. He must phone his mother. As soon as they let him go he would phone her.

The officer sighed. "We'll let you go this time. But if you want to stay in the United States, you must keep out of trouble. Keep away from the Academy. This is a country of law and order."

"I haven't broken the law, sir."

"You came awfully close. You're lucky the charges are withdrawn."

"What charges, sir?"

"Keeping a bawdyhouse, involving a juvenile," said the interrogator, but when he saw Ferdinand raising his hand in protest, he added, "There's no complaint against you any more. You're free to go - on condition that you will not contact students at the school. If you do, you will be deported."

19

Dennis and Ferdinand took their studies seriously. After the brush with the law, they appeased the landlord by paying him a full month's rent for the girls' room. On Mondays and Wednesdays they attended the Junior College evening courses in three major subjects that would make them eligible for admission to a first year college program if they passed the examinations. Ferdinand had never been so busy in his life. Dennis was used to the rigors of a college course, but for Ferdinand it meant bridging the gap between high school and serious adult studies with a minimum of teacher guidance. Not only did he manage, but when the first examinations were held in June, he found himself in the upper ten per cent of the achievement scale at the college. And all that with a full load of work at McDolly's. While he filled paper cups with Coke or coleslaw and wrapped hamburgers 'to go' in the restaurant, his mind was on mathematics and physics, and he found that in the evening he had clarified a number of problems and was ready to tackle his assignments promptly.

Dennis had been told to keep away from St. Cecilia's. But he didn't want to risk being recognized by a nun as one of the seducers of their students. He grew himself a smart moustache and asked for another delivery route. Barbara had phoned to tell him about her lessons at the Conservatory. So, every Thursday evening, after her vocal training, Barbara met Dennis clandestinely for a half hour, while Joan Bommelstring was still with Signor Mascagni.

Ferdinand was looking forward to these Thursdays just as much as Dennis was, because Barbara had become the most reliable postal service for a regular letter exchange with Jenny. Ferdinand made sure that his homework was done before Dennis came home from the Conservatory. Then he had the whole evening for reading Jenny's letter again and again.

Evening school was very demanding, and you needed a special kind of dedication to keep it up. Most students were rather mature and had to make a living at the same time. Ferdinand and Dennis doggedly pushed their way through never-ending assignments. Ferdinand had just finished a quiz in physics when Dennis delivered another letter from Jenny. Dennis withdrew into his books and left his friend to himself.

"Dear Ferdinand,

I'm sitting in the library. The nun is reading the big Bible at her desk. Her lips are moving, but you can't hear her. Every now and then her eyes sweep over the half dozen students working quietly in here. Joannie is coming in. She's giving me a big smile. She knows I'm writing to you. When my letter is finished, I'll give it to her. You'll have it tonight.

Isn't it awful that I have to be so clandestine about writing to you? Barbara says she's glad she doesn't have to write letters to Dennis. She's not a letter writer, she says. I love to write letters to you. But, of course, I'd like to see you too. Will that ever come?

You are the only person in the world I write letters to. I don't count the letters to Mom, because I always know somebody is reading every word I write before Mom gets it. I always have a feeling that somebody in a black robe is leaning over my shoulder when I sit down to write a letter to Mom.

So you are the only person in the world to whom I can speak freely and with honesty.

You are my real friend. If you can't speak freely to a real friend, that's awful. Makes you feel you're in prison. After what you wrote about your night in prison, I can imagine how it is. Prison must be unbearable if you're not guilty.

Oh, I forgot to mention that I got an 'A' in my English essay. I expect to do well in all my subjects. I've come to like physics too. Our teacher says the Church is not inflexible. It goes with the times, she says, because God makes the times. That's plausible, don't you think? Maybe one day Gregor Mendel will be sainted. Then you can become a Catholic. Sometimes I think it would be nice if you and I could kneel in Church and receive Holy Communion together.

Joannie is throwing a question mark at me with her eyes. I better finish. I could write on and on. It feels like talking to you. Now I would like to say something very nice, but I can't. I don't know how to.

Goodbye for now,
Jenny."

Mathilda Bauers was now resigned to her son living across the border. She was hoping to see him in the summer. Her work at Austen and Blimp and the letters from Buffalo kept her going.

The phone call from Ferdinand after his release from Precinct Five's cell had scared her.

Coming home from work, she found another letter from her son. She read with flying fingers:

"Dear Mom,

I want you to know I'm not coming home for the holidays. McDolly is giving me ten days. I passed all three courses with an 'A'. I'm telling you that because I know you will be proud of me. I want you to be proud of your son. I'm going to take two more credit courses during the summer. If I make it, I'll be a full-time college student in the fall. The manager at McDolly's wants me to go to their management school. But I'm sold on genetics. T.B. hasn't contacted you, has he? When I phoned you after the hearing, I didn't want to scare you. I now think the nuns that spied on me -maybe they still do - wanted to impress the police and get rid of me. They must have been fully briefed by their sisters in Toronto. So I don't think T.B. crossed the border that day. God knows where he is. We'll probably never know. And we don't really care, do we?

Now that I have a clear goal and an excellent chance of getting there, I am very happy, Mom.

Hope you're well. One of these days I'll make the trip to Toronto.

Love,

Ferdinand."

20

The leaves on the maples along Denver Road were full and lush again. The first summery days had followed a long and dreary winter and a spring that went almost unnoticed.

Dennis had just left for his Saturday work at the post office and Ferdinand had settled into the armchair for some reading when somebody knocked at the door.

It was Tom Dudston from Toronto.

"Hi, Ferdinand," he said with a broad grin.

"Tommy Dudston, what a surprise! Come in, Tommy. How did you get into the house?"

"The door was open. So I came up and knocked at the first door."

"It's good to see you, Tom. It's been a long time."

"Half a year. Let me look at you. You haven't changed much."

"You look like a Students' Council President."

"How are you doing these days," said Tom sitting down on the sofa.

"Want a Coke? After that bus ride you want a Coke, don't you?"

"No, thanks. I came by car. Dad let me have it for the trip to Buffalo. By the way, best regards from my parents."

"Thank you."

"Don't you miss good old Toronto?"

"I have my work here, Tom, and I'm doing well at the college."

"Your mother told me. That's great. I have to grind through another year before I can go to university."

Ferdinand said, "Come over here, and you'll save a whole year. You don't need Grade thirteen."

"I'm a Toronto boy," said Tom. "Do you get the Toronto Star here in Buffalo? Do you keep up with the news from home?"

"No, I don't. What's new?"

"Your name was in the paper."

Ferdinand had a sinking feeling. Did the police affair spill over to Ontario? Or did Tim Bauers show up after all?

Tom pulled an envelope out of his pocket. He showed him a paper clipping with two look-alike boys pictured, one holding a pigeon, while the other spread out one wing of the bird to show the snow-white feathers.

"Frankie and Freddy," said Ferdinand.

"Read the caption," said Tom.

"Frank and Fred Fabrini of the St. Boniface Separate School were First Prize winners of the competition of the Canadian Animal Breeders' Exhibition. Their blue-and-white pigeons were recognized as a new race."

"They did have the gene. I knew it was somewhere in there," Ferdinand was triumphant.

"Read on," said Tom.

Ferdinand read about an interview with the boys. They told the reporter that a certain Ferdinand Bauers had discovered this breed first. The reporter had then interviewed Mr. Malcolm of the public school who remembered Ferdinand as an outstanding student of science. Mr. Malcolm had then directed the reporter to Mr. Smith at Humber Collegiate. Mr. Smith also confirmed that Ferdinand Bauers was a top student and had been awarded the Science Plaque for his excellent achievement. "He moved to the United States," he added.

"How are the Fabrini boys?"

"They're having trouble in school," said Tom. "Their school doesn't offer them enough science, they say. And they have been told not to read the books on evolution and genetics that they get from the public library."

Ferdinand laughed. "You can't suppress knowledge. What else is new, Tom?"

"Nothing much. I guess you haven't changed your mind about coming back to Humber Collegiate?"

"I'm a Buffalo boy now," said Ferdinand.

"I won't even recommend your coming back to Humber now."

"You have changed your mind too?"

"We've got a new Principal."

"What's wrong with the old one?"

"Promoted upwards."

"On the basis of performance, I presume." Ferdinand grinned.

"On the basis of seniority and a smooth running school."

"Still rewarding door-to-door salesmanship?"

"Yep."

"And creating school spirit on the bleachers."

"That too."

"Are the Vikings winning?"

"Almost, as always. Their uniforms cost us more than all the other items on the school budget together."

"So you don't think I could swallow all that?"

"You probably could, if you had to. But you couldn't live with the new Principal, Mr. Bulnik."

Ferdinand shook with laughter and Tom joined him.

"Did he distribute ash trays in the classrooms?"

"Not yet. But give him time. In anticipation of such bulnikation I have resigned as President of the Students' Council."

"I like that. . .bulnikation. . ." They burst into laughter again.

"And guess who's Vice-Principal?"

"Don't tell me. . .How many guesses do I have?"

"One."

"McNelly."

"You guessed it."

"He hasn't even been Department Head."

"There are compensating features." They laughed again.

"So now you have given up Students' Council work."

"I want to concentrate on my studies," said Tom seriously.

"What are you going to take up at university?"

"Biology, of course."

"Medicine could be called biology of man."

"I think I will specialize in genetics."

"No more bellybuttons?"

"No more bellybuttons. A propos bellybuttons. You haven't asked me how Tina is."

"How's Tina?"

"Pregnant."

"What?" Ferdinand was staring at his friend, mouth open.

"She quit school long ago. She's in her ninth month by now. It was bound to happen. It happens to all the Tinas. There's a lot of giggling in the school. And of course the guessing game is on. Who's the father? For a while they were even suggesting you were the father. Can you imagine, Ferdinand Bauers, father of an illegitimate child? Ferdinand, the straight, the top science student, a man of the highest principles? Of course, nobody believed it. But you know how it is, rumors are persistent. Then they said Warren Potomac was the father. A Don Juan like Potomac could have been, with his record in such matters. Potomac, by the way, was the one who insisted he had seen you in Tina's house on the night of the prom. It was Warren Potomac who started the rumor that you are the father. Can you imagine that? You of all people! I'm lucky, I guess nobody knows <u>my</u> adventure with Tina. I bet they would extrapolate from my experience with Tina's bellybutton into the present time. It's so easy to get carried away by your fantasy."

Tom didn't notice that Ferdinand had sunk into his armchair with an expression of bewilderment on his face. He kept talking. "Lizzie Brown finally put an end to all the guessing. Her uncle has a cottage next to the Huttings in Muskoka. Tina has spent several weekends at the cottage with a young man, she said."

"When?" said Ferdinand.

"We were thinking about that too. Lizzie knows for sure she was there in October, the weekend before the prom, and again after the prom. Each time Lizzie saw a blue Jaguar at the Huttings cottage, and she saw Tina and the man driving away."

"That settles that, doesn't it?"

"Poor Tina," said Tom. "I feel kind of sorry for her."

"She's a good girl," Ferdinand agreed.

"Yeah, she didn't deserve that. But isn't it interesting, it seems to run in the family."

"You mean illegitimacy is inheritable?" said Ferdinand.

"Well, you need a certain lack of responsibility, a degree of looseness of morals, maybe a weakness of character to do a thing like that."

"What about the circumstances? The situation could be tempting. Circumstances are not inherited."

"Sex drive is," said Tom.

"There are two people involved. Maybe the man is to be blamed."

"Even if the woman is utterly attractive," said Tom, "the man should put the brakes on. I agree, he's responsible."

"Maybe it isn't such a disaster," pondered Ferdinand. "A child can be a blessing."

"It wasn't for Mrs. Pavarone, or for Mr. Teitelbaum. It took many years for the community to stop whispering and to finally accept the situation as it was," said Tom. "Now they're whispering again."

"A child should have both parents. They should get married."

"They probably will. A man with a Jaguar is a man of means."

"But he may be a jerk."

Tom laughed heartily, but Ferdinand sat there glumly.

"Let me take you out to a good restaurant, Ferdinand. You're probably sick of McDolly's French Fries."

"You've said it. Good idea, Tom. But I have to report for work at two o'clock. I know a little Hungarian spot downtown. You have the car. We might as well have a bite there."

So the two friends drove to the Csardas and had a hearty goulash. The red table cloth, the candles and the well-dressed clientele cheered Ferdinand up. He told Tom about his embarrassing brush with the police, his night in jail, his possible encounter with his father, and his guilty feeling about dragging Jenny into the mess.

"You are in love, Ferdinand."

"Everything I do now is with Jenny in mind. When I study calculus, when I dish out hamburgers, when the ghost of my father catches up with me, when you tell me about home, I always think of Jenny."

"Life is hard. Complications are awesome. You've had your share, Ferdinand."

"Yeah, but. . .Tommy, it's all worth it. I love her so much, it hurts when I think of it. But it's a beautiful pain."

"I envy you, Ferdinand."

"It'll come to you too. There's nothing one can do about it. It rains from the sky."

"We'll see," said Tom with a smile. "Oh, before I forget: your mother got her five hundred dollars back from Mrs. Potomac."

"Great ! I don't go around kicking out other people's teeth." He grinned.

Ferdinand didn't see Dennis because he started working at McDolly's after he had said goodbye to his friend from Toronto. He was thinking of Tom. It had been such a pleasant visit. Every little bit of manipulation here at the counter was mechanical. It didn't require his thinking. He was quick and efficient, but his mind was on something else.

He remembered the night in Tina's house. How she had shoved the mocha chocolates into his mouth, how he had watched her hands when she cut the Italian layer cake, how he had closed his eyes and breathed in her mysterious fragrance.

And suddenly he saw her with a little baby in her arms. Her large eyes were resting seriously on him, Ferdinand. The baby looked just like her, Italian and so pretty in its innocence. Ferdinand felt curiously attached to the picture of mother and child.

He didn't hear the cash register ring. A customer handed back a ten dollar bill. "I only gave you a five," he said.

"Thank you, sir," said Ferdinand, wiping his forehead. Then he shut the drawer of the register, went to the manager and asked him to let him go home. He wasn't feeling well. This was the first time it had happened. There was no problem.

Dennis was writing an essay on the young Gaugin. He was surrounded by books. Ferdinand opened his calculus text. But after a while he snapped it shut. He brushed his teeth and went to bed.

"Something wrong?" asked Dennis, looking up from his writing.

"Nothing, just tired."

Dennis worked till deep into the night. He finally closed his books and tip-toed to the door.

"Dennis?" he heard Ferdinand saying.

"I thought you were asleep."

"I think I won't go to work tomorrow."

"What's the problem?"

"I don't feel right."

Dennis came back and sat down at Ferdinand's bedside. "What is it?"

"I think I'm getting the flu or something."

Dennis held his hand on his roommate's forehead. "You've got a fever."

"Sometimes I feel hot, sometimes I freeze."

"Maybe you ate something wrong."

"I didn't eat at all after lunch."

"Tell you what. I'll give you an aspirin, and, if it isn't better in the morning, we'll get you to a doctor." He got up and shook a pill from the aspirin bottle. He came back with a glass of water and propped up his friend. "Take that. It won't do any harm and it keeps down your fever."

Ferdinand gulped. "Give me another glass, please."

He poured down the second glass of water.

"You're thirsty."

"I feel awfully weak, Dennis, but I have to go to the washroom."

Dennis helped his friend out of bed and supported him out into the hall.

"I can manage, thank you," he said and proceeded to the toilet on his own.

Dennis returned to his room, changed into his pyjamas and began brushing his teeth. He looked at his watch. Two-thirty. Rinsing his mouth, he was startled by a thumping noise in the hall. He rushed out and found Ferdinand lying on the floor, face down and arms sprawled.

"Oh, my God," he whispered. He turned him around and held up his head. "Ferdinand, wake up !"

Ferdinand's eyes were closed. His body was limp. Dennis let down his head gently, gently. Now he became frightened. He ran through the hall and knocked at all the doors. "Somebody help !" he shouted.

Several people opened their doors and rushed to the scene.

"What happened? Is he dead? Is he breathing? Is there a doctor in the house?"

"Stay here with him," said Dennis. "I'll get an ambulance." He ran down to the phone. As he came back up, the roomers were bending over Ferdinand. A young woman was crying.

"Such a nice man," she said between sobs.

"The ambulance will be here in a few minutes," said Dennis. He had three men help carry Ferdinand into his room and lay him on the sofa. He placed a pillow under his head.

"What happened?" said one of the men.

"I don't know. He went to the washroom and collapsed."

Two women stood in the door. The sobbing one said, "I hope he's all right."

"Do you know him?" said the other.

"I've met him in the hall many times. He's got such a nice smile."

"Will somebody please open the door downstairs for the medical people?" said Dennis. The men immediately obliged.

Now Ferdinand opened his eyes. He was pale, and sweat pearled on his forehead. "What's the matter?" he said feebly.

"You blacked out coming from the toilet."

"Oh," he said almost inaudibly.

Now there was a commotion downstairs.

"You'll go to the hospital. They'll see what's the matter with you."

A train of people rushed up the stairs. Two men in grey uniforms carried a stretcher into the room, moved Ferdinand skilfully over and asked Dennis to get dressed and come with them to the emergency department. The roomers still stood about as Dennis locked the door and followed the stretcher down.

At the hospital they decided to keep Ferdinand for observation. They wouldn't say what the problem was.

"I'll see you tomorrow," said Dennis to his friend as he was wheeled into room 104. Ferdinand smiled thinly.

Three days later Ferdinand was still in hospital. Dennis

visited him every day. Room 104 had two beds, but the other patient had been released that morning.

"I'll phone your mother," Dennis said, pulling up a chair beside Ferdinand's bed.

"No, don't," said Ferdinand. "I have eaten a little today and the fever is almost down. I don't want to scare her." His face showed the strain. His cheeks were hollow, and there were shadows around his eyes. Dennis didn't believe his friend would be released soon. It was a disturbing thought that the doctors had not found a cause for the problem.

"The fever has to come down before they let you go."

Ferdinand stared at the ceiling, and Dennis didn't know what to say. He put a paper bag on the side table. "Two oranges," he said. "You can eat oranges, can't you?"

"Yes, thank you," Ferdinand replied absent-mindedly, still looking at the ceiling. Then they were quiet for a while.

"Dennis?"

"Yes."

"I know what my problem is," said Ferdinand. His voice was weak.

"You do? Did you tell the doctor?"

"No. I won't."

"Why not?"

"It's psychosomatic."

"But you have a real fever."

"The symptoms can be bodily, just like in any other disease."

"How do you know."

"I read about it."

"But if it's psychosomatic, why didn't you get it right in the cell at Precinct Five?"

"That wasn't it, Dennis. Something more serious has come

up."

"But everything has gone so well since then, Ferdinand."

"No, it hasn't. I told you about Tom Dudston visiting me."

"Maybe it was the goulash at the Csardas!"

"It wasn't physical. Tom told me I'm going to be a father."

Dennis moved his chair closer. He placed his hand on Ferdinand's forehead. "You still have some fever, Ferdinand. Don't talk so much. Just take it easy, real easy. Promise you'll relax and just take it easy. I'm going now. I'll be back tomorrow."

"Wait." He raised his hand a little.

Dennis sat down.

"She's in her ninth month now. . .I'm the father."

"Who is in her ninth month?"

"Her name is Tina, Tina Huttings."

Dennis was speechless.

"It's not what you are thinking, Dennis. She's a good girl."

Ferdinand had his eyes closed. "She's a good girl, and she needs a father for her baby."

"Well," said Dennis, "that's no disaster. Don't worry about it, Ferdinand. Such problems can be solved, you know, all over the world, all the time. . .dammit, how could it happen to you?"

Ferdinand ran his tongue over his parched lips. "Give me a glass of water, please."

Dennis helped him with the glass, holding up his head.

"Thank you."

"I repeat, Ferdinand, it's not a disaster. You must recover first and get your strength back. Then you and I will tackle the problem. There are lots of options. There's really no reason to worry."

"But I love her so much." He still had his eyes closed.

"Then there's no problem whatsoever. So many men are forced into marriage without any love by an accident like an illegitimate child. If you love her. . ."

"I love Jenny."

"Jenny? I forgot about Jenny."

"I can never forget about Jenny."

"Listen, boy. I see your problem now. We'll talk about it tomorrow. We'll work it out together. I'm sure we can." He rose and walked towards the door.

"Dennis?"

"Yeah?"

"I'm glad I have you."

"Okay, Ferdinand. What are friends for? Don't forget your oranges. See you tomorrow."

Dennis went to the counter where the nurses on duty read the Readers Digest. "Excuse me," he said, "My friend in room 104, Ferdinand Bauers, you know him?"

"Sure I know him. The one with the fever."

"Can I see his doctor, please?"

"Dr. Granatstein will be on duty tomorrow morning at ten."

"Can I have a talk with him then?"

"He's very busy."

"I'm sure he is. I only want two minutes."

"Be here at ten sharp."

"Thank you."

The nurse made a note.

It was Thursday. He saw Barbara in the evening at the Conservatory.

Next morning Dennis caught Dr. Granatstein in the hall before he started his round. He told him about Ferdinand's opinion that his troubles were caused by an emotional upset.

The doctor listened with interest. "What was it that upset him?" he said.

"Oh, a family matter. He might tell you about it, he might not."

"It is well established that emotional upheavals cause physical disorders. We have done a series of tests on your friend. Clinically, there's nothing wrong with him. He may well be right with his own diagnosis."

"What can be done, doctor?"

"He might be better off at home, unless that's where his trouble originates."

"No, his home is in Canada. I am his roommate here."

"Can you look after him? He should be ready to go home tomorrow."

"Sure, doctor. That's what I had hoped you would suggest."

"We'll release him into your care tomorrow morning."

"Thank you so much, doctor."

"Good luck." They shook hands.

Dennis rushed to check in at the post office.

Twenty-four hours later, Ferdinand's temperature was back to normal. He was cheerful now and eager to go home. Dennis ordered a taxi and gently helped his friend up the stairs in the Denver Road rooming house.

There were three roses in a vase on the table. Ferdinand said, "Lovely flowers."

"From the lady next door, for your home coming."

"I don't know any lady next door." He picked up the card and read, "From your neighbor Susan."

"She knows you. She said you had such a nice smile."

Ferdinand grinned for the first time since he had collapsed in the hall. "I didn't know I could impress anyone with my smile."

"She even cried when you lay there on the floor."

"Don't you have to go to work, Dennis?"

"I took three days off. Don't worry about me. I just get a shorter vacation. McDolly was good to you too about your sickness. So, we're lucky. Want to lie down?"

"I feel much better. I'll sit right here in the armchair."

"I saw Barbara last night."

"Any letter for me?"

"Better than that."

"Two letters?"

"Much better. I told Barbara about you. She'll bring Jenny over to see you."

"Oh, Dennis, I don't think that's good."

"It's the best medicine Barbara and I could concoct for you."

"I don't think I want to see Jenny. How can I tell her about Tina?

"You don't tell her about Tina. In all of the United States of America you and I are the only people who know about you and Tina."

"Even in Canada, only Tina and I know about it."

"And you aren't talking. But Tina might."

"I have to talk to Tina. I can't face Jenny before I have talked to Tina. I'm almost twenty, I can shoulder it."

"Shoulder what?"

"Fatherhood."

"Don't be silly. You don't have to marry her."

"I told you, she's a good girl."

"I once heard a Swedish philosopher say: 'Marry only out of love !' "

Ferdinand sighed. "I'm always thinking of Tina. She must be crying every day, and with much better reason than the lady next door."

"Have you ever thought she might want to give up her baby for adoption?"

"Are you crazy? She can't do that."

"Why not?"

"It's my baby too."

"But you couldn't marry her even if you loved her. You can't support a family working at McDolly's. And what about our studies? No, you're too young to get trapped, Ferdinand."

"I don't have to become a scientist."

"You don't throw that away, just because a girl you don't love is having a baby. I bet she's just as guilty getting pregnant as you are. Let her bear the consequences."

"I have to be honest with Tina. I have to make my decision with her. Last night, after you left me in the hospital room, while I peeled an orange, it suddenly became crystal clear to me: I won't desert the mother of my baby. She's an illegitimate child herself. She still sees her natural parents even although they've gone their separate ways. No, Dennis, that's not the way my child will grow up. Don't you see, Dennis, my child, my own flesh and blood! I love him already, and he may not even be born yet." Ferdinand had regained some color in his face.

Dennis smiled. "Did you notice, you said you love him?"

"I don't care. If it's a girl, she will have very dark eyes with long lashes, almost black hair, a beautiful complexion and full red lips, like her mother. All dominant features."

"Tina must be beautiful."

"Oh, she's beautiful. Very attractive. The boys in the school were crazy about her."

"Then she'll have no difficulty getting married in spite of her child. The child will have her biological mother and a father too. Do you think children know the difference between the real father and the one in whose arms they grow up? If I were you I wouldn't touch the thing with a ten foot pole. Leave everything as it is and see what happens. Where's Tina now?"

"I don't have any idea. I could find out."

"Don't find out. Let fate take its course. For one thing, you're safe here in the United States. I don't think you owe her anything, particularly not across the border."

"You don't understand, Dennis. I want to play it straight with Tina."

"Has she played it straight with you? Has she ever contacted you and warned you about what happened and what was going to come nine months later? If she had told you in time, something could have been done about it."

"What do you mean?"

"There's nothing wrong with abortion. Teenagers aren't ready for parenthood. You could have helped her getting an abortion. It costs money, but it could have been done, and the whole problem could have been solved before it became a big one."

"Dennis, that's where I think differently. I have never before thought about such complicated matters. But my instinct tells me I want to be the father of that boy so much, I would begin to love his mother for giving me a child. Would you believe, when I looked into the pigeon nests and saw a baby bird break through the egg shell, my heart beat fast? It's creation, Dennis. Birth is creation. I get a kind of religious feeling over that. And now, here, this is mine. I'm in it. And through the baby I'm carried into the future, long after I die. Isn't that something great? It's awesome, when you think of it."

"You're actually thinking genetics."

"Any ordinary human being should get religious over becoming a parent."

"These are big thoughts, noble thoughts almost. But don't get lost in the clouds. You said yourself you will never forget Jenny."

"Maybe time will heal it all."

"I tell you what. You just mull it over. There's lots of time. It will get clearer in your mind every day. And maybe I can learn something too from a mess like this."

"But I don't want to see Jenny, please."

"All right, I'll call it off. And now let me make dinner."

For the summer, Barbara Kalinski rented the room next to Dennis Neelson and Ferdinand Bauers. There's nothing wrong with renting a room on Denver Road. The landlord didn't care if a single young lady slept next door to young men as long as she paid the rent. And she paid for the months of July and August ahead of time. You wouldn't expect a landlord to watch over the moral behavior of his tenants as long as nobody complained. As long as the police and those austere sisters from the Academy didn't snoop around, everything was all right. How was he to know the pretty young lady with the elegant leather suitcase was a student at St. Cecilia?

Barbara took her studies with Signor Mascagni very seriously. It was so much easier to apply yourself with élan to a subject in which you have already won recognition, than to those stuffy school subjects. The situation was ideal during the summer. Classrooms at the school were closed. Barbara practised two or three hours a day in the rooming house. No one was disturbed by her scales and arpeggios because all the young people in the house were working in the daytime. Even Dennis and Ferdinand spent many hours at the Junior College in their summer courses.

The only times she didn't sing during the day was when Dennis stayed home. Her blue plush slippers with the tassels on top were now under her own bed, in her own room.

Ferdinand found himself studying alone in his room most nights.

"Women are distracting," he said one day after supper.

"It all depends," said Dennis. "They can drain away your energy and at the same time build you up and give you strength."

"Oh, but there are so many hazards."

"There are hazards in everything we do in life," said Dennis. "The secret is to master the hazards and enjoy what you're doing at the same time."

"You can't plan it that way."

"That's probably true. You've got to have luck too," said Dennis.

"And I haven't had much luck lately," brooded Ferdinand.

"If I were you, I would write a letter to Jenny."

"It's out of the question. I can't tell her about Tina. It would destroy our relationship."

"You don't have to tell her anything."

"Oh, Dennis, you can't begin to fathom the kind of feeling I have for Jenny. Nothing but absolute honesty would do. If you knew the girl, you would understand. She is as pure as gold. I would never lie to Jenny, never !"

"You didn't tell her about your adventure with Tina, did you?"

"I would have, if there had been a chance. We have never been alone together since my fling with Tina. Do you realize that, Dennis? I have not held her in my arms, ever. I have never kissed her. I haven't even said anything of importance to her. The only thing she has ever said to me that made me shiver was, 'I'll give you a call.' "

"That's not exactly a declaration of love. And she never called you, did she?"

"Oh, but I'm so sure about Jenny, you see, and I don't want to hurt her."

"Why can't you write a nice letter without going into the matter of Tina's illegitimate baby? You don't <u>know</u> if it's your baby, and you don't have any direct knowledge from her personally. Maybe it's all just a story. You've heard it second hand. Why don't you find out for sure? In the meantime, don't leave Jenny hanging. At least answer her last letter. I have met her too. I don't claim that I'm so much more mature and experienced than you are, Ferdinand. Well, not much more anyway." He grinned. "But I think Jenny is a lovely girl. I've seen her blush. I know she loves you. Don't lose her."

"Maybe some time later, when we've finished the summer courses." They made lunch together.

21

The final examinations had been written at St. Cecilia. Now it was the night before the graduation exercises. Barbara and Joan had been practising hard for the musical part of the celebration. The girls had made substantial progress at the Conservatory, and the school rules had been bent to allow for rehearsals at odd times.

Jenny was in awe every time in the dormitory or even in the washroom, when the singers went through their duets. Oh, to be a singer! Instead of crawling under the bedcovers right after the evening prayer Barbara sat on her bed and practised breathing. Her breasts were bulging under her nightie. Then she sang scales, me, me, me. . .mo, mo, mo. . .up and down, up and down. Then the same in chromatic scale. Even a simple thing like a scale made the girls in the room sit up and watch. Yes, singers are privileged people.

But the nun on duty cut all that out by switching off the light. Barbara and Joan would then cover their heads with their blankets and still hum a little theme from their Handel part. Surely, God would forgive them. It was all in His honor.

Jenny was promoted to her senior year at the Academy together with Barbara and Joan. Her report card was something to be proud of since she was first in the whole school, even with a rather poor mark in religious studies. She had shocked her teacher one day by asking him to tell the class something about other religions. He had mentioned Islam as another monotheistic faith and, with some derision in his voice, added, "They say Mohammed heard the voice of God and wrote down what he heard. And now they call that the Koran."

Jenny had raised her hand and asked the teacher, "In what language did God speak to Mohammed?"

"It wasn't really God he heard," said the teacher. "It was what they call Allah. Allah is their God. The Koran is written in Arabic. There you have it, their Allah speaks Arabic." He smiled as if he were forgiving the poor pagans.

"Is there one God for us and another for the Mohammedans?" asked Jenny.

"No, there's only one God," said the teacher.

"Then their Allah is not God."

The priest looked nervously around the room. "Of course not," he said. He found students like Geneviève Fabrini uncomfortable and slightly suspect. But of course he wouldn't swim against the stream and give her a failing mark in 'religion'. So, in spite of the low mark in this subject, she had an average of over ninety per cent.

The festivities had been uplifting. Brother Vincent, the Methuselah at the organ, filled the hall with a glorious tumult that shook the listeners through and through. The presence of the Bishop in his splendid silken robe and his dignified miter had given special significance to this event. After the celebration Jenny was introduced to him together with Barbara and Joan. They genuflected and kissed his ring as they had been taught in 'religion'. It was a proud moment for her and the two soloists.

Anna Fabrini, in her pew among other parents and the rest of the school, had tears of pride in her eyes.

The school provided a bus to the railway station and to the Greyhound terminal. Jenny said goodbye to Barbara who was staying for studies with Signor Mascagni, and to Joannie who was going to Los Angeles for her father's fourth wedding.

The janitor had opened the big gate for the bus. As it drove out, an ambulance silently rushed in and stopped at the chapel. The travellers were spared the sadness of witnessing Brother Vincent's final trip. He had collaped after his last concert. They found him with a smile on his withered face. It couldn't have been a more sublime ending for the oldest member of St. Cecilia's Academy.

Anna was happy to have her daughter back home. Jenny's school work was a source of pride for her mother, and her two brothers told anyone who would listen, "Jenny's home. She's the top banana in her school."

Jenny insisted she wanted to work during the summer to make some money. She had talked to Anna on the bus about her chances of getting a job.

"I could teach you how to sew. There's really not much to it, and Mr. Teitelbaum needs help all the time."

"I want to try McDolly's."

When Anna heard the name of that restaurant, she recoiled. "Why McDolly of all places?" She had been told that the reason for all the difficulties in Jenny's life was Ferdinand Bauers and she knew he was working for McDolly's in Buffalo. She had decided not to stir up the embarrassing memories of the police action right after Christmas. She had been lucky not to see her daughter expelled. Now Jenny had brilliantly pulled through her troubles. The Church had exercised truly Christian forgiveness, had not revoked the scholarship, had on the contrary encouraged Jenny to continue studying at the famous school. They had been so right keeping her daughter from seeing that unfortunate young man with the dubious background and such godless ideas. Now she wanted to work at McDolly's.

"McDolly's on Queen Street? It's a long way from home."

"They are good employers."

"You don't want to be a waitress, Jenny."

"Waitress isn't any worse than seamstress."

"But it isn't a good restaurant."

"They are good to their employees. And I don't have to come home for lunch."

"You don't want to eat hamburgers every day."

"They have other things too. Anyway, I'll go and talk to them."

Anna realized her daughter did her own thinking now. Maybe that's the way it was going to be with all her children. They were growing up. Not so in Italy. She knew for sure she would never be able to pick young men for her three daughters and tell them to marry their mother's choice. Things were different now, maybe even in Calabria.

The next day, early in the morning, Jenny took the streetcar to McDolly's, was hired on the spot, outfitted with a uniform and kept all day long to learn the special McDolly tricks. She phoned her mother at noon, sounding happy to make money for the first time in her life. When she came home, she was so tired she could hardly answer all the questions from Freddy and Frankie. To them she looked like a breadwinner. She felt like one, too, went to bed and set the alarm clock for seven thirty.

In a very short time Jenny became the manager's prize worker at McDolly's. She was quick, neat and cheerful. It didn't escape the manager either that she was very pretty in her blue uniform with the tiny bonnet on her curly hair. Customers like to be served by pretty girls.

When she received her first pay check, she placed it in the centre of the kitchen table. The whole family sat around the table and stared at the check while the dinner sizzled in the oven. An appreciation of hard-earned money was natural to immigrants and their children.

"Wow," said Frankie, "do you get a check like that every month?"

"Every two weeks," said Jenny.

"Oh boy ! What are you going to do with it?" said Freddy.

"I don't know yet."

"You should put it in the bank," said Mary. She already had a little bank account from her baby sitting.

"I don't make much more than that myself," said Anna. "We are lucky Mary got a scholarship for the Abbey, otherwise she couldn't go to school."

"She could go to Humber Collegiate. It costs nothing," said Jenny.

"You get what you pay for. I'm glad I haven't been forced to send any of you to a school like that."

"There are lots of Catholics going to Humber," said Jenny.

"How do you know?"

"One of them is working at McDolly's. He told me."

"He can't be a good Catholic," said Sophie.

"Does he go to church?" Freddy wanted to know.

"I don't know," said Jenny, "it's none of my business. He's a nice guy."

"Tommy isn't Catholic. He's a nice guy too," said Frankie.

"You don't have to be a Catholic to be a nice guy."

"What's the use of being a nice guy, if you can't go to Heaven?" said Freddy.

"Our teacher says there are no Moslems in Heaven." Jenny sounded a little facetious, thought Anna.

"Moslems aren't Catholics," explained Freddy.

"They could be nice guys though," said Frankie.

"How do you know? You've never seen one."

Anna rose. "That's enough talk now. Set the table, boys. We'll have dinner."

Jenny took her check and everybody went through their roles in putting the dinner on the table.

"Wash your hands," said Anna, placing her big lasagna dish on the mat in the centre.

When everybody was seated, she asked Mary to say Grace. Then Anna watched her children dig in. She had a motherly feeling of satisfaction.

"Mom," said Jenny, "there's nothing like your lasagna."

There couldn't have been more important praise than that for Anna. Jenny was the daughter who had travelled far, all the way to the United States. They obviously couldn't match her lasagna in Buffalo.

"It's not like McDolly, is it?" said Sophie.

After dinner the dishes were washed in a few minutes. Everybody knew his role. They had done it hundreds of times.

Now they heard a car door slam on the driveway.

It was Mrs. Pavarone.

"Come in, Signora," said Anna.

"It smells good in here. I heard Jenny is in town. How are you, Jenny? My, you are a big girl!" She sat down on the sofa near the aquariums.

"I've taken a summer job," said Jenny proudly.

"A hundred and fifty dollars a month," shouted Frankie.

"Not quite," said Jenny.

"And she can drink as much Coke as she wants," added Freddy.

"Well, well. Money isn't everything," said Mrs. Pavarone. Anna poured her a cup of tea.

"Thank you, Anna. I see everything is going well for you."

"And how is it going for you, Signora?"

"Eh," the matron said in her Italian way, one hand sweeping upwards, "meno male, so so. Could be better."

"We all have our burdens to carry," said Anna. Although she knew that Mrs. Pavarone had some dark areas in her past, she did not know of the recent developments and she had no inkling that there were reasons for her depressed way of talking. Mrs. Pavarone was a real pillar of society, working tirelessly for the Church. She had earned the esteem of the authorities and the gratitude of the people. Nobody asked for details of her relationship with Tina Huttings and her father any more.

The Signora sighed heavily. "If I had the choice now, I would become a nun." Frankie snickered. It was embarrassing. Anna gave him a warning stare.

"I know it's too late now, but I could be living happily in a convent. When I had the choice I went the earthly way. It's too late now."

"You had your children," said Anna.

"They are gone, Anna. Yours will go too. Then you're alone."

"But you have the Church, Signora."

"It's not the same thing. I should have taken the vows when I was young. In the convent you are in a family. You don't get into trouble if you're in a family. I don't have a family."

"Mom will always have us," said Freddy, "eh, Mom?"

Anna gave her son a warm look.

"Is Jenny thinking of a holy life?" said the visitor, out of the blue. "This is her last year at school, isn't it?" She directed the question at her mother, as if this were the natural thing to do. But Jenny answered, "I haven't decided. I'll probably go to university."

"She's the top banana in her school," said Frankie.

"Don't say banana," objected Jenny.

"She's tops," corrected Frankie.

"They need bright nuns too. You could be a scholar in the convent," said Mrs. Pavarone.

"I want to study biology or maybe physics."

"Why don't you talk all that over with Mother Monica at Holy Cross Abbey? She mentioned your name just yesterday. She knows you came first in school. She's just a wonderful person, and she's a scholar if ever there was one. You can pour your heart out to Mother Monica."

"She gave you the scholarship," said Anna.

"I don't understand. Why should I go and see Mother Monica?"

"Nothing particular. But talking with such a person is good for anyone. Not everyone gets invited to see Mother Monica. She can tell you a lot about life in a convent. And about everything else, too."

"I can't just go storming in to the Principal's office at Holy Cross?"

"Of course you can. She told me she would love to see you. I'll give her a call and tell her you'll come and see her."

"No, thank you, Signora. I'll call her if I want to talk to her."

"My Aunt Francesca became a nun," said Anna. "Mother was very proud of her when she left home and went to Rome. We never saw her again."

"Why not, Mom?" said Mary.

"Oh, it's a sad story. I never told you about it."

"What was it, Mom?" asked Sophie. All the children looked at their mother. Why had she never talked about Aunt Francesca before?

Anna hesitated.

"Well, it's time to go home," said Mrs. Pavarone. She emptied her cup and rose with some difficulty. Anna accompanied her out.

"Thanks for the tea, Anna. You know," she said, with the door knob in her hand, "Jenny is such a bright girl. She would make a good contribution to the convent."

"She has to make up her own mind about that," said Anna.

"You said the same thing about going to Holy Cross Abbey, Anna. But don't you see, we did the right thing for her? She will be happy in the service of the Lord."

Anna went with her down the walkway to the car. "Things are different now," she said.

"You still have a responsibility for her well-being."

"Not quite," said Anna with a smile, "she's grown up."

"Say, what was it that was so sad about your Aunt Francesca?"

"She died in the convent."

"Oh, but they now have excellent medical care."

"She just withered away."

"Oh, mamma mia. Why?"

"My mother never told me, but the rumor was that she had gone into the cloister only because she fell in love with a man."

"That's not a good reason to become a nun."

"She had a child from that man, an illegitimate child."

"Oh, that's a terrible sin. And then she made it worse taking the vows. What happened to the baby?"

"It died. She didn't feed it properly, they said. And then she went to Rome. But she didn't get over it."

"The guy should have married her."

"He couldn't. He wasn't Catholic. A Moslem, they said."

"How could she ever ! A pagan ! The Lord punished the poor soul."

Jenny really enjoyed working at McDolly's. She was halfway through the summer and had already deposited over a hundred dollars in her bank account. It was good to be productive. Looking at her bank book gave her the same uplifting feeling as holding her school report card in her hand. Both money and marks are the result of hard work.

What had Mrs. Pavarone said? Money isn't everything? She was right, of course. But there's something positive about it, something wholesome. Money is even collected in church, a lot of it. And the Church is selling real estate in several places in town, for money of course. Anna had said that Joe Fabrini had a hard time dealing with the priests who were especially assigned to handle real estate. They were tough, he said. Money isn't everything. But everybody wants it, the more the better. There's nothing wrong with it, as long as you put it to good use. The Church has bought the corner lot near the Fabrinis' bungalow. It's an ideal corner for a service station, they say, some time in the future.

Maybe one day, when she makes money as a biologist or a physicist, her bank account will grow to the point where she can buy a piece of land too, as her father had done after years of work. Maybe she'll have a house built on it as well.

A house? What for?

Why doesn't Ferdinand write? In her last letter, Barbara said 'the boys' are both working hard for the examinations, so they can go to university in the fall. But surely there's time for writing a letter?

It was good to be busy and not to think too much about Ferdinand. At least he should acknowledge her letter. Barbara writes Dennis has always had time for her. Of course, it's a little different with Barbara and Dennis. They're as good as married. Why don't they get married? What they're doing is wrong. One day they will have to account for what they're doing. The final judgement is inescapable.

Dennis is probably not even Catholic. Oh, poor Barbara!

But she's a singer, a person with entirely different standards. She shouldn't really be in a convent school. Isn't she constantly sinning, without ever repenting?

At four o'clock she drank half a glass of Coke, took off her McDolly cap with the logo of two dolls holding hands on it, stuffed it into her pocket, said goodbye to the boss and started walking to the streetcar stop.

The young man who had told her that there are lots of Catholics at Humber was already standing at the stop. He also wore the blue McDolly uniform. He looked rather smart in it, thought Jenny. His blond hair was partly covered by the McDolly cap he was still wearing.

"Going the same direction?" he said. He was somewhat taller than Jenny. His blue eyes rested on her bare arms. "The uniform looks good on you out here in the street too," he said.

"I'm getting out of it when I get home. You don't want to be a McDolly person all day long."

"That's for sure," said her colleague. His eyes were still riveted on her arms and neck. Now the streetcar arrived, and the young man helped Jenny up the steps, grasping her from behind at her waist. Jenny felt very uncomfortable as his finger tips supported her breasts.

She chose a window seat and her colleague sat beside her.

"Where do you get off?" he asked.

"Humberlane."

"Do you live around there?"

"Yes."

Now she felt his hand on her arm. "How come I've never seen you around here?"

She withdrew her arm. "I'm out of town most of the time," she said coolly.

There was no more conversation for the rest of the trip. When Jenny got up and passed by her neighbor's knees, she felt his hands grabbing her again and guiding her into the aisle. "I have two more stops to go," he said. "See you tomorrow."

Jenny went to bed early. She included Ferdinand in her prayer, as always.

Ferdinand had never grabbed her around the waist.

The next day, her colleague was conspicuously near her all day. Jenny didn't know what to think of it. He wasn't bad looking and he wasn't really obnoxious, even if he did seem a bit pushy in his approach. She had shuddered when he touched her. But maybe she was overly sensitive. She told herself she had not had any experience with boys. Her upbringing in a girls' school was probably restricting her normal development. There isn't anything wrong with touching another person. Oh, she wished Ferdinand was in Toronto. She would talk it over with him. Or would she?

They were riding the same streetcar home again. This time he got off with her at Humberland. "I'll walk you home," he offered. Jenny didn't know whether to be flattered by his chivalry or annoyed by his persistence.

When they reached the privet hedge, he said, "Can I come over after supper? Maybe we can go for a little walk through High Park."

"No, I don't think so."

"Say yes," he said, grabbing her hand.

"Is that you, Jenny?" shouted Frankie from the door.

"Coming," said Jenny. She ran inside, leaving the disgruntled young man in the street.

"Who was that?" said Frankie.

"A guy working with me at McDolly's."

"Any good?"

"What do you mean, any good?"

"Tall, handsome, clever and Catholic."

"He's Catholic," said Jenny with a smile.

Jenny began to be annoyed by the constant attention from her blond co-worker. But her feelings were mixed. The young man did not seem to be attracted to the other girls at McDolly's. At least, that was her impression and it gave her a faint feeling of satisfaction. She wasn't conscious of it but she was feminine enough to enjoy being the object of a young man's desire. He didn't come near Ferdinand's image. She couldn't help comparing the two. But she was hurt by Ferdinand's silence. Maybe he had forgotten her. It made her down-hearted to think Ferdinand would forget her. Did he have a girlfriend in Buffalo?

Suddenly she froze behind the counter. She remembered Barbara talking in her letter about Joanie Bommelstring having been impressed by Ferdinand's good looks when they met on Thursday afternoon at the Conservatory. Could it be that Ferdinand. . .? No, Barbara would have reported it. She says she's no letter writer. But when she writes, she's so talkative. Maybe she didn't want to hurt her. Maybe Ferdinand writes letters to Los Angeles now? Jenny didn't really like Joan Bommelstring. In fact, she hated her. Yes, she did. You can't trust a singer, not even Barbara. But Barbara had her Dennis. It was fortunate Joan had travelled all the way to the west coast to see her father and didn't stay in Buffalo for the summer. Imagine her father getting rid of his third wife in Germany and now marrying the fourth ! Actors are no better than singers.

She decided to be nicer to her colleague. It was just in time, because the manager snapped his finger in front of her face. "Hey," he said, "you're dreaming. Don't you see there are people waiting?"

Jenny worked efficiently for the rest of the day.

It was Friday and rush hour when they boarded the streetcar. It was so crowded, they almost did't make it up the steps. Now they stood squeezed in between potbellied men and parcel-carrying women. They were facing each other, pressed together. Jenny felt the young man's breath on her forehead. His hands clasped her around the waist. He took advantage of the situation. She couldn't escape it, even if she wanted to. And after a while she didn't want to.

It was a beautiful summer day in late August. Jenny appreciated the weekends more now than ever after being on her feet all day, five days a week, and every second Saturday too. Today was her Saturday off.

None of the three sisters had ever had a date. Jenny had one today. She was going to see a movie with her new friend. He was going to pick her up at six. The whole family was excited. Jenny was going out with a gentleman! What was he like? What were they going to do?

She stood in front of the mirror in her room. She put on a pretty cotton print dress and a white cardigan. She then clasped her gold chain with the cross around her neck. She hadn't worn it for some time. Oh, it was such a pretty chain, the only piece of jewelry she possessed, Ferdinand's Christmas present. Why couldn't she go out with Ferdinand? She unclasped the chain lock and put the necklace back into the drawer.

The phone rang. Anna picked it up.

"Who?" she said. "Warren Potomac? Oh I see. . .yes, I'll tell her. All right, Mr. Potomac. Goodbye."

Anna came into Jenny's room. "It was your colleague from McDolly's. He's going to get gasoline. He'll be here at six fifteen."

"Thanks, Mom. He didn't tell me he had a car."

"Now, Jenny, don't stay out late. The movie won't last more than an hour and a half."

"Maybe he'll take me to a restaurant or something."

"That would be another hour at the most. You should be home no later than ten."

"You can't predict the exact time, Mom."

"Well, no later than ten. This is your first date. Don't overdo it. And take care of yourself. Bring him in for a cup of coffee when you get home."

"Okay, Mom."

They all congregated in the livingroom, from where one had a clear view of the driveway.

"Nobody has asked me for a date," said Sophie.

"There's no hurry for anything like that," Anna explained. "I had my first date with your father when I was Jenny's age."

"Of course," said Mary. "Dates end up in marriage."

"In my case it did. Dad had practically no choice. If he hadn't married me after Father Domenico had arranged for a date, I would have been sent all the way over the Atlantic Ocean back to Calabria. What an embarrassment that would have been."

"I don't understand how they could make you marry Dad without. . .you know. . .without love," said Sophie.

"We loved each other very much," said Anna.

"But how is that possible? You didn't know each other."

"We were lucky. Love came after God had put us together."

"You mean Father Domenico put you together," said Frankie.

"Father Domenico was God's instrument. He told us after the wedding he felt like a heavenly broker."

Jenny did not take part in the conversation. She looked out of the window. Her mind was far away. Ferdinand was probably working hard at his summer courses. In the fall he would be a university student. How time flies! She saw him sitting in his room at Denver Road, bending over his textbooks. Or was he writing a letter to Joan Bommelstring?

Someone honked a horn three times. A car, shaped like a bullet, swept up the driveway.

"A Studebaker," said Freddy. He sounded disappointed.

"He could have washed it," said Frankie.

"Look at the dent in the door. What a heap of junk!" said Freddy, as if his sister was too good for a ride in an old Studebaker.

The driver didn't come out. He honked three times, drawn out, reproachfully.

"Okay, coming," said Jenny.

"Bye, Jenny, have fun," they said.

"Drive carefully," added Anna.

They looked out the window to get a glimpse of Jenny's escort, but he didn't bother coming out. The car backed out and screeched away. Anna was cringing. Drive carefully, she had said.

"What kind of guy is he?" said Sophie.

"He didn't wash his car," said Frankie with contempt.

"He didn't open the door for Jenny," said Mary.

"Why didn't he knock at the door and ask for her?" said Anna. "Horn honking makes me nervous."

At ten o'clock Anna cleared her sewing gear away and put a kettle of water on the stove. Mary was still up, reading. At ten-fifteen she poured herself the second cup of coffe.

"What are you reading?"

"A Russian novel."

"Russian?"

"Translated into English, of course."

Now Anna saw Mary's eyes were red, as if she had cried. "Are you reading it in school?"

"No, of course not."

"Why do you say 'of course not'?"

"Mom, if you want to read something really good, you get it from the library."

"How can it be good if it makes you cry?"

Mary wiped her eyes. "Does it show?" She smiled.

"Can't you read Canadian stories?"

"I have read some of the stuff on the Holy Cross List of Recommended Books. It's awful. I read in school only what I have to read, no more."

"Why do you call it 'stuff'?"

"It's all about saints and saintly people. Take Father Brebeuf. He's the good guy and the savages are the bad guys."

"Don't call a priest a guy, Mary."

"Why are all the Indians bad and savage, and why is every missionary sent by God to make Catholics out of savages?"

"Oh Mary, what got into you?"

"I'm not the only one that talks like that."

"I think Mrs. Pavarone was right when she said the world is falling apart."

"Mom, if you could read this book, you would cry too."

"I cry enough without reading a Russian novel."

"But it's the kind of crying that makes you feel good. The world isn't falling apart. It's all so interesting, Mom, even if it makes you cry."

"I don't have much time for reading." She looked at the clock.

"Mamma mia, it's ten-thirty. She should be home."

Mary yawned. She closed her book. "Maybe it's a long movie. Some movies go on for hours. I'm going to bed. Good night."

"Good night, Mary."

Even if it was a long movie, they should be home by now. The young man should have come in when he picked her up, and Jenny should have introduced him to her mother. As it was she had no idea what kind of man her daughter was going out with. All she knew was that he worked at McDolly's and that his name was Warren Potomac. And she knew that he was a Catholic, thank God. But there are so many young people now who call themselves Catholic, yet don't go to Church any more. To call yourself Catholic nowadays doesn't mean what it used to mean.

She poured herself another cup. She knew she wouldn't be able to sleep with so much coffee. She took a blouse from Teitelbaum's cardboard box and tried to thread a needle. Were her eyes getting old? She didn't get the thread into the needle's eye, not in a dozen attempts. The thread was trembling. Maybe it was the coffee. Coffee makes you jittery. She heard Mary brushing her teeth in the bathroom. She stuck the needle into the cushion and folded the blouse back into the box. She had done enough sewing for today anyway.

Eleven o'clock. She switched on the radio, turning it low. The World News. She wasn't listening, but the announcer's voice was soothing. She stood up and looked out of the kitchen window. It was a dark night. No stars were showing. The boys had once led their mother out into the garden to show her the planet Venus competing in brightness with the Dog Star. They had been so proud to see her admire the beautiful Orion too. They had stayed up late to share their knowledge with their mother. Then they had seen a shooting star streaking across the sky. It had made them hold their breath. The boys told her that it was a celestial body entering the earth's atmosphere. She had learned from the boys, and it was exciting. She had never heard of such things. The only thing that disturbed her that night was the fact that the boys hadn't learned it in school. They were reading books from the public library, as were the girls.

Now she paced up and down in the kitchen. She turned off the radio. The children were growing up, and that meant new worries and problems coming up every year. Today was the first time she was worried about her almost grown-up daughter who was out with a man she didn't know.

It was going on midnight.

There was nothing she could do but wait. This was only the first time. How many more times would she have to sit up in fear of the unknown? And she had two more daughters growing up. What kind of worries were ahead? And then the boys. Somehow she didn't think boys were so much of a problem.

How she missed Joe now! Father Domenico had told her that she had done an admirable job taking her five children to the point where they were now. Maybe the real difficulty was still to come? The children had given her boundless happiness, but the loneliness of her widowhood weighed heavily on her.

One o'clock. I must call the police, Anna told herself. She picked up the phone. Then she put it back on the hook, trembling. Tears were welling up and trickling down her cheeks. She mopped her face with a kleenex. Finally, pulling herself together, she picked up the phone once more.

"Operator, give me the police please."

The seconds were running. How long does it take the operator to make the connecton?

She heard the front door opening. She hung up and rushed into the hall.

"Oh, Jenny !" Anna embraced her daughter with the abandon that comes from total relief. "Where have you been so long?"

Jenny looked animated. Her face was flushed.

"I had a good time, Mom." They walked into the kitchen.

"But you're so late."

"I'm sixteen, Mom. I had a good time."

"How was the movie?"

"We didn't go to a movie."

"Then why did it take so long?"

"First we drove around, along the lake. Then Warren said, 'Let's go to High Park.' "

"Why High Park? It's dark there in the evening."

"It was a balmy night, Mom. We walked and walked." With that she picked a thistle burr from her cardigan.

"I'm going to bed, Mom."

"You have never been up this late."

"I know, Mom. This was the first time." She walked out of the kitchen. Anna saw three more burrs on her skirt and one on her cardigan. She also noticed mud on the white wool and on her heels.

"Good night, Mom."

"Good night, Jenny."

Mary stood in the hall in her pyjamas, with sleepy eyes. "You're late," she said drowsily.

"I know," said Jenny. "Good night."

The two girls went into their rooms and Anna stood in the kitchen, woodenly staring out of the window. It was quiet in the house now. She sat down at the table and buried her face in her arms.

22

The Fabrinis were ready for Sunday Mass, everybody except Jenny. In the Fabrini family Sunday Mass was as routine as sunrise. They were in their Sunday best, ready to go, waiting at the door. Jenny had not come out. Anna went back into Jenny's bedroom.

She shook her daughter by the shoulder in an outbreak of rage. "Cattiva! Infida meschina!" she yelled. A torrent of long forgotten Italian words broke out of her. "You need to go to church today, you sinner!" Her fury filled the bungalow. The children had never heard their mother speak so much Italian, and never had they seen her lose control of herself so completely.

Jenny guessed what the words were about. She turned on her side, pulling her blanket over her shoulders. "I'm not going," she said.

"Jesu, Maria, Giuseppe," Anna screamed hysterically. "The Lord will punish you!" She stormed out into the hall. Her other four children were huddling at the door. "Let's go," she said. She led her flock to church.

Jenny couldn't sleep any more after that. She got up and took a shower. She dried herself in front of the tall mirror. She hadn't paid much attention to her body before. She wondered why Warren Potomac had tried all evening to touch her skin. She was satisfied with what she saw in the mirror. It was her own body and not Warren Potomac's. And the stuff he had whispered into her ear! She felt blood rushing into her face just thinking about it. It had been embarrassing. And ever since he tried to slip his hands under her dress, she had wanted to go home. She had been surprised how strong she was holding him away from her. And when he wrestled her to the ground in the thick underbrush in High Park, she had managed to stun him with a blow from her elbow in his face before running out to the road past the old Studebaker and back home. She had looked back for the car to catch up with her, ready to jump aside and hide in the shrubs but after she heard the car start, it drove away in the other direction.

He didn't have to behave like that! She had begun to like his presence. At the lake he had been talking about Humber Collegiate and his prowess on the football team. They had parked the car at the beach, opened the window and breathed the fresh breeze from the lake. Then he had kissed her, and she had wondered what all the fuss was about. Kissing certainly wasn't the exalting experience Barbara had always boasted about. How could anyone write a poem about kisses? It wasn't repulsive, of course, but really nothing to get worked up over.

Then they had to close the window because it became rather chilly and Warren suggested going to High Park. There he had become so strangely aggressive, she had to walk out on him, all the way home through the dark, on foot.

She put on a white blouse and a navy blue skirt. Now she took the gold chain out and held it around her neck. She was going to wear it today. Suddenly she thought Ferdinand's lips looked different from Warren's. But Ferdinand was so far away.

She regretted having been so rude to her mother. But she wanted to make her own decisions now. Mom had to admit that her daughter was growing up. She had recently shown signs of change in her patronizing attitude. But her outbreak this morning had been terrible. Why couldn't Jenny decide for herself when to go to church?

The phone rang.

"Hello."

"Jenny? This is Warren. Sorry about last night."

"It's all right."

"I'd like to see you again, if you don't mind."

"Do you want to go to church with me?"

"To church? You kidding? Any place, but not to church."

"Where do you want to go?"

"Just for a drive."

"Okay."

"See you in five minutes."

Five minutes later the Studebaker pulled into the driveway.

"Your father lets you have the car whenever you want it?"

"It's my car."

"It needs a wash."

"It's beyond washing."

"Why do you want a car at all?"

"So I can drive you around."

"Is that all?"

"And so I can drive to work."

"I thought you take the streetcar to work."

"Only when I want to meet you."

"You are only a high school student. Why do you have to work?"

"So I can drive the car."

"You drive the car so you can work, and you work so you can afford a car."

"Never thought about it that way," said Potomac truthfully.

Jenny thought she noticed a slight speech defect in Warren.

She hadn't noticed it before. The 's' didn't come out right.

"Where are we going?"

"High Park."

"Not again," she said. "Let's go to the water."

"I have to find my teeth."

"What do you mean?"

"You knocked out my teeth last night. With your elbow, remember?"

He bared his teeth like a grinning chimpanzee. The two upper front teeth were missing.

"Oh my God," said Jenny. She stared at him with a mixture of pity and fear. "Did I really?"

"And now we have to find the spot where it happened."

"Oh, I'm so sorry," said Jenny.

"Just don't hit me again."

"We won't find your teeth in High Park. And if we do, you can't put them back in." Jenny was fearful of what was going to happen.

Potomac grinned. He looked awful with the black hole in the mouth. Oh, what had she done! She should have gone to mass this morning. Her mother was right. More than ever she needed to go to church. Now she remembered she hadn't left a note to say she had gone out and would be back in an hour or so. Her big ideas of growing up and making her own decisions! Mother was right. Mom was always right.

They had reached the spot where one could drive the car into a group of hazel bushes. It looked so different in daylight.

"This is the place," said Warren Potomac. "If we find the teeth, I can put them back in. They're artificial." As he said 'artificial', Jenny felt his spit landing on her face. She was sorry for him. At the same time she wished she had never met the man.

"Did you lose your teeth before?" she asked.

"I once got into a fight over a girl. This creep at Humber Collegiate was a kind of bum, you know, nothing scared him. He tried to get fresh with my girl. There are creeps like that. He hit me in the face before I disposed of him." He looked at Jenny to see what effect his story had on her. He was proud of the word 'disposed'.

Jenny wished she had not gone on this weird Sunday stroll.

"Of course he had to pay for it. Artificial teeth are expensive." He waited for Jenny to ask how much the aggressor had to pay. But Jenny was thinkng of how to get out of this situation.

"We took him to court. He had to pay five hundred dollars. On top of that he was thrown out of school. The jerk is now a waiter in the United States. Left the country, scared stiff."

If it hadn't been such a terrible story, it could have been funny. Jenny wiped her face after he had said 'scared stiff'. Then, suddenly, with her eyes wide open, she shouted, "You're not talking about Ferdinand Bauers, are you?"

Potomac stepped on the brakes. Jenny had to brace herself against the windshield.

"Are you?" she screamed.

He was speechless.

"If you're talking about Ferdinand Bauers, you're a liar." She opened the door, jumped out of the car and ran. But Potomac was a football player. He leapt out of his car and tackled the girl from behind. He had learned the manoeuvre in Mr. McNelly's expert coaching class. They fell into the dense weeds among the bushes. He held his hand over her mouth and muffled her screams, panting through his gaping mouth. His face was red. "Don't tell me you're Bauers' girl too," he said between gasps. "His other girl just got pregnant by him. That creep escaped over the border, and his baby is in Canada."

He ripped open her blouse and grabbed her breast, holding her pinned down with his whole body.

A dog barked furiously, pulling his white-haired owner on the leash around the hazelbush. The leash was taut and the owner used all his might to restrain the German Shepherd barking furiously at the pair in front of him.

"Are you all right, miss?" said the man as the two scrambled to their feet. Jenny was terrified but the dog kept barking only at her attacker ignoring the victim. Potomac said, "Keep your dog off me."

The gentleman repeated, "Are you all right, miss?"

Jenny held her torn blouse together with one hand. She nodded. "I'm okay, thank you."

Potomac said, "We'll go home now. Let's go, Jenny."

The man calmed down his dog, patting him with affection. "Do you want anything, miss?"

"Can you walk me home?" said Jenny.

"Sure can."

Potomac sneaked into his Studebaker and drove away.

"Thank you so much, sir," said Jenny. The dog wagged its tail.

"I remember his license number," said the gentleman.

"It's okay, I know the guy," she said.

Anna came home from church. She had been rather absent-minded during the service. Her children had stayed behind to help in the next mass. Where was Jenny? She had made her bed before leaving. Anna was beginning to worry when she heard

Jenny outside, "Goodbye, sir. Thank you again." Then she ran inside and fell into her mother's arms, sobbing violently.

Anna waited patiently. She sat down beside her daughter on the sofa and let her cry. She knew tears can wash away so many troubles. She held her tight, stroking her head. What are mothers for?

Jenny dreaded going to work at McDolly's after her two disastrous outings with Warren Potomac. She gave notice to the manager two days early. To get ready for school, she told him. She picked up her last pay check, and the manager told her she was welcome any time to work at the restaurant, part-time or full-time. "You've done a good job. Good luck to you, Jenny," he said.

She had avoided Potomac whenever she could. But in the crowded eating place it was impossible not to bump into him once in a while. He even seemed to seek such encounters.

Oh, how she hated him! What a liar he was! To say an untruth like that about anybody was cruel and tasteless, but to say it about Ferdinand was so wicked, she couldn't find words for it. She couldn't believe any of it, not a shred. But it hurt her so much, she almost forgot his physical brutality in High Park.

And then his story about his teeth. What a liar! But the story about Ferdinand being the father of an illegitimate child! Every time she recalled this accusation coming through the hole in his front teeth she buried her face in her hands and said, "no, no, no." She did that lying in bed and even in daytime when she was by herself. She couldn't get rid of the picture of Ferdinand cradling a baby in his arms. What a terrible lie! She couldn't have worked one more day at McDolly's. How could people like Warren Potomac live with themselves? Such fabrication must ultimately destroy its inventor. God have mercy on Potomac!

But there remained a sting in her heart, a nagging fear, vague and fuzzy, but lingering, painfully.

She had tossed sleeplessly for nights after that Sunday when she had refused to go to church. She had promised her mother to go to mass next time. It was the last Sunday before she had to return to St. Cecilia.

When Jenny phoned Mother Monica, she didn't have to explain why she wanted to see her. She was invited with great warmth to come over any time at all, say at two o'clock that afternoon?

The Holy Cross Abbey was deserted. Jenny rang the bell. A young nun opened the door with a pretty smile. Jenny was expected, she said. She led the way. Their steps echoed in the high-ceilinged hall. It smelled like blackboards, cleaning material and just old age. All schools smell the same, thought Jenny. She was not excited by the thought of meeting the Principal; she was a little tired and worn out.

The nun knocked at the Principal's door.

"Come in."

The nun smiled at Jenny and let her in, closing the door behind her.

There were three people in the office.

"Hello, Geneviève. How nice to see you," said Mother Monica. "I don't have to introduce you to Father Domenico and Mother Theresa, do I?" The priest and the Principal of St. Boniface were sitting in comfortable chairs around a low oak table. All three church leaders smiled benevolently. Jenny was offered one of the remaining chairs and Mother Monica took the other.

"You certainly have grown up, Geneviève," said Father Domenico.

But Mother Theresa saw trouble in Jenny's face. Something must worry the girl to seek this interview with the Abbey's Principal. "Have you had a good summer?" she asked.

"Yes, thank you. I have been working at McDolly's."

"Why did you choose McDolly's?" asked Mother Theresa.

"It's a good place to make money."

Mother Monica cleared her throat. "Nice of you to come and see us. You have your roots in Toronto, don't you?"

"I suppose so." Jenny wondered why there were three people here. Did they happen to come by, just drop in? Hardly.

Mother Monica seemed to guess what was on Jenny's mind. She said, "I never got to know you well, Geneviève. Mother Theresa and Father Domenico have known you for all these years, and whenever you name came up, I noticed they were warmly interested in your development. So I invited them over for our little talk."

"You certainly have been one of the finest students we have ever had at St. Boniface," said Mother Theresa. "Naturally, we are most interested in your welfare. There's nothing more gratifying for an educator than to see the seed grow and to prove to the community that the school was on the right track in its endeavors, and that all the daily efforts year in, year out are eventually rewarded by success."

"Speaking of success, Geneviève," said Father Domenico, "Our hearty congratulations on your excellent showing at St. Cecilia."

"Thank you, Father."

"You see," added Mother Monica, "when we recommend a student for admission to another school, we are very anxious to see that student justify our confidence in her. You have been a credit to our schools, our Church and, yes, Canada, by achieving what you have achieved in Buffalo."

Now Jenny smiled shyly, "I never thought of it that way."

"One should pursue one's education without the pressure of forced gratitude to anybody," said Mother Monica. "You did the right thing, Geneviève. You are only young once, and you have to live to the fullest. Of course there's nothing wrong with remembering that the Church has made your studies at St. Cecilia's Academy possible by granting you such a substantial scholarship."

"My mother is very grateful to the Church," said Jenny. "She couldn't have afforded the fees at St. Cecilia."

"And you are grateful too, aren't you?" said Mother Theresa.

"Of course," said Jenny. She was thinking of Humber Collegiate. It would have cost her nothing. And Ferdinand would probably be there. But now the whole Potomac misery fell over her again and reminded her why she had asked for this meeting. She would have preferred to talk to Mother Monica alone. She liked the motherly warmth coming through her soft dark voice and her kind eyes.

"I'm glad you came to see us, Geneviève," repeated the Abbey's Principal. "Was there anything particular you wanted to ask?"

Jenny sighed deeply, shifted her position in the soft chair and said, "I would like to ask a few questions about a nun's life."

She noticed a smile on each of the faces around her. How much more one has to study the faces of men and women of the cloth in order to get some impression of their personalities and emotions! Their clerical black habits don't express anything but austere uniformity. The nuns even cover their hair and most of their foreheads. Their gestures are sparse and measured, not spontaneous or exuberant as in most people, particularly in those of Italian origin. Now all three showed pleasure at the reason for Jenny's visit.

Instinctively Anna Fabrini knew her daughter had gone to see Mother Monica to find out whether a nun's life was something she should consider, as Signora Pavarone had suggested. She also knew this sudden interest had something to do with Warren Potomac. She sensed that Jenny had come through the affair without harm and, if as a result of that encounter, she decided to enter a monastery, that would be just fine with her. It would be a life of ultimate service to God, a life of dignity and tanquillity, highly respected by believers and secretly admired by non-believers. It meant of course a fundamental commitment to the principles of the Church and severance from the pursuits of worldly goals, but it was entirely up to Jenny to make that choice.

Anna would be happy to have her oldest daughter enter a religious life. The whole family would look up to her, and her connection with them would not be totally cut. Her own motherly love for her child would be widened and elevated. She saw Jenny in a black nun's habit, her face smiling, surrounded by the white rim under the black hood. Now Anna had tears in her eyes. Whatever it was that made Jenny consider a nun's life, it was not an escape like the one of Aunt Francesca. Anna was grateful for that. A mother has to leave the decision entirely to her daughter, of course. Jenny had another whole year to make up her mind.

When Jenny came home, Tommy Dudston was in the kitchen, catching an angel fish with a little net out of the aquarium. Frankie and Freddy helped him. Anna was sewing buttons on Teitelbaum's blouses.

"Hello, Tom," said Jenny.

"Hi, Jenny." Tom was shaking a large angel out of his net into a water-filled marmalade jar. "He's eating his own babies."

"He's already eaten half of them. They were only born this morning," said Frankie.

"The father eats his own babies, isn't it awful?" complained Freddy.

"Some men leave their babies too," said Jenny. "It's not only animals that do that."

"But they don't eat them," said Frankie. Everybody chuckled. Even Anna smiled.

"Some men leave their children," continued Jenny. "They run away from their duty to look after them. And they know what they're doing. Your angel fish doesn't know what he's doing."

"That's right," said Frankie, "he's not sinning if he doesn't know what he's doing. Animals can't sin, can they, Mom?"

"No, they can't."

"Then they all go to heaven? Rattlesnakes, skunks and hyenas?" Everybody laughed again.

"You have to ask Father Domenico about that," said Anna.

"Father Domenico doesn't have all the answers either," said Jenny. Anna searched her daughter's face. She had noticed a bitter undertone in what Jenny said.

"If you think, Mother, you can get the answer to everything from our religious leaders, you are mistaken." Jenny certainly didn't sound like a future nun to Anna.

Tom Dudston said, "There are many things we'll never know. But we are getting more and more answers. Thousands of people are asking questions every day, and thousands are working hard to find the answers."

"That's called science," said Freddy.

"Science doesn't explain everything either," said Jenny.

"What does?" asked Frankie.

"Religion does," said Jenny. It puzzled her mother. Was that the same Jenny who had just said that our religious leaders don't have all the answers?

"I think you're right, Jenny," said Tom. "If you have faith, you find all your answers in your faith."

"And it doesn't matter what science says, it doesn't matter what anybody says. If you believe, nothing can shake you," said Jenny firmly.

"It must be beautiful to have a sound religious belief," said Tom, implying that he had no such belief and that he regretted it.

"There's nothing more beautiful than to believe in the Lord," said Anna. "I have felt that all my life."

"What about the angel fish?" said Frankie.

"Yeah, what do we do with the sinner?" said Freddy.

"We just said he's no sinner. We'll have to leave him in this jar till his babies are too big to eat." That was Frankie's solution of this problem. The bigger problems would have to be left to another time and to other people.

"Have you heard from Ferdinand?" asked Tom out of the blue sky.

Jenny blushed. Her mother saw it. It disturbed her.

"From Ferdinand? Should I?"

"I thought maybe he had written to you. He doesn't write much, you probably notice that."

Anna packed her blouse into the box. "Tom, are you going to have a cup of tea with us? You are finished with the fish, aren't you?"

"Yes, we're finished. Thank you, no, I'd better get going. Where's Mary?"

"She's in the library with Sophie," said Freddy.

"They're reading big books by Russian writers," added Frankie. It wasn't clear whether there was a criticism in his tone. "Mary promised to get me the book by Goldschmidt on chromosomes. There's a guy in my class who has it. It's fantastic. You should read it, Tom."

"I have it at home. I'll loan it to you, if you want me to."

"Thanks, Tom. Can I come with you and get it?"

"You stay here, Frankie. Sorry you have to go, Tom. It was nice of you to come over." Anna rose.

Tom rose too, and the boys accompanied him out.

"Goodbye, Jenny," said Tom. "Can I write to Ferdinand that I have met you and that I've had a nice talk with you?"

"Jenny, let Tom go now," interrupted Anna. "He wants to go home, don't you see?"

"Goodbye Mrs. Fabrini," said Tom.

"Goodbye," said Anna, and Jenny followed the boys to the door. She wanted to ask Tom so many questions. But, not knowing what to ask, she could only open her mouth. She watched her brothers escort Ferdinand's friend through the privet hedge into Humberlane.

"Hey, Mom," shouted Frankie from the hall as they came back, "Tom's a really nice guy, don't you think?"

Anna didn't answer. Why had he asked for Mary?

"He sure is," echoed Freddy. But when the twins entered the kitchen there was their mother embracing their sister and stroking her hair. Jenny's shoulders were shaking.

"What happened?" asked Freddy. But then the boys realized that mother and daughter wouldn't answer. The women weren't sure they knew what was happening either.

23

Ferdinand and Dennis were both accepted into the freshman program at the University of Buffalo, Ferdinand in science and Dennis in arts. With those excellent marks in their pre-college courses they were even given an entrance scholarship that would keep them afloat with some income from part-time work. They were both successful in cutting their work time in half at the post office and at McDolly's, and there was enough flexibility to avoid interference with their academic schedule.

Ferdinand had recovered fully. He had been right, time did heal all. He could now think about Tina and her baby without painful remorse. He had not lost the warmth of his feeling about the young mother and her baby, his baby.

In August he had received a staggering hospital bill for a hundred and fifty-two dollars. It had demonstrated to the two young men how vulnerable they were in their lack of financial security. They had pondered about the best method of paying the bill. Dennis wrote a letter to the hospital administration, asking them to spread the payments over the next twelve months. He described the situation of the two budding university students in all details. They mailed the letter. Ferdinand said he didn't want any financial help from Dennis.

"What are friends for?" said Dennis.

"I'll pay for it, even if I have to work full-time."

"No, you won't. I have a better idea. Leave it to me."

In the first week of September, both friends survived the registration procedure at the university and were about to begin their lectures, when Dennis came home one Thursday night with a happy grin on his face, waving a check in the air and laying it in front of Ferdinand on the table. "It's for you," he said. It was a certified check, made out to Ferdinand Bauers for the exact amount of the hospital bill, one hundred and fifty-two dollars.

Ferdinand held the check in his hand, looking with a puzzled face at Dennis. "I can't read the signature," he said. "Looks like Stan. . .Stan who?"

"Stan Kalinski," said Dennis.

"Who's Stan Kalinski?"

"A millionaire out West."

"Sending me a check for the hospital? Why? Who is he?"

"Barbara's father."

"You asked Barbara to have her father pay my hospital bill?"

"No, I just told her about it and the dire straits you're in."

"Wow ! Do you think I should take it?"

"Can there be any doubt? He's got so much dough, he doesn't know what to do with it."

"I can't get over it. Why would he do that?"

"Love."

"He doesn't know me."

"He loves his daughter, dummy."

"And Barbara doesn't know me either."

"But she loves me. It's a chain reaction."

The next day Ferdinand went to the hospital to pay his bill. He was elated. It was a good feeling to be able to get rid of one's debts, especially if they were painful and debilitating, and when a check covered the whole thing. He handed the check together with the bill to the lady at the counter. She fingered through her file, withdrew a folder, took the two papers that Ferdinand had submitted, and said, "Excuse me a moment." She knocked at the accountant's door.

What's wrong? thought Ferdinand. Obstacles, obstacles.

After a minute or two the accountant emerged with the lady. He held the ledger card in one hand and the check in the other. "Mr. Bauers?"

"Yes."

"You owe us nothing. The bill has been paid."

"I don't think I paid it," said Ferdinand. "In fact, I know I didn't, because I didn't have the money, to tell you the truth. Not yet."

"Well, it's been paid. That's all we are interested in."

"There must be some misunderstanding. Who would pay my bill?"

"A lady by the name of Geneviève Fabrini."

Ferdinand rushed home.

"The Kalinski check bounced," he shouted, interrupting Dennis at his studies. "You'd better take it back to Barbara."

"It bounced?"

"Not really. But they didn't want to take it at the hospital because a lady by the name of Geneviève Fabrini had already paid my bill."

"Jenny paid your bill? She must be back at St. Cecilia's. Why would she pay a hundred and fifty-two dollars for Ferdinand Bauers? No, it's obvious why she did that. But where did she get the money?"

Dennis did not succeed in giving the check back to Barbara Kalinski. Barbara argued that her father's accountants would find it difficult to reverse their bookkeeping procedures. Her father had without doubt forgotten about the check long since.

Barbara also insisted she had nothing to do with Jenny's decision to pay Ferdinand's hospital bill. It was a big surprise to her. She had told her friend about Ferdinand's staggering hospital bill and that her father would pay for it. But obviously Jenny had immediately gone down to the hospital and paid the bill. Ferdinand put his signature on the back of Mr. Kalinski's check and told Dennis to take it to Jenny. He couldn't accept a gift from a girl he felt he had betrayed. But Jenny refused to take the money. So Ferdinand wrote her a letter.

"Dear Jenny !

I want you to know that I have put the check into my bank account with the understanding that it is your money. The opportunity will come to spend it on something worthwhile, and we will make that decision when the time comes.

Dennis tells me you have been working all summer. And now you have put all your earnings into the hospital for me. I don't dare take your action as a sign of what it appears to be. But I want you to know that it makes me utterly happy to think of that possibility. It makes me happier than anything that ever happened in my life.

I have been silent so long, and I am still torn between pouring my heart out to you and withdrawing completely. There is something I have to clear up in my life. I will work on that, and then I will write you again.

Until then

I am yours

Ferdinand."

Ferdinand was successful at university. His first tests in all five subjects had been deemed excellent by his professors. He was able to concentrate on his studies and to keep his worries about Tina and Jenny at arm's length as long as he worked. He also had developed the ability to put his mind to work on a problem while he filled plastic cups with Coke or apple juice and put hamburgers and frankfurters with French fries on cardboard plates. It was all routine. He even handled the money automatically. Four hours of McDolly every day, six days a week was not too much effort for him. It didn't interfere with his main work, his scientific studies. The two friends followed their different daily schedules and they had little time together.

Ferdinand had surrounded himself with books and made himself comfortable in the old armchair. The phone rang downstairs. Someone would answer it. He didn't expect a call. It kept ringing. He finally went down.

"Hello."

"Is that you, Ferdinand?"

"Tommy? How nice to hear your voice. Haven't heard from you for quite some time."

"No wonder. You're not exactly a letter writer."

"That's true, Tommy. But I'm very busy. I've never been so busy in all my life."

"Your mother tells me you're quite successful. You see, some news about you trickles through to good old Toronto."

"Any news on the home front?"

"Well, that's why I'm calling, Ferdinand. Very good news indeed. Tina had her baby."

"She did? Is it a boy?"

"Yes, it's a boy. Eight pounds six ounces."

"Where is she?" Ferdinand exclaimed.

"She's on a farm near Aurora. Her father owns the farm."

"I'm coming to Toronto on the weekend. I've got to see him. Can you drive me up to Aurora?"

"Why do you want to see Tina's baby?"

"Well, yes, why should I want to see her baby? You're right. It's the biologist in me, I guess. I bet he looks like Tina."

"He might. Maybe he looks like his father. God knows who the father is."

"And sometimes they look like their grandparents," said Ferdinand.

"Maybe he looks like Mr. Teitelbaum."

"God forbid !"

"By the way, Tina's getting married."

"What? So fast?"

"She's marrying a tycoon."

"A tycoon? How did that happen?"

"He's probably the father of her baby."

"Well, that's nice, isn't it? Who's the tycoon?"

"I don't know. It's only a rumor."

"You mean the whole thing may not be true?"

"The baby is a fact. It was in the paper."

"I see. And how are you, Tommy?"

"Fine. School is a drag, though."

"I bet it is."

"Warren Potomac is our new Students' Council President."

"Congratulations !"

"He looks funny with his front teeth missing. He says he lost them in High Park. The whole Students' Council went out looking for them. Now, every day after school he goes looking. How crazy can you get !"

"He'd better find them. They cost five hundred dollars."

"Are you coming over for the prom, Ferdinand?"

"Not likely."

"I didn't think so. If Jenny were here, we could all go together."

"Who is all?"

"You and Jenny and me and my girl."

"Who is your girl, Tommy?"

"Mary Fabrini."

"You're kidding. You never told me."

"You never asked and I didn't know it until last week."

"Tommy, I like that, I really do. They're a nice family."

"We're both in good company. Aren't we lucky?"

"Well, Dennis, nice talking to you. Best of luck."

"Are you coming on the weekend? Do you still want to see Tina's baby?"

"No, I don't think so. Thanks for calling, Tommy."

"Goodbye, Ferdinand."

Ferdinand jumped up the stairs, two steps at a time. He was in no mood to continue with his books. He opened the window, letting in the fresh air and the noise from the street. He sucked in the breeze, spread his arms wide and yelled out a cry of relief and abandon. A man looked up and stopped in his tracks, probably expecting the young man at the window to do something foolish. Ferdinand laughed and yelled and yodeled like an Austrian mountaineer. The man shook his head and went on walking.

He heard a knock at the door behind him. It was the lady who had been so concerned when he blacked out. Before she could say anything, he took her in his arms and kissed her on the mouth. She blushed.

"Sorry," said Ferdinand, "you're Susan, aren't you?"

"Yes. I wondered whether you were all right."

"Of course. Sorry again. Did I sound silly?"

"If not silly, somewhat unusual in this quiet rooming house. May I come in?" she entered the room and sat down on the sofa. "Don't you want to close the window?"

"Of course, excuse me." He shut the window and drew the curtain.

She smiled at him. "You look very happy."

"I could embrace the whole world."

"I noticed that."

"I know I shouldn't have done that. I'm sorry again."

"I didn't mind," she said with an impish look in her blue eyes.

"I always wanted to knock on your door and thank you for the flowers after I was released from hospital."

"You could have done that any time."

"I'm a slob when it comes to social graces. There are people who think I'm downright anti-social."

"They're nuts. Tell them I said so. Now you paid me with a kiss. We're even. What made you so happy that you had to scream out of the window?"

"Oh, that's a long story."

"What's her name?"

Ferdinand laughed. "I haven't told you anything. What makes you think there's a girl?"

"I can see it in your face. It's written all over it."

Now Ferdinand became serious. The smile disappeared. He said almost solemnly, "Yes, Susan, it's written all over me, in me and through me."

Dennis came in. He saw the visitor on the sofa and then, noticing Ferdinand's radiant face, he said, "Look who we've got here. Well, well!"

"I have to go," said the girl. She rose and turned to Ferdinand. "I wish you well. You've been a good neighbor, very quiet - up to today." She looked amused. "Good night, gentlemen," she said and left.

"What was she talking about?" said Dennis.

Ferdinand poured out the big news from Toronto. It was three o'clock in the morning when they went to bed.

"I have to see Jenny," said Ferdinand, switching out the light.

"I'll ask Barbara to think up something. I'm going to see her Thursday at the Conservatory."

"Today is only Friday. No, it's Saturday, isn't it?"

"There isn't <u>that</u> much hurry, is there?"

"Yes, there is, Dennis, I'm ready to bust !"

When Dennis returned from his Thursday meeting with the singer, he reported that Barbara had promised to arrange a meeting between Jenny and Ferdinand. The following Thursday he brought a letter from Jenny.

"Thank you, Dennis," said Ferdinand, putting it in his pocket.

"Don't you want to read it?"

"I will." Ferdinand didn't tell his friend that his heart was pounding his ribs and that he wanted to be alone to open the letter. That opportunity came only much later.

"Dear Ferdinand,

Thank you for your last letter. It was a good idea to put Mr. Kalinski's money into the bank. As you say, maybe one day you can find a good use for it.

Ferdinand, this letter will be a first and a last letter. The first thing I want to tell you is that I went to the hospital to pay your debts because I had this strange urge to help you get out of the calamity. I did it because I thought I loved you. It was an impulse. I was confused.

One of your schoolmates, Warren Potomac, worked with me at McDolly's on Queen Street. He told me about your other girl and about the baby. Of course I didn't believe him. But then I remembered your letter where you say there is something in your life you want to clear up before you contact me again. I think I understand what you mean.

So this is the first letter to ever tell you that I loved you. I can tell you that because I'm over it. And it will also be my last letter to you because I have just yesterday received a reply to my application for admission to St. Luke's Convent. I have been accepted and I will be happy to dedicate my life to the service of the Lord, now and forever.

I wish you lots of happiness.

Jenny Fabrini."

Ferdinand stuffed the letter back into his pocket. "No !" he yelled. He longed to open the window and shout it into the street, "No, no, no !" But he sat down and pulled up his knees, clasping his arms around them. He brooded. He heard the bell ringing at St. Cecilia. It was nine o'clock.

Dennis came home from the library. It was dark and Ferdinand was still sitting in his chair, his head on his knees.

"What's the matter?"

Ferdinand didn't answer and Dennis interpreted his silence as love sickness. He opened a book and started reading. Then he looked up. "By the way, Barbara told me Jenny was crying when she gave her the letter."

Minutes passed in silence.

Finally Ferdinand said, "I'll go for a walk."

"Where are you going?"

"Just for a walk. Get some fresh air."

He walked down the stairs, locked the house door and went briskly to St. Cecilia's Academy. What was there to do?

In the post office across the street, they were switching off the lights. He walked alongside the school fence. The gate was closed. Why do they always shut themselves off from the world? Why build a wall between groups of people? There was the window where Dennis had looked for the ruler leaning against the glass. Why had it been necessary to play such infantile games with letters dangling on ropes?

He walked down the long front of the building. The girls still had the lights on. Somewhere there behind the curtains was Jenny. She had done her prayers.

Suddenly he felt Jesus was his enemy or at least his rival. He clenched his fist around Jenny's letter in his pocket. What was this mysterious power radiating from Christ after twenty centuries? It must be real. It couldn't be just in the minds of some religious fanatics. With so many highly intelligent people devoting all their lives to this magnetic God-man, and pure and beautiful souls like Jenny being pulled into his orbit, there must be more to it than he could understand.

He tried to open the gate. No, it was locked. What would he do if it were open? He looked up at the window and suddenly he felt with absolute certainty that Jenny was thinking of him, of Ferdinand Bauers. It wasn't his imagination. There must be such a thing as telepathy. Wasn't there some movement at the curtain? Did he see Jenny's silhouette ever so faintly? He rattled at the gate. Then he came to the maple with the branch stretching over the fence. He jumped and pulled himself up until his feet reached the top of the fence. Swinging himself over, he stumbled and caught his thigh on a spike. His own weight impaled him on the sharp spike and he ended upside down, groping with his hands at the wrought iron. He didn't want to scream. He clenched his teeth but the terrible pain in his thigh made him groan.

Blood drained to his head and everything became black and huge and tumbling.

When he came to, the scene was bathed in torch light. Firemen were trying to free him. A semicircle of murmuring people surrounded the spot on the outside and a group of nuns watched on the inside. All the windows at the Academy were bright and girls in nighties were staring down. The fire engine's diesel was rumbling. An ambulance shot blue flashes over the faces of the onlookers.

When they finally got him loose, they placed Ferdinand on a stretcher. The janitor started washing blood off the fence.

"Prowler Caught Breaking into St. Cecilia's" said the Courier on the front page. A gory picture showed a man dangling upside down from the fence with three nuns watching two firemen prying him loose. The report said the police had apprehended an intruder, a freshman at the University of Buffalo. It was the second time he had been taken into custody. The young man, a Canadian, was now in the General Hospital in satisfactory condition with injuries sustained in his break-in attempt. He faced deportation.

Dennis carried the front section of the newspaper in his pocket when he entered the hospital. But when he saw Ferdinand's pale face, he decided not to show it to him.

"What are you doing here again?" he said, trying to sound carefree.

"I don't know what got into me," said Ferdinand. Then he told Dennis what had happened.

"How bad is it?"

"I lost a lot of blood. But they gave me a transfusion. I have a flesh wound in the upper left thigh. The doctor told me it's nothing to worry about. Nothing vital was injured. I'll be out in a couple of days."

"Thank God. You should leave fence-climbing to desperate postmen."

"Then I must rest for a while, the doctor said."

"Just don't ride a horse."

"That's about it."

There were two more visitors that day for Ferdinand, both of them quite unexpected.

At ten o'clock, a white-coated man with a well-trimmed black beard came in and sat down at his bedside.

"Oh, hello, Dr. Granatstein," said Ferdinand. "Are you on my case again?"

"No, I'm not, but I heard about the prowler who got caught at St. Cecilia, and I found out we had met before."

"I'm causing a lot of trouble."

"And this time it's not psychosomatic. The disease is not imagined. A sizeable cut near your testicles and twenty stitches to close the hole, those aren't symptoms cooked up in your mind."

Ferdinand thought that over for a while.

"In a way they are, Doctor. I think I'm in your hospital the second time for the same reason as the first time."

"How's that?"

And now Ferdinand told the doctor about Jenny and Tina and the baby that, thank God, wasn't his. And then Jenny's commitment to a life of religious seclusion. There was no other patient in the room and Ferdinand let it all out. He felt good talking to this doctor.

Dr. Granatstein listened with patience. "You are in a lot of turmoil for your age," he said.

"It's nice of you, Doctor, to listen to my story. It makes me feel much better when I unburden myself."

"You see the value of confession."

"Are you Catholic, sir?"

"No, I'm Jewish."

"Jews don't confess, do they?"

"Why should we? We don't sin." His sonorous laughter was contagious. Ferdinand joined in, only to stop abruptly with a grimace. "My stitches," he said.

A nurse peered through the door. She smiled and withdrew when she saw where the laughter came from. There hadn't been a good laugh in the hospital for some time. Laughter didn't quite fit here.

"It says in the paper you're a freshman at the University. What are you studying?"

"Science. I want to go into genetics."

"There'll be none of that if they throw you out. It says in the Courier you will be deported."

Ferdinand told the doctor about his bawdyhouse affair and the humiliating night behind bars. And about his father, the fugitive. "They warned me I would be deported if I had any more dealings with St. Cecilia students. I don't know why I bother you with all this, Doctor."

"We've got to get you out of this," said Dr. Granatstein. "Do you know you're under arrest?"

"What?"

"You are in custody right here in the hospital. But I think I can get you out of it. Leave it to me."

He rose and left. "I'll see you tomorrow," he said from the door.

"Thanks, Doctor."

Ferdinand ate well at lunch time. He fell asleep. There was a lot of catching up to be done.

The nurse opened the door. "He's asleep," she said to a man in a blue trenchcoat looking over her shoulder. "You can't talk to him now. He's under sedation."

"We have to get his version of the story," said the man.

The nurse put her finger on her lips. She whispered, "Pssst, not now. This is a hospital, not a police station."

"I'll be back tomorrow morning."

"Fine," said the nurse, closing the door.

Something touched Ferdinand's hand. He opened his eyes.

It was Jenny, smiling as he remembered her, with dimples and sparkling white teeth.

"Ferdinand," she said. Her hand was still resting on his.

"Oh, Jenny!" An avalanche of emotions rushed through his chest. They were silent. They had never touched each other before. Her hand felt so good. He was afraid she would withdraw it if he moved. How could one arrest time? How could one make the moment last?

Now Jenny sat down at his side, took his other hand and said, "Does it hurt?"

"Not any more."

"We didn't sleep all night after your accident. Barbara said it was the mailman hanging on the fence. But why should he want to climb over the fence?"

"It's a terrible fence," said Ferdinand. They were still holding hands.

"Then a nun said it was you. She had taken a letter from your pocket, my letter to you. I cried all night, Ferdinand."

"Bend your head down, Jenny."

"Why?"

"Please do. I want to say something in your ear."

She obeyed with a smile.

"I love you," he whispered.

She straightened up again. Her face was flushed and her lashes covered her eyes.

"I don't know what made me climb over the fence. I wanted to tell you, what my schoolmate at McDolly's told you about my past, wasn't true. That's why I did it. And then, I just couldn't take it any longer. I wanted to be near you." He watched her face. Did she know what he was talking about? "I don't have an illegitimate child," he said. Again he couldn't see any reaction in her face.

"I know," she finally said.

"How could you know?"

Jenny sighed and looked straight into his blue eyes. "You wouldn't do that to me, Ferdinand."

"I wouldn't want to hurt you for anything in the world, that's true."

"Can I say something into your ear, Ferdinand?"

He smiled and turned his head sideways. She bent down and whispered the sweetest words a young woman coming into full bloom can say, "I love you too."

But then he remembered that Jenny had taken the first decisive step towards entering a religious order. And she had been accepted. He studied her face. No, never, he thought. Never, never!

"I know what you're thinking," she said. "I told them this morning that I withdraw my application. They were quite upset. Then I demanded my letter back. Here it is," she took a sheet out of her pocket. "It says here that I love you, after my visit to the hospital. Today is the second time I walked to the hospital. I love you even more now."

The loudspeaker in the hall said, "Visiting hours are over."

Jenny bent down again and kissed him on the mouth.

Dr. Granatstein found a happy patient smiling at him when he entered Ferdinand's room. "How is it going?" he said.

"I ate well, I slept well and I went to the bathroom."

"You will be out of here in no time. Did the police talk to you?"

"No, they didn't. Should they?"

"Not any more. You will not be prosecuted. I told the Police Inspector that I know you well and that you had no intention of trespassing. He had already had a phone call from St. Cecilia's, he said, telling him they didn't want any more publicity about the matter. It had been upsetting enough for the girls in the school, they said. The Inspector said he'd drop the matter, although he didn't understand what you were doing in the dark on that fence. He said he never understands young weirdos like you. And he was even more baffled, he said, when your biology professor told him on the phone that you are a student of great promise."

Ferdinand was moved. "Thank you for all that, Doctor."

"It's nothing. A doctor has to look after his patients, particularly when the case is complicated by psychosomatic interaction." He smiled through his beard.

"Doctor, are you married?"

"Yes, I am. With two healthy children, thank you."

"When you got married, were you engaged first?"

The doctor smiled. "Yes, we were engaged first. Now you're going to ask me whether we had a child before the wedding."

"No. But you did get engaged?"

"What are all these personal questions about?"

"Sorry, I don't want to be indiscreet."

"Yes," said the doctor, looking out the window, "my wife and I got engaged one sunny September day in Niagara Falls. We were looking over the railing into the thundering gorge. But I didn't hear the water, I didn't see the Falls at all. I only saw Esther's face. I could hardly hear her voice over the din. But I'll never forget the words she shouted into my ear."

"I know those words," said Ferdinand. "But she whispered them into mine."

Dr. Granatstein understood. "You don't have to go to Niagara Falls for that. It can happen anywhere."

"Even in a hospital room."

Now they were smiling together as they had been laughing together when the doctor insisted Jews don't sin.

"Did you find that the world looks different after that?"

"Yes, I did, very much so."

"And that there's a golden shimmer on everything?"

"On everything."

"I'm engaged, Doctor."

"I know." They shook hands.

Ferdinand received a sad letter from his mother. The first thing he pulled out of the envelope was a cutting from The Toronto Star.

"Toronto Fugitive Found Dead in Oklahoma" said the headline. Then it reported that Tim Bauers had died in the gutter on skid row with no identification in his pockets except two paper clippings from The Toronto Star. One carried a picture of two pigeon-breeding boys and an interview with Ferdinand Bauers' two science teachers. The name Bauers had triggered an investigation in the right direction. The other clipping, also from the Star, reported the death of the President of Wilson Lumber, Inc. where Tim Bauers had been an employee before his conviction. Final identification of Ferdinand's father had been made with fingerprints.

For a minute, Ferdinand sat quietly with the letter in his hand. Then he read:

"Dear Ferdinand,

I thought you should know. That's why I'm sending you this. We lost your father several times. Each time it hurt, but after all these years, this final news comes like a relief. I will admit I shed one tear when I read the paper but only one, Ferdinand. Don't worry about me. I cried a lot when I heard about your accident. I see those awful spikes on the fence and I shudder when I think of it. I'm glad it's all over

and you're back in your studies. Next time we come
together, you'll have to tell me what the dickens you were
doing on that fence.
Yours with love,
Mom.
P.S. Dr. Granatstein wrote me a comforting letter. Seems
to be a very nice gentleman. It cheered me up and I feel
much better now."

Ferdinand felt drained. All his life he had thought he was
incomplete without a father. But time was smoothing things
over, he had told himself. Now tears welled up. Death was so
utterly final.

Dennis was teasing when he said, "You have to make up your
mind now whether you want to marry Jenny or Susan. At least
Susan sends you flowers."

Three half-opened roses stood in a vase on the table. And
the card beside it said, "Whenever you come from hospital, I'll
present you with flowers in the hope that you will pay me back.
Love, Susan."

"I'll tell her I'm engaged," said Ferdinand.

"An engagement doesn't mean much any more."

"It means everything to me." Ferdinand spoke with such
sincerity, it touched his friend. "And I know what it means to
Jenny," he added.

"Without flowers?"

Now Ferdinand smiled. "Without flowers. But I think I'll
buy a ring for her."

"Rings are expensive."

"What's money for?"

"You don't have any," said Dennis.

"I have a hundred and fifty-two dollars in the bank."

"That's Jenny's money. Have you thought of the new hospital bill?"

"To tell you the truth, I had forgotten about it."

"So you'd better pay the hospital bill first."

"I'll go right away."

"I'll come with you."

They couldn't believe their ears when the accountant at the hospital said with a grin, "Mr. Bauers, you are a lucky person. This bill has also been paid for you."

"By whom?" said Ferdinand.

"By Doctor Granatstein."

Ferdinand linked arms with Dennis as they left the building.

"Do you think gold with a little diamond will do?"

They went to a jeweller on Main Street.

Jenny wouldn't mind spending the money on such a noble cause.

24

There hadn't been a double wedding like this at the Church of the Blessed Virgin for as long as Father Domenico remembered. And the christening of John Nathan Wilson was scheduled the same day right after the double wedding.

An unusually large crowd filled every seat in the nave. It was a triple event, unusual in many ways. There were at least a dozen middle-aged men wearing skullcaps, some made of black silk, others fancifully woven and stitched in different colors. The Italian community had come too. And the whole School Board was present, Catholic and Protestant alike. So were the management staff of Wilson Lumber, Inc.

Jenny Fabrini and her mother were among the guests. Ferdinand Bauers and Tommy Dudston occupied seats in the last pew. Even Dennis Neelson had come from Buffalo. He had accompanied Barbara Kalinski and Joan Bommelstring who were to adorn the ceremonies as soloists, a fine gesture from St. Cecilia's Academy to the Church of the Blessed Virgin in Toronto.

Tommy craned his head to find Maria Fabrini in the choir. Frankie and Freddy acted as altar boys.

Travelling expenses and hotel accommodation for out-of-town guests were paid by the two grooms. They had rented the prestigious Town and Country Hall for the festivities after the church service. The two grooms had made a very substantial donation to the Church, a sum that would remove any doubts about the propriety of it all. A smaller donation was also promised to St. Cecilia.

It was, to be sure, an auspicious occasion matched by the splendor of the proceedings.

As always, when the organ and the choir thundered their first hymn through the huge edifice, the audience was at the same time subdued in awe and elevated in jubilation. That was the function of music.

Father Domenico joined in Holy matrimony Mr. Nathan Abraham Teitelbaum and Mrs. Paula Christina Pavarone. The groom wore his tail coat with a red rose in his lapel, and his bride a simple white silk gown that seemed to amplify rather than subdue whatever there was, and there was ample. The groom in comparison looked undernourished, at least as seen from the rear. His best man was Mr. Bulnik, Principal of Humber Collegiate. The maid of honor nobody knew.

Of all the unusual circumstances and procedures, the most startling on this great day was the fact that the couple, after they had exchanged rings, did not walk back through the centre aisle in solemn procession but took the seats that had been reserved for them in the front row. The choir and the two soloists now came to the musical climax of their rendition of a stirring cantata by Buxtehude. When the final chord had rung out and some people in the pews felt a twitch in their hands to applaud, the Chairman of the School Board walked back along the red carpet in the middle aisle and, as the organ intoned the familiar wedding theme, led his daughter forward to Father Domenico. His shrivelled face looked happy, perhaps even slightly amused. He nodded to Mr. and Mrs. Huttings who were seated next to the aisle.

Tina wore the full white veil of a first-time bride. Her glowing eyes burned through the white gauze. Ferdinand looked at her. Yes, she was beautiful, but somewhere there in the crowd was Jenny. He knew it and let out a sigh of relief.

But then came Warren Potomac. He looked as if he hadn't quite made it. His black suit didn't fit and his bow tie was askew on his old-fashioned collar. He smiled broadly, baring his newly fixed, expensive teeth. He was accompanied by a truly imposing man of about twenty-four with a manly moustache. Yes, it was Chuck Wilson, portly and secure. Chuck was the recently appointed President of Wilson Lumber, Inc., a solid figure in the community. One could foresee President Wilson one day becoming a member of the School Board, President of the Chamber of Commerce and Honorary Chairman of the Society for Crippled Children. He had already been made a Kinsman even before returning from his studies in the United States. When his father died, he had to quit playing football and studying, a decision that was made easy by the fact that he had not passed his academic year. And it had taken him only six hours to make up his mind to become the master of assets of at least twelve million dollars, not counting the Wilson holdings in the British Columbia forest products industry. Yes, Chuck Wilson was a tycoon all right.

After the 'I do', more beautiful music was offered and then Tina picked up a sky-blue bundle from the arms of Signora Pavarone, now Mrs. N.A. Teitelbaum. She flipped back her veil before the towering former quarterback of the Vikings bent down to kiss her. Now she cuddled her little son in his pale blue wrapping. It was a touching moment. Then she handed him to the godfather, Mr. McNelly, the groom's former coach and now Vice-Principal, and at that moment all hell broke loose in the church. A piercing scream rose from the little bundle, echoing from the pillars and arches of the dignified edifice. Mr. McNelly didn't seem comfortable. He rocked the baby, but the screams persisted through the baptismal ceremony. The congregation smiled.

"What a voice !" whispered Ferdinand.

"He's got it from his father," said Tommy.

Father Domenico officiated unperturbed. Behind him a stained glass window depicted the Lord Jesus and a ray of sunshine fell obliquely down from His haloed face on the red carpet in the aisle.

Now Tina took the baby out of his godfather's arms. The screams immediately subsided. She cuddled him and walked with her husband back up the aisle, followed by two sweet little flower girls.

All the ceremonies were over and the main actors followed the Wilsons.

As Tina walked through the shaft of sunshine from the Lord's face, little John Nathan Wilson was bathed in golden warmth. He gazed contendedly at his mother, his left eye veering slightly inward. Was he cross-eyed?

Ferdinand waited in the vestibule. He remembered that cold Christmas morning when he stood here watching the congregation pouring in from the cold, their breath rising like steam.

How he had longed to see Jenny coming through that door ! And she had been in Buffalo all the time. Now he was facing the other way. Jenny was sure to come out of the nave. She knew he was waiting out here. Everything was so simple now, so beautifully simple.

There she was. He took her hand and led her down the stairs. They saw Mr. and Mrs. Wilson driving off in a blue Jaguar. Mr. Teitelbaum helped Mrs. Teitelbaum into a black limousine. The stairs were covered with confetti. The two young people stole away from the crowd, down Linden Street, past the Bauers' house. The sidewalk was clean. There were no pigeons flying from the hole in the gable. They passed Wong's grocery with the big Coca Cola sign over it. They were still holding hands. Now they started to run. Out of breath, they reached the embankment. Ferdinand picked up a stone and threw it at the solitary linden tree.

"Of course !" said Jenny as he hit it. And they laughed in the sunny autumn day. They scrambled down the embankment. Ferdinand took a tiny box out of his pocket. He opened it, took out the ring and slipped it over her finger.

"The goldenrod is blooming again," said Jenny.

"And the Canada geese are honking."

"Where?"

"Somewhere way up there," said Ferdinand, holding out his hand.

She flew into his arms. He would never let her go.

THE BALTIMORE CONNECTION

by

Wolfgang E. Franke

Alex is a German teenager who is thrown into the war in Italy in 1945. His special assignment is to interrupt the supply lines to the communists in the Balkans by the assassination of the British agent who directs the flow of arms to Tito. Alex is terrified and resists his assignment in vain. He parachutes behind enemy lines, but falls into the hands of the communist guerillas who beat him mercilessly. Through the Baltimore connection and with the help of the agent he was sent to kill, the story evolves.

Forthcoming - Fall, 1983

ABOUT THE ARTIST:

Alan Wilson was born in Ireland in 1940 and came to Canada in 1957. He graduated from the Ontario College of Art four years later and has had regular one-man shows of his paintings and his photographs in Toronto. His work is in private collections in Canada, Australia and the United States including Chicago, Boston and the Vincent Price Collection in California.

His work has been reproduced on record jackets and on posters and in the industrial field, includes recently the design of logos for a large international electronics company.

Mr. Wilson lives in Toronto.